HATE NEVER
FELT SO GOOD

HATE STORY

NICOLE WILLIAMS

NEW YORK TIMES BESTSELLING AUTHOR

PROLOGUE

I didn't know anything about the man other than his last name. That, and what his last name meant.

Storm.

As a noun, storm was defined as a violent disturbance of the atmosphere. As a verb, it meant to move forcefully in a specified direction.

He came into my life just like that.

Maybe I should have anticipated that, given our situation. Maybe I was naïve to assume anything less than a storm could ensue between two people as different as he and I were. I should have known, and maybe if I had, I would have done things differently.

Maybe I would have done *everything* differently.

Maybe I would have done *nothing* differently.

This story wasn't about the maybes and the what-ifs. This story was about the details and the destruction that came.

This wasn't a love story. Nothing close to a romance. A happily-ever-after knocked on its ass. True love bashed on its fragile head. A fairy tale no one tells their children.

This was the other kind of story. The kind not punctuated with contented sighs and skipping hearts.

This was a story of a storm—the storm that eviscerated everything in my whole entire world.

This wasn't the story of how I grew to love him—it's the account of how I came to hate him.

That was where this story leads. The path I found myself on which wound down many trails until it came to an abrupt end.

This is our hate story.

ONE

Nina

Second thoughts. I was having them.

Experiencing these any time before stepping into the lobby of the swanky hotel I was meeting him at would have been helpful.

"Sure you're ready for this?" my best friend, Kate, asked, surveying the lobby like he was going to be lurking there with a sign hanging above his head.

"I'm sure."

It was a lie. I wasn't sure I was ready, but I didn't have a choice. The bills had gone from a pile to a pillar, and if I didn't do something soon, I would lose the house. I couldn't lose the house. Not ever. It was the only home I'd ever known.

"You don't have to do this, you know? There are other options. When I mentioned this a few months ago, it was just a far-off suggestion, not one I thought you'd actually run with." Kate slowed down as we got closer to the hotel lounge where he was supposed to be waiting.

"There are no other options that include me keeping the house. At least not ones that are any less illicit than this one." I licked my lips out of nervousness. With the way things had been lately, it was a miracle they hadn't turned into sandpaper.

"You know you could go to jail, right?"

My tongue touched my lips again. "Only if I get caught."

Kate shook her head, and her light hair whipped across her shoulders. She was everything I wasn't. Tall, rail-thin, straight blond hair that cooperated, skin that looked like she'd been gilded in something ethereal, and dressed like life was one endless party. Our personalities were a stark contrast as well. She was effervescent, where I fell somewhere closer to the jaded end of the scale. She wrung the life out of each day, loved like she'd never been hurt, and laughed like she'd never known sorrow.

What she saw in me that kept our friendship enduring, I didn't know. I just hoped she hadn't hung around when others bailed because she felt obligated. I didn't want to be anyone's pity penance.

She snagged my arm when I walked in front of her, braking me to a stop when I was a few steps from the lounge's entrance. "Do you know what he looks like?"

I tempered my irritation before glancing at her. She was coming from a place of concern, but I was committed. I just needed to get this over with already. "No."

"About how old he is?"

My armpits were starting to sweat. I hadn't even seen him yet and I was already pitting out. "No," I answered, lifting my arms a little for ventilation.

"Do you know what he's going to be wearing tonight?" Kate glanced over my shoulder, almost glaring into the lounge.

"No." I twisted from side to side to create as much of a breeze as I could. I so should have splurged for the clinical strength deodorant instead of this cheap dollar-store junk that was probably going to give me cancer one day. If my budget hadn't been worked out to the last quarter, I would have.

"Do you know anything about him?" Kate sighed, motioning at me like I was the lamb who'd just brayed as the first volunteer for the slaughter. "Other than, you know . . ." She swallowed. "What he wants?"

My stomach rolled. I definitely knew what he wanted. "I know his name."

Kate waited a moment. "And his name is . . .?"

"Sturm."

Her nose wrinkled. "What kind of a name is that?"

"Sturm's his last name. I don't know what his first is."

Kate's nose went back to normal, but a high eyebrow took over its job of disapproving. She was especially expressive. That was another way we were different. Kate seemed to have no desire or inclination to hide what she felt, whereas I had every desire and inclination to hide.

"So what is he expecting you to call him? *Mister* Sturm? Because this twenty-first-century feminist is so not okay with one of her best friends addressing this guy like that."

"Yeah, neither is this twenty-first-century feminist." I flapped air in the direction of my armpits because they were only getting worse.

"The same feminist agreeing to marry a man for money?" Kate drew her hand up to her hip and stretched into every inch of her nearly-six-foot frame.

The word still sucked the air out of my lungs, but it had lost some of its potency. "Exactly—agreeing to marry him for money instead of lame reasons like love or feelings or to grow old together. How much more feminist does it get?"

Kate looked down at me. "Eh, how about instead of marrying him for money, you could turn him into the authorities for trying to commit green card fraud?" She peeked over my shoulder and craned her neck to look into the lounge. "Besides, what is a million dollars really? That chick in that *Indecent Proposal* movie got a million and she only had to spend one night with him. Plus if you factor in inflation, since that movie's almost as old as I am, you are getting the proverbial and literal shaft. In the ass."

I gave up the armpit sweat battle and hung my arms at my sides. Why did I care if this guy's first impression of me was as a profuse sweater? I wasn't asking for his approval or even expecting it. He was a business transaction to me. I was a means to an end to him.

A case of two people embracing the capitalist spirit of America.

"Yeah, but she had to sleep with the guy. That's not part of our deal," I argued. "But if it was part of the fine print, believe me, I'd ask for a hell of a lot more."

We had an agreement. Kind of. It was more a rough draft that had just as many amendments as it had bullet points, but I preferred having everything ironed out in advance. I wanted to know exactly what I was getting into before sinking up to my neck in it, which I was minutes away from doing.

"So you're saying you *would* sleep with him if the price was right?" Kate's other hand flew to her hip.

I gave her the most indifferent face I could. I might have been able to look the part, but I certainly didn't feel the part. "Hey, Morality Police, I'm already agreeing to marry a guy so he can get a green card. Give me a break."

Kate's phone chimed in her clutch. She'd wrangled up a couple of friends to meet her at this lounge tonight so she could keep an eye on me. I guessed she was worried the guy might not be on the up-and-up and might be using a green card as a cover for wanting to sell me off for internal organs or into the sex trade. I wasn't worried about that, but I was thankful she was here for support if nothing else.

After punching in a quick text, Kate circled her phone at me. "And what are you wearing? Did you think there was going to be a ribbon handed out at the end of the night for the most colorful outfit?"

I glanced down at myself. I liked color. Lots of it. Living in a place like Portland, Oregon, a person had to find a way to fight off the perpetual gray. This was my chosen method.

"I wanted to make sure he knew who I was," I said, just barely peeking inside the lounge. Dozens of bodies, all of them different shapes, sizes, and colors, and all of them were dressed like they'd conspired to match. "If I'd known everyone would be in some shade of gray or blue, I wouldn't have dressed in a green polka-dot dress, fuchsia shoes, and a blue checked scarf."

Kate bit her lip to keep from laughing. "You're a fashion intervention begging to happen."

I stopped rubbing at a wrinkle in my dress. If an iron hadn't been up to the challenge of smoothing it out, my thumb wasn't going to do it. "I don't care. I'm not here to impress him or earn his approval."

"Yeah, that's obvious," she mumbled just loud enough for me to hear. When I went to give her a little shove, she slid out of the way. "And if you're not trying to impress him, why are you wearing the first dress I've seen you in since, god, probably when you wore that very one at spring fling of our senior year?" Kate was looking inside the lounge now, her gaze skimming the space like she was looking for something. Her friends must have already been there because she waved at someone before lifting her finger in a just-a-minute kind of way.

"Because I didn't think this place was a holey jeans and sneakers kind of place," I argued, wondering why I was defending my wardrobe choices to someone who dressed by the less-is-more standard.

"Let's hope *Mister* Sturm is fashion blind." The way she said it earned her another little shove.

"He's a single, foreign man who's paying someone a hell of a lot of money to marry him." I crossed my arms at her as she kept peeking into the lounge. "I think it's safe to say I'm not about to come face-to-face with a guy who spends his nights flipping the pages of *GQ*. And if you call him Mister Sturm again, I'm going to pull your hair."

Kate winked at me. "My scalp's a little sensitive from the hair pulling last night."

I rolled my eyes. "Alexander?" The last man *du jour* she'd mentioned to me.

"Trenton." She kind of sighed his name. Actually, it held the hint of a moan. God. I could never imagine sighing-slash-moaning some guy's name. Ever. The closest I'd ever gotten to a sigh-moan was over the peanut butter pie my grandma had made for my last birthday.

"Fine," I said, interrupting the last notes of her moan. "Then I'll slap your ass if you say it again."

She flashed a wicked smile my direction before giving her hips a shake. "Just as sensitive."

"God, fine," I groaned. "Just stop. Your sex life nause-ates me."

"Jealous is not a good look for you. Besides, someone needs to make up for your lack of it." Kate waved at me like my sex life was visible for all to read.

"At your rate, you're making up for the entire city's lack of sex life."

She nodded solemnly. "You're welcome."

"Besides, sex is not all it's cracked up to be." At this point, I was stalling, but I was nervous.

"Believe me, with the right person who knows what they're doing, it is all, and more, it's cracked up to be." Kate bounced her brows. "Some guys just know how to use their dick better than others."

I frowned. "Wow. I'm about to orgasm all over the place."

Kate laughed as she slid in front of me and teased my hair with her fingers.

"Oww," I whined as she ripped and pulled at my hair. "And I hope you washed your hands with bleach after the last dick you touched."

She responded by smearing her hands down the sides of my face. "Most action you've ever seen." She scrubbed them down my face one more time. "You're welcome."

I stepped out of the reach of her filthy little paws and waved her toward the lounge.

"I'll be right there. Just give the signal if the guy turns out to be a serious creeper, okay?" She waited for me to nod, then she kissed the air in my direction. "Go get him, tomcat."

I didn't know how to reply to that, so I went with an okay signal.

I waited a minute after Kate had disappeared into the lounge. Then I waited one more before forcing my feet forward. It wasn't like my dwindling courage was going to find its way back the longer I stalled.

Taking in a slow breath, I pictured my house. The one I'd grown up in. The one that had housed a Burton for sixty years. The one that would probably be gutted or ripped down and replaced by whatever rich a-hole bought it at the foreclosure sale. I pictured relief from the stack of bills, the freedom to have choices, and a future that wasn't already painted with bleak hues and dark strokes.

Then I moved inside the lounge and took my first step toward my future husband.

TWO

Nina

I couldn't stand out more even if I'd stripped naked and dipped myself in hot pink paint.

The lounge kept in the hotel's theme of being expensive-looking and meant for an upper echelon I was not a member of. I didn't belong there. I felt it as much as I sensed the few stares from people thinking the same thing. There might not have been a list of rules stapled outside the door, but it was clear there were plenty of unsaid ones.

Like one shall not step foot into this space unless their net worth tips the seven-figure boundary. Or one shall not breathe this air unless they drive a car that costs as much as a modest house. Or one shall not rub elbows with the rest of the inhabitants unless they have so many prospects, they've become an inconvenience of their own.

But since no one was guarding the entrance or about to toss me out for forcing my presence on the place, I moved deeper into the room.

It wasn't as large as I'd expected it would be, but that could be due to the number of bodies already filling the lounge. It was early by a Friday night's standards, but this place seemed like the kind of spot a person needed to make an early claim on. Above the bar was a giant stained glass window of a peacock, and the rest of the room followed the same theme. Rich colors, showy accents.

It wasn't my kind of place at all. I preferred the local hole-in-the-wall or dive. If this pretentious space was *his* kind of place, then this marriage wouldn't just be difficult because of our illegal arrangement. If this was the kind of place he felt comfortable in—the type of people he fit in with—then we were polar opposites.

Because this whole thing needed to be more complicated . . .

I scanned the room for someone flagging me over. He knew what I'd be wearing tonight, but I didn't know what he would be in. If the room was any indication, he was probably parading around in a suit that cost more to dry-clean than anything in my wardrobe had cost brand new.

I continued to just stand there, doing another room scan. I didn't know what he looked like. How old he was. What nationality he was. His hair color. Height. Skin color. Nothing. I knew his last name and that he was willing to pay me a million dollars to marry him. That was all I needed to know to say *I do*.

Some people exchanged sex for money. I was exchanging marriage. Go ahead and judge me. God knew I'd done plenty of it on my own.

Okay, still nothing. How much longer was he going to keep me standing here feeling like an outcast in my kaleidoscope of colors and cotton?

Kate was at a table with her friends, trying not to make it obvious she was watching me as though she was waiting for this Sturm guy to come stick a knife in my back like she'd convinced herself he'd already done in figurative terms.

A bunch of couples were clustered close together, kissing, touching, whispering . . . one couple, in particular, had me guesstimating how long it would be before the woman was spread out on the closest semi-private surface with her legs in the air. The guy didn't seem as enthusiastic about the prospect, but she didn't look like the kind of girl who heard no often. If ever.

I was half considering coming to Mr. Stiff Back's rescue and mentioning something about his male lover running a few minutes late, but that was when I noticed, from the corner of my eye, someone's arm lift.

I swallowed. It was him.

I gave myself one moment to prep for anything, so when I did look at him, nothing that hinted at surprise was present. If I acted surprised by the way he looked, then that led to the conclusion that I'd set expectations, and I didn't have any.

No expectations. An exchange of vows. A million dollars. That was it. Nothing else. Nothing less. Certainly nothing more.

A business deal.

When I did look at the man with his arm extended, I felt nothing. No disappointment. No pleasant surprise. Nothing.

When my attention settled on him, he waved me over to the empty seat in front of him. He'd somehow wound up with the best spot in the whole room—a couple of deep-seated chairs positioned across from each other beneath a glowing chandelier.

As I passed Kate, she didn't make it subtle that she was staring at the man I was moving toward. I didn't have to check her face to know she was wearing some combination of a glare and a gape.

Even though *I* had no expectations, I knew Kate had arrived with some, and this guy definitely tipped toward the old end of the age scale. It was hard to say in this light, but he could have easily been my father, if not my grandfather.

I swallowed again. Okay, so he was old. So what? It wasn't like I had to service his shriveled balls or anything. Marriage for money. Simple. If age wasn't a factor for falling in love, then it definitely shouldn't be for falling in fake love.

When I was a little way's back, the man rose from the chair and painted on a conventional smile. It wasn't warm. Nothing resembling friendly. It looked more forced than anything, like he was fighting every emotion to keep it there, which kind of baffled me. He was the one who'd set this whole marriage of mutual benefit into action.

Then it hit me—I was looking at the man I was going to marry.

I guessed the emotions dicing my gut into confetti were not the same feelings other women had when they looked at the guy they were about to exchange vows with.

"Miss Burton," he said, motioning at the chair across from him.

"Mr. Sturm." I made myself look into his eyes so he could see I wasn't intimidated. I wasn't some weak thing he could bend and twist to his liking. I needed him to know from the start that I might have accepted the position of his future bride, but I wasn't giving up my identity in exchange. I wasn't giving up the most microscopic sliver of it.

"Please, have a seat." His gaze dropped to the chair I was positioned in front of.

I didn't move. "You first." I indicated the chair behind him and waited.

His brows came together, but after holding out for another minute, he took a seat. I stayed standing until he was fully situated.

"Would you like a drink?" His eyes darted to the bar.

I dropped into the chair slowly, reminding myself to think before I spoke. *Every* time I spoke. I didn't want to start our relationship with him ordering me a drink. It was too much like a real relationship. Too traditional.

"No." I shook my head and crossed my ankles. "Thank you."

I could feel him looking at me, examining me. I wondered if he'd come into this arrangement with the same notions. No expectations. No room for disappointment. No margin of error for surprise.

I hoped so. I didn't have a self-confidence issue, but I was also a realist. I knew I wasn't the traditional Venus men wanted to take a piss on to mark their territory. I wasn't a head-turner, the body a guy pictured as he jacked off. I wasn't the first girl asked to dance . . . or the second or third.

Some might have said what I lacked in the looks department I made up for in the personality one. Society might have followed that up with a sympathetic pat on the back, but I took immense pride with my disposition.

Looks dimmed with time. Wit sharpened.

He leaned back into the chair, watching me like he was considering making a purchase. Hadn't he already bought me? Hadn't the price already been settled on? The longer his stare went on, the harder it became to not shift.

Like hell. I was not going to squirm in front of this man. I was not going to lead him to the assumption that I could be unsettled by something as small as a penetrating stare.

"Why are you doing this?"

I gave myself time to think before answering even though this answer was as basic as they came. "I need the money."

No reason why. No explanation as to what had happened to shove me into this corner.

"As much as I need my green card?"

I didn't look away. "Yes."

He was quiet, contemplating my answer or scheming a way to get out of this now that I was sitting across from him. I didn't know what he was thinking, but that was part of the beauty of this kind of arrangement. I didn't need to know what he was thinking or try to guess or mold my next moves to whatever may have been on his mind. I had no reason to withhold honesty because I just didn't give a shit what he thought about me.

And no, the irony of honesty being a perk of such a dishonest arrangement was not lost on me.

"And what happens if you suddenly decide to walk away from this?"

His voice held no hint of an accent, and he looked just as "American" as I did. Brown eyes, dark hair washing out to silver, average height and weight, a general apathetic tenor to his voice.

"That won't happen," I replied when I realized he was still waiting for my answer. American-looking or not, he was the one who wanted a green card badly enough to drop one million one dollar bills for it.

"How do you know?"

I was sitting across from the guy I was going to marry. I should feel something. I should feel some kind of emotion other than . . . resolve.

Damn. I really was as ice cold when it came to men as Kate had been telling me for years. Ever since Bryant Collins asked me to senior prom and my answer came in the form of a carton of milk spilling over his head.

I might have failed to mention to Kate that I'd overheard Bryant mentioning to a group of his friends that he was going to ask me so he could cross "popping a cherry" off his bucket list. You would have thought a guy with that lofty of a list would have been a bit more discreet with his virgin conquering plans.

So yeah. I'd been Ice Queen from that day on, and I'd fully embraced my title.

He was waiting for my answer. Again.

I needed to stop meandering down memory lane before he took his million somewhere else.

"Because I know exactly what it feels like to have people break their promises, and I will never do that to anyone." I scooted a little toward the edge of my seat. "I won't make a promise I can't keep. And I expect the same from you."

Maybe it was something in my voice. Maybe it was something on my face. Maybe it was a flatulence issue that had just been resolved, but he visibly relaxed. Almost like he'd just been read the negative results of a biopsy after waiting on edge for weeks.

"And you can promise to follow this through?" he asked, his gaze shifting just over my shoulder. It was faint, but I didn't miss his nod. "To its end?"

I wanted to glance over my shoulder to see who he'd just signaled, but not before I answered him. I wanted to make sure I was always looking him in the eye when I answered. "I can promise you that."

He nodded once more, but this time, it was aimed at me. "Then, Miss Burton, I'd like to introduce you to someone."

My eyebrows pulled together. Had he brought a friend to play lookout like I had? Shit, was he some undercover detective who'd baited me into this whole illegal affair? The guy now standing across from me definitely looked more like some hardened detective nearing retirement than some wealthy foreigner in the market for an American wife.

"You'd like to introduce me to who?"

That was when someone came up beside me. This was not the someone I'd expected. Not at all.

Shit again. I hadn't had any expectations, remember?

The figure looming beside me exchanged places with the older man. *Holy . . .*

"Your future husband."

THREE

Nina

Where was the abort button?

Not that I could punch it if it magically appeared in front of me anyway because my condition was, by banks' standards, dire. All the overtime in the world couldn't save me. Getting my body siliconed the hell out and grinding my ass up and down a pole couldn't even save me. Nothing short of a windfall of money would save me, and I didn't have the luck to win the lottery. As far as I knew, this was the only person making me that kind of an offer.

He hadn't stopped smiling at me, and it wasn't the friendly kind of smile. It was the kind that made it seem like he was in on some secret I wasn't privy to. The kind of smile that made me feel like I was being trifled with and made the punch line of a hundred jokes I had yet to hear.

I wanted to wipe the cocky smile off his face, but that would have required touching him and even I wasn't gutsy enough for that. A woman did not touch a guy like him unless she wanted him to be her undoing. Nope. You didn't play with fire. You didn't touch it. You didn't even come close.

Fire. That was all I saw when I looked at him. I was playing with it by agreeing to this kind of arrangement with him. I'd rather have the grumpy-faced grandpa back.

Even the way he lounged in the chair was smug. Like it was his throne and he was just waiting for minions to come bow before him.

"You're younger than I thought you'd be." He broke the silence first.

Though it was faint, I could just make out an accent. It was European, but I couldn't nail down the country. To look at the bastard, you'd think he was Scandinavian—blond hair, blue eyes, commanding frame—but his accent was too sharp to hail from the land of Vikings.

I was tempted to glare at the tipped smile aimed at me, but I didn't want to lead him to the impression I cared. I gave him my version of the same smile, abandoning my "no expectations" policy for the prospect of pissing him off. "You're older than I thought you'd be."

His smile shifted into the realm of a smirk, like he knew I was lying. So yeah, maybe I was lying about thinking he was older, but I wouldn't give him the satisfaction of confirming his silent accusation. He was older than me, but not by much. He might have been closing in on thirty, but he wasn't past it.

He leaned forward in the chair. When his gaze circled my face to my fiery red hair, his brow elevated. *Yes, I am the stereotype. Be warned.*

"Prettier too."

I stiffened. He was fucking with me now. I'd already agreed to marry him. How much more did he think he could screw me over?

I gave him a cursory glance and kept the unaffected look on my face. "Uglier."

He cocked a brow like he knew better. "And the personality of ten women rolled into one."

"Intimidated?"

His head shook once. "Intrigued."

"Irritated?"

His eyes investigated me again. It felt intrusive, definitely not cursory. "Impressed."

"As impressed by me as the woman in heat who was just mauling you over by the bar?"

"You mean the woman who gave me this?" He pulled something out of the inside pocket of his suit jacket and set it on the small table between us.

It was a hotel card key. With a lipstick kiss pressed into it.

"Classy place, this five-star hotel." I glanced back at the woman at the bar. She was still there, watching him as though he was the height of the male species. "Did you tell her the reason you were here?"

His attention stayed on me. "Yes, I told her I was here to meet the woman I was going to marry."

My stomach wrung. This was the man I was going to marry.

Holy shit.

"And she didn't ask for her room key back?" I asked.

"She didn't give it to me until right after I mentioned that." His stare was intense. Too intense. I felt like every secret—every piece of who I was—was strewn out on that table for him to see. "Women love a man who isn't afraid of commitment. It's like an aphrodisiac."

"You know what else women like?" I didn't pause for an answer because I guessed he didn't have a clue. "A man who's humble."

He fought a smile and leaned back in his chair when a server approached with a couple of drinks on a tray. "No, they like to think they do, but they don't." His head shook authoritatively. "They like the cocky bastard who goes after what he wants and doesn't take no for an answer."

Because the server was shielding some of me from his view, I allowed myself to shift. I was getting fired up, and if he kept saying the same kinds of things with the same kinds of looks on his face, that drink was going to wind up in his face.

That was when I noticed what the server had set in front of me. A tumbler with something amber in color. The same thing she was setting in front of him. Although from the curve of her smile, she was offering to give him a blow job on the side, compliments of the house.

"What is this?" I asked. Him. Her. Whoever wanted to answer.

"Scotch," he answered, ignoring the server lingering between us.

My nose curled at the drink.

"Expensive scotch."

"I don't care if it came from the fountain of youth. I won't drink it."

His forehead creased with what appeared to be irritation, but I couldn't be sure. Maybe it was confusion, like he couldn't decide what to make of me. "You would have me believe you wouldn't take a sip of that if you knew it would give you eternal life?" When I shook my head, his head tipped. "Why?"

"Because I value my free will far more than long life." I pushed the drink away until it clinked against his. "I'd rather live one day free than an eternity in a cage."

He was quiet for a moment. The server stayed between us, staring at him, waiting.

"Then why are you here?" he asked me finally.

I leaned forward and hoped my stare was as powerful as his. "Because free will is expensive."

He let that hang between us, never looking away. He wasn't used to being challenged, having people push back. I understood why. He didn't just exude confidence, he defined it. He didn't just garner respect, he demanded it.

Of course one of the few men in the world who had probably been a world ruler in some other life would be about to marry one of the few women in the world who had likely been a Joan of Arc figure.

Irony? You suck.

"Well?" He waved between the server and me. "She's not just lingering here for her health."

I considered mentioning that no, she was waiting for him to take her up on the BJ offer, but better judgment caught me just in time. It was rare when that happened.

"Water," I said to her, staring at him. I would not be intimated by a stare. I would not let him slate himself in the top spot by crumbling beneath his confident façade. "I'll have a water please."

"A water?" the server repeated, like she'd never heard of it. In this place, where inebriated seemed to be the theme, maybe she hadn't.

"You know, that stuff that comes out of a faucet? All clear and cold? Chemical symbol $H2O$? That stuff we're supposed to drink eight eight-ounce glasses of a day?" I paused when I noticed him fighting another smile. "That's what I'd like. Please." I might have been strong-minded, but I had manners.

Unlike the person sitting across from me, still fighting a smile that was dripping with amusement.

Once the server left to hopefully fill my drink order, I scanned the room. It was filling up. Kate and her friends were stationed at a table behind me. She was positioned so she could see us, but it wasn't me she was watching. And she wasn't appraising him like she was looking out for her friend's best interest but like she was contemplating how to make him hers.

Of course I knew better because Kate and I held to the Girl Code that friends didn't date each other's boyfriends or, I guess in this case, future husbands. However, if I were someone else sitting across from this guy, she'd be making her play, probably in the form of her panties dropping in his lap. Kate didn't do anything half-heartedly.

"You don't have any problems with women." I turned back around in my seat when I counted at least another dozen women making frequent, if not continuous, looks his way. "So why pay one a million dollars to marry you when I bet half of the women in this bar now would agree to marry you free of charge?"

When I looked at him, I found his stare still leveled on me. I wondered how he could keep that kind of concentration when half the room was giving him *Take Me Now* eyes

"Commitment is never free," he answered, looking away for the first time. His gaze landed on the floor. "Believe me when I say a million dollars is a better deal. Twice as much would be a better deal."

It was the first time I'd witnessed a shadow of emotion from him that didn't tip the confidence scale. "Why?"

His eyes narrowed for a moment before they returned to mine. They were hardened almost. "Because attraction comes with complications, and I need this to be complication free. I need this to be a business transaction. You do something for me, and I pay you for it. No feelings. No emotions. Simple."

The server returned with my water. It had ice and everything. I thanked her with a smile. She thanked him with a Fuck Me smile.

"You're afraid of commitment," I stated because it was one of the few truths I knew. Men, as a species, were afraid of commitment. Incapable of it. Humans as a species were incapable of it.

"Not afraid," he said, reaching for his drink for the first time when I lifted my water. "Just know better now."

I took a drink of my water. "You were burned."

He finally took a drink of his scotch, that peculiar flash of vulnerability rolling through his expression again. He took another drink. "To ashes."

The way he said it—the way he looked when he said it—made something in my chest squeeze. I knew that feeling. I'd learned that traits the human condition was trained to lean toward were usually the things we should be leaning away from. Commitment. Trust. Love. All conditions that should be replaced with caution, skepticism, and reason.

When I should have been keeping a wall between us, I found myself on the verge of commiserating with him. His damn good looks didn't help the confusion either. I might have hardened myself against the species known as man, but I was not immune to them.

"Who was the man just here?" Twisting around in my seat, I searched the room, but he was gone.

"Ezra," he said.

Waving, I waited.

"I've known him for a long time and trust him implicitly, so you don't have to worry about him turning us in for what we're discussing. He's been a friend of my family's since before I was born and serves as a sort of right-hand man for me now. In all facets of my life."

"I wasn't worried. Just wanted to know who he is." I shrugged casually.

"And now you know."

"Now I know Ezra's name. But not yours." From his accent and the way he looked as though he had descended from some Nordic king, Axel and Sven seemed like plausible options. From his personality, I would happily call him Jackass.

"You know my name."

"Yeah, your last name."

He cocked a brow like he was questioning why I needed anything more.

"Since you're clearly the kind of guy who thinks he can just order a woman a drink and she'll take it with a smile, let me clue you in on the type of woman I am." I leaned forward, encouraged by the fresh anger I felt pulsing through my veins. He was less attractive when he was pissing me off. It encouraged me. "Not the kind who's ever—*ever*—going to call you Mr. Sturm."

He swirled his drink, back to studying me. "No?"

"Never."

He set his drink down and slid it against my cup of water. He was testing me. I knew it, but I kept my water where it was. He could get his glass all up in my glass's business for all I cared—that's the only business of mine he'd be getting in.

"Well, *Miss Burton*, my first name is Max."

Something spilled down my spine when he said my name like that. Like it was both a promise of something to come and a challenge.

"Max?" I said, not tempering the doubt in my voice.

He was in a suit that probably cost more than most people's cars. He towered far above the average man. He looked like a fairy tale princess and a Greek God had gotten it on and he'd popped out nine months later. He oozed confidence that bordered on conceit, and I doubted it was the fake kind most men pretended they had. His confidence had been earned. Like hell he was "Max."

"My given name is Maximilian Hans Xavier Sturm." He cocked that same right brow at me. "However, my friends call me Max since the alternative is a bit of a mouthful."

My thumb ran down the side of the water glass. "We just met. I'm not your friend."

"You're going to be my wife, so you can call me Max." His mouth twitched at the same time his eyes flashed. "Or Mr. Sturm."

"Funny," I said with a fake smile. "*Max*."

When he smiled, it did something to me it shouldn't. I felt something tighten in my chest, and when his eyes slid back to mine with that smile still in place, I felt something else tighten farther south.

Shit. Not him. Not now. Not ever.

"Now that we've met, is there anything you'd like to ask me? Anything you'd like to go over?"

Besides everything?

We'd "met" online through a super-secret site you had to know a friend of a friend of a deity to know about—Kate had been my hookup in this instance. We'd communicated back and forth for the past couple of months, but about nothing too personal. It had felt more like a test of my commitment to following through with this than an actual attempt to get to know me. Other than knowing he was willing to pay a million bucks for a green card and that his emails were painfully formal, Max Sturm was a mystery to me.

Our emails back and forth had been focused on the guidelines and timeline of our "arrangement" instead of the getting-to-know-you facet. All business.

I supposed there were a million things I could have asked him about our arrangement. A million more I could have asked him about himself. But only one question was on my mind.

It hadn't been much of a concern until coming face to face with him. Now? It was Concern#1.

"Just to clarify . . ." I felt like the chair seat had been stuffed with broken glass and nails. "There is no expectation, anticipation, or remote possibility that we would have sex. Right?" I had to look away. I couldn't keep looking at him with the way his expression was changing. From business to pleasure in point two seconds.

"Why?" I heard the same change in his tone. "Have you changed your mind on that bullet point now that we've met?"

That welcome surge of anger flooded my system again. I liked it. I needed it where he was involved. When my narrowed eyes landed on him, he was grinning. Almost gloating. Cocky fucking bastard.

"No," I said slowly. "Meeting you has only solidified my 'no' under that bullet point. I'd rather sleep with the first guy I met than you."

"Ezra?" He laughed a few beats. "You'd rather have sex with a man in his sixties who's attracted to men?" Another short laugh. "Well, good luck getting him to reciprocate the sentiment."

My blood was heating. It encouraged me on. "A man twice my age who likes men is more my type than yours is, how about that?"

Max's brows pulled together. "*My* type?"

I leaned forward, not blinking. "Yeah, the kind that believes anything and anyone comes with a price tag."

He leaned forward too, until his face was so close I could detect the heat of the scotch on his breath. "Well, you're the one agreeing to marry me for money." He didn't blink either. "You must be of the same mindset."

It took all of my willpower to keep my hands to myself. "I kind of hate you, you know that?"

His eyes challenged that. "I'm asking you to marry me, not like me. Hate me all you want."

FOUR

Max

This wasn't the woman I'd thought I'd find myself sitting across from tonight. There wasn't a shadow of that fictional woman in the real one before me.

She was like no one I'd ever met. In this country, my home country, or any of the dozens I'd visited. She was attractive, but not in the way that screamed to be noticed. Her beauty made a person want to lean in to take a closer look, to inspect the details that made up the whole.

Her sense of style was unusual, for sure, but I had yet to determine if she just didn't give a shit about style or if this was her way of expressing it. Her clothes were bright. Her more-red-than-auburn hair was bright. Her eyes were bright. Even her skin, as pale as it was, was bright.

In here a hundred people, a thousand distractions, all of them pining for attention, and I couldn't take my eyes from her.

I didn't know why. I wasn't attracted to her in *that* way. At least, I didn't think I was. She didn't fit the mold of the girls I'd been with, and she certainly didn't talk like them—firing insults instead of flattery.

Maybe that was why I liked her. Or found myself . . . *drawn* to her. She was making me earn it. Her respect. Her approval. Her friendship. She wasn't like the others who had let the way I looked or dollar signs dictate their approval.

I was fascinated by her in a way that didn't stem from how to get her below me in bed as quickly as possible. It came from some place else. A place I wasn't sure I could name if I had a year to dedicate to the task.

I was staring at her again. I was pretty sure she was taking it as some play to assert my dominance, but it wasn't—I simply couldn't *not* stare at her. It would have been like staring at the wall above Mona Lisa. A person just didn't not look at something that unique and different when it was right in front of them.

She was staring right back too. Though her stare was definitely an attempt to assert her own dominance. Now, *that* . . . that was one hell of a turn-on. In *that* way.

"Why are you doing this?" I reached for my scotch to distract myself, not because I actually wanted a drink.

She folded her hands in her lap and sat up straighter. "Because if I don't, I'm going to lose my house."

I nodded, trying not to show my surprise. Most young women who would sign up to marry a man for money had other plans for spending that kind of money. "And this is a bad thing?"

Her hands squeezed a little tighter together. "Yes. If you consider losing the only home you've ever known a 'bad thing.'"

I took a sip of the scotch. I didn't taste it. "Will you be able to commit to this? It will take three years to see this through." I already knew her answer, of course—I'd spent the last few months confirming it with her online—but I had to hear her say it. I had to watch her say it.

"Yes."

I wasn't sure I'd heard or seen anyone so convincing. This woman was committed to making this unusual relationship of mutual convenience work. I didn't doubt it.

"You won't be able to date anyone else while we're together," I said, repeating something we'd already gone over. Again, I needed to hear it confirmed with her sitting five feet in front of me.

"That won't be a problem." She sat up straighter.

I rolled the glass between my hands, wondering what she meant by that. "Why?"

She didn't pause to consider her answer. "Because dating someone would imply me meeting someone dateable."

I felt myself wanting to smile again, so I tried to stop it. My smiles seemed to irritate the hell out of her. "And this is unlikely?"

Her shoulder lifted. "Only if you take my history into account."

I shifted in my chair, constructing a follow-up question that wouldn't earn me another glare she seemed to have no qualms about firing my way.

That's when she tipped her head down the bar. "That woman's still staring at you."

I didn't turn around. I couldn't even remember the color of that woman's hair. "Probably wondering if I'm going to take her up on her offer."

"Her offer of sexual relations?" She was teasing me—I could tell from the way one corner of her mouth was twitching.

"That woman had more than sexual relations in mind." When she lifted a brow at me, I continued, perhaps against my better judgment. "She would have let me flip through every last page of the sexual kinkery handbook, and she would be an eager and willing participant."

Her throat moved when she swallowed, then the faintest color spread up her neck. If she didn't have such fair skin, I never would have noticed. I'd rattled her. Teased her right back to the point of making her blush.

Good. My blood heated with the acknowledgement that she wasn't as immune to me as she let on.

"Yeah, well, out in the lobby"—she stuck her thumb over her shoulder—"there was a guy who was all over me. You should have heard the things he said he wanted to do to me." She kept stabbing her thumb over her shoulder, and I had to take a drink to keep from smiling again. "Yeah. Totally wanted to do . . . things . . . to me."

She didn't shift. Her eyes didn't dart away. She didn't bite her lip. She didn't give any sign that she was concocting the whole story, though I guessed she was. Not because I didn't doubt some prick would hit on her wherever she went, but because she was innocent. I could tell. I'd gotten the faintest hint of it from our correspondence, but I could see it clearly with her sitting right in front of me.

"What kind of things?" I set my empty glass down and scooted to the edge of the chair.

She shot me the faintest glare. She knew I was calling her out on lying. "*Things.*"

Now I was thinking about how many men she'd been with. What way she liked to be taken. What she sounded like when she . . .

And shit. What is happening to me?

Thinking with my dick was off-limits, especially with this woman. I couldn't mess this up. I couldn't let things like urges and emotions get in the way.

She was the one who was going to help me earn my freedom in the country I loved. The place that was home.

Stop thinking about her mouth and her sexual prefer-ences and get your fucking head in the game, Max. This whole arrangement needed to be approached from as emo-tionless of a standpoint as possible. This was a business deal and should be treated like all business deals—with confi-dence and cool removal.

"Well, I promise I won't do 'things' to you," I told her, giving my inner sexual deviant a chance to speak up. He didn't, and I felt my whole body relax. There were plenty of women in the world. Plenty of them willing to share their body with me for a night. This woman could not be one of them.

"Like you even could do 'things' to me," she huffed, gracing me with a look that led me to believe she thought me quite the Quasimodo.

"Believe me." I waited for her eyes to meet mine again. When they did, the green in them actually looked molten. I didn't blink as I stretched closer. "If I wanted to—if I put my mind to it, my body into action—I could do all kinds of things to you."

Her face remained composed. But her body gave her away. Her chest started rising and falling faster, and that was when I knew she wasn't immune to me at all. In fact, she was so not immune to me that was the whole reason for this cold act.

It made my chest move a little faster too. It made some-thing else react. She was drawn to me in some primal way like I was drawn to her. Humanity had been trying to ascribe a word to this kind of attraction since its inception, settling on terms such as fate or soul mates, but that was a load of bull. There was no such thing as being fated to be together. No such thing as soul mates. I'd seen enough of life, lived enough of it, to know better.

Not that any of that attraction mattered since neither of us could act on it. Desire was natural, but that didn't mean we had to give in to it. It didn't mean we ever could.

She had been well on her way to hating me before I let my worse judgment get in the way. I needed to let her hate me. A lot. She needed to despise me or else I'd fuck this up. She needed to hate me for this marriage to work.

Those green molten eyes of hers narrowed at me even more. "Not before I could do *things* to you. Like kneeing your balls into your stomach."

Good. She was back to the start. She was back to hating me.

FIVE

Nina

What had I gotten myself into?

Not that it really mattered because it wasn't like I could get myself out of it. Consequences of having a crapload of debt and little-to-no cash flow.

Maximilian Hans Xavier Sturm. I'd just met the arrogant asshole, had a total of one conversation that included actual verbalized words instead of the typed version, and I already knew him better than I'd known most people.

That was the result of reading a damn bible of all things, Max.

At the end of our "meeting" last night, he'd left me with a folder the size of my old high school calculus book. Inside were pages of questions and answers—basically a biography—of the first twenty-nine years of Max's life. It went over everything.

Everything.

I'd never known such intimate details about another person. Not even my grandma, the person I'd been closest to in my whole life.

I understood the point of it, but it still felt like some giant invasion of privacy. Like I was sitting behind a one-way mirror and observing someone else's life.

I now knew what country he was from originally— Germany—what he did for a living—he was a day trader . . . whatever that was—and just about everything else. He'd grown up in Bavaria with his parents, Hans and Anya Sturm, and had one younger brother. He went to private school, was top of his class, and was captain of both the hockey and swimming team (which no doubt had exacerbated his arrogance, if not being the root of it), studied business on a student visa at not one, not two, but three Ivy League schools here in the States, before graduating with his doctorate at the age of twenty-four. So the arrogant a-hole was an overachiever too.

Awesome. Just fucking awesome.

Page after page it went on, until I flipped to the last section . . . which made me promptly slam the folder closed. There was such a thing as TMI, and he'd crossed it when listing his first sexual encounter as being with his former nanny at the ripe old age of fifteen. I couldn't decide it I was more grossed out or appalled by that factoid.

I'd stayed up most of last night thumbing through the Encyclopedia Maximilian—save for that final part I'd sectioned off with imaginary red tape—so I didn't know why I'd brought it into work with me tonight. I told myself it was so I could memorize as much of this stuff as I could. When we had to sit before the review board before he was issued his green card, our stories needed to be as watertight as a frog's butt. That wasn't really it though.

It had more to do with how fascinating I found his life. How astounding I found it that he wasn't thirty and had lived as full a life as he had. How he'd already visited all seven continents, shaken hands with three Nobel Peace Prize winners, published a book on commodity trading, and attended Shakespeare in the Park every summer since he'd come to the States.

Sure, I was six years younger, but even if I turned on the turbo boosters and had an endless stream of money at my disposal, I'd be lucky to accomplish a tenth of what he had by his age.

Reading about his life—his accomplishments—made my life seem small and insignificant. I wasn't ashamed of my life or anything, just kind of depressed that it amounted to so little after working so hard. Realizing how people could exert the same amount of effort and commitment and come out with two totally different results was sobering.

A pounding on the door of The Busy Bean made me jump so badly, I spilled the cup of coffee I'd been sipping while pouring over Max the Great's life story.

I automatically reached for the bat the owner kept propped in the corner for these kinds of situations, also known as some bum, meth head, or thug looking to score a quick and easy hundred bucks from the till. This part of Portland wasn't known for its low crime rates. That and the stand's twenty-four-hour-a-day schedule equated to a higher than average robbery rate.

"Hey, fräulein. Open up the damn door already," a familiar voice shouted with another pound.

I left the bat where it was and swallowed my heart back into my chest. I'd been working the night shift a few months ago when some kid in an ancient Oldsmobile rolled up to the window and demanded all of the money in the till. He said he had a gun, but I never saw it. He probably didn't, but I wasn't going to call his bluff over forty-one dollars.

"You know, second to cancer, heart disease is the leading cause of death in women," I said after unlocking the cheap door and opening it. "Thank you for ensuring I'll wind up in that statistic one day."

Kate puckered her shocking pink lips at me before hopping inside. "Thank *you* for not answering your phone when I called you fifty thousand times today."

I locked the door and grabbed a towel to mop up the spilled coffee dripping onto the floor. "Sorry. Kind of hard to answer a phone that's been shut off due to non-payment."

Kate was already rummaging through the fridge, digging around for the half and half to make her peach Italian soda. "Those corporate slugs. Always thinking of themselves first. Kind of like all of the men I've dated. Sure, we'll give you that, if you give us this first." Kate slammed the fridge door and made a face. "You know I'm always here whenever you're ready to ask for help. I might not make the kind of bank the future Mr. Nina Burton does, but I make enough to keep a girl's phone on."

I wiped up the coffee on the counter first before kneeling beside the mess on the floor. "Thank you, but no. Besides, other than the bill collectors, you're the only one who calls me and I see you almost every day anyway."

"Not to mention you'll be getting the hookup soon." Kate glanced at me as she dished a scoop of ice into the largest cup we sold. "Cha-ching."

I focused on getting every last drop cleaned up. "Yep."

"How's it working again? Five hundred grand now, five hundred after?"

I rose and tossed the dirty towel into the hamper. "First half on our wedding day. The second half the day he gets approved for his green card."

"Nothing until you exchange vows? Really?" She poured a load of peach syrup over the ice. "He can't even throw you fifty grand after the first date or something? Maybe after the first good fuck?"

"Kate . . ." I snatched a fresh towel from the pile and lobbed it at the back of her head.

"What? It's true. Men write their checks with their dicks, not their hands. Remember that."

"That's not part of our arrangement. We've *both* agreed on that."

"Yeah? And how long are you two going to have to be exclusive to make this thing convincing to the federal government?" She poured more half and half than soda water into the cup then gave it a quick stir.

I shrugged. "A few years."

She popped a lid on and stabbed a straw through it. "And no sex?"

I checked the drive-up windows just to make sure a customer wasn't waiting. "Nope."

She rolled her eyes. "He's expecting sex."

"No, he's not."

"Yes, he is," she argued before taking a sip of her drink.

"He never said that." I glanced at the folder. No sex. I'd made sure of it. I'd quadruple-checked.

Kate lifted her eyes to the ceiling again. "No, the million singles said that."

It did? No, it didn't. The million said, "Marry me so I can legally get away with committing a crime."

"Well, I'm not having sex with him." I crossed my arms.

"Why not? Hell, I'd pay him a million bucks to have sex with him. You know, if I had that kind of money lying around." Her eyebrow peaked, and she got that far-off look that meant she was having another filthy fantasy right in front of me.

Another towel sailed at her face. "Kate."

"What?" She chewed the end of her straw. "You know he's hung like a frickin' sperm whale."

Her mentioning that part of his body made me think about that part of his body . . . which made my stomach feel something it shouldn't. "Eh, no, I do not." I curled my nose and tried to shudder. Weak attempt on my part. "With those huge hands and feet, he's probably hung like a hamster."

Kate huffed. "You are clueless."

"Yeah, and I'd like to remain clueless when it comes to that part of his anatomy, so scoot. I've got a mess of homework to complete." I waved at the other thick folder and bit my lip. Sure, there were a thousand pages of questions and ample spaces for me to answer, but I'd only need one page to list my whole life story of twenty-three years.

"How far have you gotten?" Before I could run interception, Kate lunged toward the folder and flipped it open. "How far have you *not* gotten." She flipped through the mostly empty pages.

"I know. I just . . . get paralyzed every time I try to fill in one stupid question." I fired a glare at the empty pages like they were the enemy, instead of me and my pathetic existence. "You read through his and it's like you're reading the screenplay for some future Academy Award-winning movie, and then you compare what mine would read like . . ." My sneakers squeaked on the weathered linoleum when I shifted. "And it's like what someone would read if they were trying to put themselves to sleep."

Kate flipped through the first couple of pages of Bible of Max before turning to face me. "So what? So you haven't scaled the Eiffel Tower with your toes. Or made enough money to support a small country. You have your own story that's just as impressive."

Both of my eyebrows hit my hairline. "I'm a twenty-three-year-old with a high school degree who walks dogs by day, works an all-night coffee stand frequented by felons, and in my 'free time,' I take photos that don't sell." I lifted my arms at my side and did a slow spin. "I'm single, swimming in an ocean of bills, and about to lose my grandma's house."

Kate set her drink on the counter and gave my arm a squeeze. "It's your house, Nina."

"It will always be Grandma's house." I kicked at the linoleum.

"You know I hate it when you get all defeatist on me." Kate grabbed a pen from the counter and lowered it to the first question on the first page. The part about family. "'I gave up my dreams to take care of a person I loved.' Edit that." She lifted her index finger. "You *temporarily* put your dreams on hold to take care of a person you loved. How is that any less impressive than all of this?" She shook Max's pages. "Making money, scratching goals off some checklist, winning awards . . . who gives a shit? At the end of the day, we all want what you've got, Nina Burton—a big heart that doesn't possess a single selfish beat."

I always got uncomfortable when she painted me as some modern-day urban Mother Teresa, so I dodged the topic. "Family." I stabbed my finger at the first thing listed. "Grandma. That's all I've got to fill in. Mom would be a lie, Dad would be a guess, and brothers and sisters? Probably, but god knows I never have and never will meet them."

Kate lifted the pen and thumped the end against my forehead. "You had the real deal with your grandma. Most people never get that. Not once. Having one person who loves you and can back that up is worth more than a million who claim to love you but come up short when put to the test."

I moved toward the empty pages waiting for me to fill them in. "I know that. I'm not ashamed of my life. I don't regret anything. I wouldn't trade a single day with Grandma for all the money in the world . . . I just feel kind of stuck, you know? Grandma's gone now, but I can't figure out what I want to do with my life. Some days I feel like I'm going to wake up and find out I've aged fifty years and am still working here and eating canned soup while sitting in front of a television all alone." I grabbed another towel to wipe down the espresso machine as a distraction.

I didn't give most people a chance to get close enough to know the real me—the person who hid fear behind strength. Kate, I'd let slip past the gate enough that she knew.

"I can't conceive of a better time to get 'unstuck' than with some hot, wealthy foreigner who's paying you a load of money to break the law with him."

The way she'd said it so matter-of-factly made me smile. "It's definitely a fresh start."

She nudged me with her elbow. "Definitely."

SIX

Nina

It was the first date I'd been on in a long time. It was the first "fake" date I'd ever been on. That had to be the reason my stomach was unleashing hell on me as I rode the elevator to the top floor of the hotel I was meeting him at.

For dinner. *Only* dinner.

After our initial meeting last week, we'd agreed on a day, place, and time to get this first date thing scratched off the relationship to-do list. Much like last week, at the other slightly less lavish hotel, I was getting looks from the time I stepped into the lobby. Kind of the way a person felt in a dream when they showed up naked at school.

I didn't fit in with the social elite. I never would. I'd never rub elbows with the wealthy or bullshit with the upper crust.

And I didn't give a crap.

People in this class of society behaved like money was their passport dictating how to experience life. They acted like anything could be bought, along with themselves. It turned my stomach . . . right until I stopped in front of the hostess stand and remembered why I was there. I was marrying a man for a million dollars.

I turned the judgment finger around on myself.

"Max Sturm," I told the hostess, guessing he was already there since I was fifteen minutes late. A person like Max didn't show up late to anything in life.

The girl didn't need to consult the sheet in front of her. "Mr. Sturm's right this way." She led me into the dining room while I refrained from grumbling over the *mister* part.

It was prime dinner hour, and the restaurant was busy. There wasn't one empty table, and from the wait out front, I doubted there would be for a while. I practically had to jog to keep up with the hostess. Twilight hung in the sky outside, and as we moved closer to the windows stretching around the perimeter of the restaurant, I let myself take in the view.

Portland was bathed in color, the great Willamette River looking as if it was filled with diamonds instead of water thanks to the lighting. The view alone was worth the price.

Still jogging to keep up through this restaurant that would not end, I kept admiring the view. Which backfired when I kept walk-jogging even after the hostess had rolled to a stop. When I crashed into her, I made a noise that was more animal than human.

"Sorry," I said, realizing a moment later that we'd stopped in front of a window table where someone was waiting.

He was looking at me in that same way again—fighting that damn smile. Although since I'd just rear-ended a hostess in front of a restaurant full of people, the smile was warranted.

"Hey," I greeted him as the hostess slid the empty chair out for me.

"Hello, Nina."

I slid off my shoulder bag and settled it on the floor beside my chair, trying to shake off the chills I felt tumbling down my spine from the way he'd said my name. "Sorry, I'm late."

I scooted the chair closer to the table and didn't know where to look. He obviously had no qualms about staring a person in the eye. Usually I didn't either, but for some reason, tonight I found it difficult to maintain eye contact.

Especially when the person I was supposed to be making eye contact with was *him*. A face meant to be worshipped, a body meant to sin, a smile birthed straight from the depths of hell. My future husband. *That* person.

He leaned across the table like he wanted to tell me a secret. "If this were a real date, I might actually be offended."

"But you're not? Since this isn't?"

His eyes dropped to my mouth, then he leaned back in his chair. "Not this time, but please try to keep in mind that I respect your time, and I hope you'll do the same with me."

Was he telling me not to be late again? Ordering me?

I knew I had a serious chip on my shoulder with this kind of stuff, so I made myself take a deep breath and calm down. He was saying he respected my time, and he had been the one here on time. He was saying that he hoped I'd do the same, which was not too much to ask.

One more deep breath and the raging feminist inside me calmed her shit.

"I should have been here on time, but public transportation had other plans." I reached for my glass of water and took a drink. I was thirsty from hustling from the bus stop to the hotel.

"You take public transportation? As in the bus?"

The way he said it, like it was an incurable disease, made me smile. "As in the bus, the light rail, and even those nifty streetcars on occasion."

"That's not safe. In this city. For a woman. At this hour." Max motioned out the window at the darkening sky, like the city was brimming with thugs and thieves just waiting to prey upon the innocent after nightfall. "I wasn't aware that was how you got around. I'll have it taken care of."

"Actually, nothing needs 'taken care of,' and the reason you didn't know I'm a fan of public transportation is because you didn't have this." I reached into my bag to pull out the Bible of Nina that I'd finally managed to finish last night with the help of a few shots of vodka. My life story didn't seem nearly as depressing when I was steeping in Smirnoff.

When I held the folder out for him, Max studied me for a minute. Half of his stares felt as if he could see through me, and the other half felt as if he was trying to figure me out. This was one of the latter stares.

"Finished?" he asked, taking the folder. He set it on the table in front of him instead of stuffing it in some lock-and-key briefcase like I'd imagined he would, given our situation.

I nodded. "Finished."

Well, mostly. That last section remained blank because no amount of vodka could make me brave enough to fill in those questions.

"Good." He reached for something beside his chair and pulled out another folder. This one was green instead of blue and not nearly as thick, but still. *Another* one? I never knew committing a federal crime would be so much work. "I've drawn up a timeline for us to follow. When you get a chance, please review the dates and let me know if you have any conflicts with the schedule."

I found myself looking around the restaurant, almost like I was expecting a few FBI agents to lunge out of their seats and haul us away in handcuffs. But no one was looking. No one cared what was inside the folders we were exchanging over dinner. I wondered if anyone would even if they knew what was inside them.

"It's important that we document our relationship as it progresses, so if you haven't already, please open up a social media account or two, so your friends and family won't be shocked when you announce you're getting married." He pulled something else out of his briefcase of goodies. "I'll be doing the same so my family and friends won't be startled by it either."

He set a white rectangular box in front of me. It had a picture of a phone on it—one of those sleek, giant new ones.

"I took the liberty of purchasing you a new phone as I noticed your current one is so old . . ." He must have noticed the warning in my expression. "It looked pre-camera-phone era."

His head turned to look out the window, but I didn't miss the smile trying to form.

"Thank you, but I can't take it."

Before I could continue, he lifted his hand. "Before you get too far, I anticipated your lack of acquiescence and am equipped with a favorable solution."

He paused just long enough to let me say something, but I stayed quiet. He was right—my phone could barely hold a call, let alone take a picture. Not to mention said phone was in indefinite hibernation.

"I could deduct the cost of the phone from what I'm paying you. If you prefer that option." He didn't glance around the room like I did. He seemed so at ease with this arrangement. So unconcerned that this could blow up in our faces. "Is your silence a sign of your agreement, disagreement, or indecision?"

I eyed the phone, thinking. He was right about documenting our relationship in the form of photos and social media posts. Not that I had one of those, but I could open one easily enough. The friends and family part would be a different obstacle.

I'd already agreed to marry him for money—what was accepting a phone in comparison?

"You'll deduct the full amount?" I asked.

"To the last penny if it makes you happy." His tone was playful.

"Deal," I said before slipping the phone into my purse. With the exchanging of folders and now a new phone, we probably looked like a couple of international spies to anyone watching us. Which no one seemed to be doing anyway.

"By the way . . ." His eyes circled me. "Nice dress."

I glanced at the dress I'd zipped into tonight. It was another old one from high school that had been barely in fashion back then. It was pretty much the antithesis of the dress that had been hand-delivered to my front door earlier today. The dress box alone had probably cost as much as my weekly grocery budget.

"Yeah, so I returned that lovely one you sent me and managed to pay off the past three months' electricity and water bills, so thank you." I ran my hands down the old dress. "I love it."

"Glad you found a good use for it."

I leaned back in my seat when a waiter came by and lit the votive candle on the table. "Me too."

I'd never been inside the store the dress had come from, but I'd thought the security guards were going to toss me out on my ass when they saw me slip through the glass doors. I held up the dress box like it was my invitation before heading to the cashier. When I found out how much the dress had cost, I gave a low whistle and promptly rushed the fresh money in my wallet to the utility company and paid what I owed.

It felt good having those bills off my hands. At least for this month.

"Is money an issue right now, Nina?"

I took another drink of water. "Money is always an issue, Max. The plight of the middle-to-lower class."

He was quiet for a minute, and I was starting to regret bringing up the whole exchanging an expensive dress to pay arrears utility bills when he shifted in his chair. "If it would be helpful, we could revisit the payment terms of our agreement. Perhaps so you receive a portion earlier than planned."

I shook my head. "No. We have an agreement."

"Yes, we do. One that can be easily amended."

I looked him in the eye. "We have a deal."

He wanted to say more. I could tell. But he didn't. Maybe that was because he could tell I wasn't going to change my mind. It was strange how we already seemed to know each other after really only just meeting. Maybe that was the benefit of approaching a relationship from a position of reason instead of emotion.

When the waiter approached the table again to take our order, I stole a look at Max while he was distracted. He was in another dark blue suit, complete with a vest and white button-down shirt. His face didn't show a hint of a shadow, like he'd just shaven, and his eyes were bright, like sleepless nights didn't make frequent visits at his place as they did mine.

He was easy to look at—handsome in such a way it was hard to glance away. He smiled easily, seemed at ease in any situation, and I sensed he possessed a brand of loyalty that was rare in this world. I could sense that in what I'd read from his biography, as well as what I'd read between the lines.

I didn't know why I felt a pull toward him, but I did. I'd accepted that. But just because I'd accepted I was attracted to the man I'd agreed to marry didn't mean I needed to act on it. Actually, I'd never been so adamant against acting on anything in my life.

I didn't care if my whole body felt like it was about to rip apart from the tension, I would not act upon that attraction. Never.

It helped that I was certain he was in no way attracted to me. Nothing like harsh reality to bring a girl back to her senses.

"Excuse me?" I called as the waiter turned to leave.

"Yes, ma'am?" He turned and waited.

"I haven't ordered yet." *Because I was too busy checking out my future husband.*

"I ordered for you. I got you the special like I got myself," Max said.

I felt my eyes narrow, but I didn't aim them at him. He'd probably like it. "I don't want the special," I told the waiter. "I'd like to order the . . ." I hadn't looked at the menu. I hadn't even seen one. What did a place like this serve? That I would actually eat? That I could pronounce without sounding like a hillbilly?

The waiter waited patiently for me.

Max, not so much. "Go with the special. You'll like it, trust me."

This time, I did aim that glare in his direction. "I'll have the hamburger," I told the waiter. "Please."

"The hamburger?" He sounded stumped.

Across from me, Max was fighting another one of those damn infuriating smiles. Arrogant asshole.

"We don't have a hamburger on the menu, ma'am . . ."

As the waiter struggled to find the right way not to piss me off, Max lifted his hand. "Talk with Jean-Luc. Tell him Max Sturm's guest would like to order a hamburger." As he said it, Max's smile went higher. "I'm sure he'll be able to figure something out."

The waiter looked between the two of us, still confused, before nodding and rushing away.

"So the Max Sturm name carries a lot of clout in this upper circle?"

He tipped his hand back and forth. "Enough to special order a hamburger at least."

"Unbelievable," I said under my breath as I folded my napkin into my lap.

"You don't even know what the special is."

I shook my head. "Nope."

"Then why did you order something else instead of asking? I eat here twice a week—I know what's good." Max settled back into his chair, getting comfortable.

"Because it was 'special' ordering it all on my own and not having someone order for me." I peaked an eyebrow and waited for his rebuttal.

"You are willfully independent."

"Good, you're figuring that out sooner rather than later. It will make our whole fake relationship that much more authentic." When I wet my lips, his eyes dropped to my mouth. An expression that looked almost painful formed.

"Your independence." He stared at my mouth one more second before diverting his stare out the window again. "Is it by choice or circumstance?"

I struggled not to shift in my chair. "Both."

He sighed just loud enough for me to hear. He was obviously not used to people responding to his probing questions with vague answers. "Let me rephrase—how did it start out? By choice or circumstance?"

Sighing, I answered, "Circumstance."

I was bracing for him to probe further down this unpleasant path when he cleared his throat. "Do you have any questions about anything you read in my file?"

I focused on the flickering candle between us. Over the past five days, I'd gone through his file numerous times. I'd reread certain parts so many times they were committed to memory. I had a million questions for him. A hundred follow-ups to each one of those.

Instead of listing them off one by one, I went with the one most pressing, and most relevant, to our situation. "Why are you so desperate to get a green card?" My eyes narrowed on the dancing flame. "Your family, your home in Germany . . . it all seems idyllic."

"I love my family and I love Germany, but here, this is home." Max motioned out the window at the darkening city of Portland. "I knew it from the first time I visited with my family the summer I was fifteen. I was born and raised half a world away, but when I stepped foot in America, it was like I'd finally come home." He was still staring out the window when he leaned in closer. "Wouldn't you do just about anything to stay in the place you call home?"

I didn't have to think about that question. My answer to it was the very reason I was sitting across from him. "I would," I said, leaning across the table as he was. "I'd even marry a stranger."

SEVEN

Max

It was strange, sitting across from the woman I was going to marry. It was strange to know I'd be spending the next few years with this person I knew very little about.

Nina was both the perfect candidate for this, and the worst. Perfect in that she was easy to be around, didn't act intimidated by me, and embodied commitment and dedication in an age where both were in scant supply. She was the worst candidate for this because, try as I may, I felt some level of attraction toward her.

Attraction wasn't a new concept for me—desire I was on a first-name basis with—but this, it was different. I'd never felt it before, so I didn't have a name for it, nothing to compare it to, and no way of knowing where it would lead.

I'd hoped for an eventual friendship with the woman I married, one that stemmed from mutual respect and dedication to the plan. I could see all of that in Nina. It was what I saw in addition to that that scared me.

The one woman in the world who was off-limits to me in *that* way was her, the woman I was counting on becoming my wife. I couldn't let emotions and feelings and all of those other things that drove people apart endanger our arrangement. Nina was, for all intents and purpose, off-limits.

We were marrying each other—that was the plan. Desire, attraction, and love were not part of that plan.

Across the table, Nina was watching me, waiting. The light flickering from the candle was illuminating her, making her green eyes glow and her hair look like it was on fire. She knew I was staring at her. Where others would have diverted their gaze moments ago, she just kept staring right back.

"Since you know my life story, tell me a little about yourself," I asked, letting my gaze shift first. Hers stayed on me though, still unyielding. I could feel it.

"It's all in the folder I just gave you," she answered.

"The folder I haven't had a chance to open yet? Humor me."

She leaned into the table. "I'm marrying you for money. How much more humor do you need?"

God, I was smiling again. I wasn't a smiley person, but I couldn't seem to control myself around this girl. "What are your hobbies? Interests? What do you do for a living? Nothing too personal, see?" I waved between her and me. "Conversation. You talk, I listen. I talk, you listen. It's nice."

She sighed, fighting a smile of her own. "I like taking pictures. It's more of a hobby than a career, but who knows? Maybe one day I'll actually sell a picture and make enough money to splurge on a bottle instead of a box of wine."

She was making a joke. I liked how I could already tell that about her. The odd sense of humor. The straight face she kept when she delivered it.

"Speaking of wine . . ." I made eye contact with our waiter and lifted my hand. When he came over, I almost wanted to order a hamburger for myself just to see the look on his face from before when Nina had ordered hers. Priceless. "Willfully Independent? Please order the wine for us."

When I motioned at her and waited, she almost looked stunned. I'd taken her by surprise.

"I'll have some . . . white wine," she ordered, rolling her shoulders back and putting on a face like she knew exactly what she was saying. Which she didn't.

"What kind of white wine, ma'am?" the server asked, glancing at me like he was waiting for me to jump in.

I lifted my hands in response.

Nina cleared her throat and sat up straighter. God, it was like the more unsure she became on the inside, the more assured she tried to look on the outside. "The kind that's . . . good."

I had to fake a cough to keep from laughing.

Nina shot a glare in my direction. She probably knew exactly what I was disguising. The waiter looked even more perplexed than he had over the hamburger order, so to help everyone out, I handed her the leather-bound menu listing the bottles of wine. Nina scanned it for a few seconds before stabbing her finger at one.

I didn't recognize the name of it, but I did notice it was the cheapest bottle on the menu. I wondered if that was why she'd ordered it or if it was sheer coincidence. Most of the women I'd taken to dinner picked the most expensive bottle listed because they could and I'd pay for it.

I didn't know what to think of Nina—the woman I was going to marry—ordering the cheapest bottle on the menu. Had she done it for my bank account's benefit or because she just couldn't comprehend spending anything more than fifty dollars for a bottle of wine?

I didn't know, and I found myself wanting to ask. I found myself wanting to ask her everything I couldn't seem to make fit because people I could read. Most people. Their motives were easy. Their choices predictable. But hers . . . not at all.

Of course the woman I would marry was the only soul I'd never been able to get a read on right from the start.

The waiter was long gone and she was still scanning the wine menu. Her eyes got wider the farther down the list she went.

"You're a photographer?" I asked, stealing another moment to admire her when she wasn't looking.

"Photographer is putting it generously. I'm more a hobbyist with a camera." She closed the menu and scooted it to the edge of the table.

"But you've got some photographs on display?'

When her eyes lifted to mine, she caught me staring. Again. Instead of the glare I was used to, her eyes shifted away like she was uncomfortable. Was I making her so? The way I was looking at her?

"I've got a few photographs on display." She searched the room like she was looking for something, but I thought that might have something to do with the way she'd just caught me looking at her.

"In what galleries?" I leaned back in my seat and tamed my stare.

"None you've ever heard of, I'm sure."

Actually, I probably wouldn't have heard of any of the galleries in the city. I wasn't the kind of guy who paid exorbitant amounts of money for a painting that looked like someone had taken their compost pile and slimed it all around a giant piece of canvas. I didn't buy things for the sake of owning them. I didn't buy things for the sake of impressing people.

I bought things because I wanted them. I bought things I liked and that had meaning to me.

When the poor waiter returned a minute later, he didn't say anything. He just opened the bottle, poured some into our glasses, and hustled away.

"Why don't you have an accent?" she asked abruptly, like it had been weighing on her mind.

"I don't?"

She shook her head and reached for her wine glass. "Not really. Every once in a while you'll sneak a v into a word that starts with w, but if I didn't know you were born in Germany, I'd assume you grew up here."

I touched the stem of the wine glass and rolled it between my fingers. "I don't know vhat you're talking about."

She lifted her eyes to the ceiling and took a drink of the wine. It was obvious she didn't like it. But she didn't say anything.

"I've lived here full-time since I was eighteen. I consider myself more American than I do German." When I took a drink of my wine, I realized why she didn't like it. It tasted like shit. "I suppose my accent feels the same way."

She took another drink of wine, and this time, she didn't show any distaste for it. It was like she'd been bracing herself for it. "Why did you let your visa expire?"

I knew she'd have questions. I was surprised by how direct she was with them. I liked that though—preferred it. Set the precedent so when it was my turn to examine her folder and ask questions of my own, she'd hopefully be as forthcoming with me as I was trying to be with her.

"Because this country is as much my home as it is yours," I answered.

"Not according to the United States government."

"I think, given our agreement, you can figure out just what I think about that."

She started to smile, plunging her fingers into her water cup and pulling out a chunk of ice. "Why did you choose me? You must have had hundreds of other interested parties." She popped the chunk of ice into her mouth. It wasn't meant to be seductive in the slightest, but she had no idea what she was doing to me as she slowly sucked on that piece of frozen water.

I had to give myself a mental ice bath before I could answer her. "Actually, I had thousands." When I heard my voice, I cleared my throat. It sounded too low, too much like how I sounded in the bedroom.

"Why me?"

I wondered why she was asking that. Curiosity? Concern? Conversation? "For starters, you lived here in Portland. I didn't want anyone to uproot from wherever they were and move here."

"Or, you know, you could have moved to wherever they were." She shifted the ice to the other side of her mouth, her lips shining from the moisture.

"No, I wouldn't leave Portland for another person. Fake relationship or real." My words came out sharper than I'd intended.

"Any other fabulous, totally unselfish reasons why I was the lucky girl?"

Nina's face stayed the same, but I heard the sarcasm in her voice. God knew I should be able to identify it since that was mostly what she directed my way.

"You were able to put together an email that indicated you hadn't flunked fourth-grade English, and you didn't use so many emojis and acronyms that I felt I was actually communicating with said fourth grader."

She bit down on the ice. "Yeah, I was an overachiever and passed twelfth grade English."

"I could tell. Although I was actually going to guess that you were an English major. Wrong guess?" I didn't realize I was taking a sip of the wine before I was swallowing it. I wrestled with another wince and set the glass down. I was too distracted when I was with her. Too out of my goddamned mind.

"Wrong guess."

"What did you study?" *Besides fucking with my mind and busting my balls?*

"Nothing." She lifted her shoulders, staring out the window without really seeming to see anything. "I didn't go to college."

I was surprised. She seemed educated. Intelligent. Determined. Not that a person had to attend college to embody those traits, but still. "Why not?"

She was silent, then she opened her mouth, but nothing came out. Instead, she sealed her lips and scooped another chunk of ice out of her glass before . . . dammit . . . she sucked it into her mouth. Next time, I was ordering water with no ice. I already had some sick fascination with her mouth—I did not need her sucking on something two feet in front of me.

"Nina?" My voice was low again.

"It's all in that encyclopedia you had me fill out. You can read more about it later."

From the look on her face, I wanted to tear into her biography and devour every word now. She hadn't gone to college, but from her affect, I could see it was something she regretted. Maybe regret wasn't the right word, but in another life . . . she would have.

What had kept her from going? A boy? God knew I understood the sacrifices people made in the name of love. Money? I might not have known the extent of her financial troubles, but I knew they were pressing enough to agree to marry someone for money.

Suddenly, I had a deep-seated need to know everything there was to know about this strange woman sitting in front of me. To know every memory she carried around. To witness every experience that had molded and shaped her into this unique creature who seemed like the strongest woman I'd ever known and, at the same time, the most fragile.

"Any other reasons you picked me? Besides the romantic notions of location and grammar?" Her voice drifted through the fog I was lost in.

Feeling this way about her was not what I'd planned on. If I'd known she would draw these kinds of deeply buried emotions from me, I never would have chosen her. Going with someone who lived on the opposite side of the country who spoke in LOLs and BTWs would have been better.

I couldn't *feel* for her. I couldn't.

It had led to my demise before. I couldn't let it crumble what I'd worked so hard to build.

She was waiting, slipping that chunk of ice around in her mouth and looking at me like she didn't loathe me as much as she had at the beginning of the night.

I had to make sure she kept her levels of despise high. Since I seemed incapable of being detached, I had to ensure she positively loathed me so that when I lost my head and leaned in, she'd lean away. So that when the time came when I couldn't restrain myself any longer, all she saw was an arrogant, selfish bastard.

I didn't just want her to hate me—I needed her to hate me.

"You seemed available," I said, finally answering her question.

"Available?" Her forehead creased.

"Yes, available," I continued, working my jaw. "Whenever I sent you a message, you'd get back to me right away. It didn't seem to matter how early or how late. What day of the week. What holiday. You always got back to me quickly."

At first, she digested what I'd just said. When she bit down on the chunk of ice, I knew she understood. Her face fell for a moment, almost like she wanted to cry, then it moved into something I was used to seeing directed my way.

"You choose me because I had no life. That's what you're saying?" Anger burned in her eyes. Disdain pulsed from her in waves, but I thought I could still see it if I looked really closely—the sadness she was disguising.

I wanted to drive my butter knife through my eye for making her feel like that, but it was better this way. She was better if she kept me at a distance.

"You seemed like you didn't have a lot of commitments, that's what I'm saying," I said. "The fewer commitments you had, the more you could commit yourself to this."

When I waved between us, she crossed her arms and looked away. With the darkness seeping in through the windows and the gentle flicker of candlelight glowing between us, it was hard to tell, but her eyes looked different now. Like she might be about to cry.

Shit. This was exactly why I wanted to keep emotions out of the equation.

I wanted to say something, though I didn't know what, then our dinners arrived. Nina barely seemed to notice the plate the waiter settled in front of her.

I needed to leave. I'd had enough for one night. If I stayed any longer, hurting her even more was inevitable.

"Would you take a picture of us?" I slid my phone from my jacket and held it out for the waiter.

From the corner of my eyes, I saw Nina's eyes narrow like I'd somehow betrayed her. When the waiter stepped back from the table, lifting the phone at us, I leaned across the table a little. Nina stayed where she was.

"We wouldn't want to forget to 'document' our first date." She didn't sound pissed, just kind of removed.

I should have wanted to sigh with relief that we were back on track. But I felt something squeeze in my chest when that cool removal hit me.

After the waiter took the picture and handed my phone back, I rose from my chair.

"I've got to go," I told her. She wouldn't look at me. That was a good thing, I told myself. "I have a meeting."

"Go ahead." She waved in my direction and folded her napkin into her lap. "I have nowhere else to be, no one else to be with, so I'll just stay and eat dinner alone. Wait for your message to come in, so I can drop nothing to get back to you. Be your beck-and-call girl. That's me."

I came around the side of the table. I was looking at her, but I knew she wouldn't look back. I'd done the job of pushing her away, and I'd done it well. "I'll call Ezra. He can drive you home when you're done."

Her jaw tightened. "That's okay. The bus works just fine. All hours too."

The thought of her on the bus, alone, at night . . . it made something that felt like a vise tighten around my neck. "I don't think so. I don't like the idea of you on the bus."

I didn't miss the way her hands curled in her lap. "Why? Because some other foreigner might try to lure me away from you to earn a green card?"

Afraid someone else might take you away from me, afraid something might happen to you, afraid you might take yourself away from me. Yes to all of it. "I need you to stay safe."

"Why?"

Instead of telling her the truth, I went with the opposite. I went with the lie because wasn't that why we were there? A lie. A falsity. A deception.

"Because I like to protect my investments."

EIGHT

Nina

*A*ccording to the Max Sturm Approved Timeline, it was time for our second date. Since he got to plan the first one at a restaurant that couldn't even get a hamburger right, I was choosing today's.

After he'd ditched me at dinner, I invited Ezra over to eat Max's dinner. A lobster tail that size should not end up in a dumpster, plus I didn't want to eat alone. I did enough of that at home. He did, albeit reluctantly, then he escorted me home as Max had instructed. On the bus, as I'd demanded.

Max was paying me to marry him, but there was no amount of money he could offer me to submit to him. I would not be ordered, instructed, or manipulated.

Dinner. Just thinking about it made me slump into the park bench a little deeper. What a disaster. It had started out great—or good, at least. It seemed like we might have been getting along, which was an added bonus since we'd be spending a lot of time together over the next few years, but then I felt like the rug was pulled out from beneath me.

He'd gone from warm to cool. From open to distant. From kind to mean. I didn't know Max well enough to determine which of those traits he embodied most, but I wasn't sure he'd let me get close enough to figure that out.

Which was a good thing, I told myself. I didn't want to get too close. I didn't want him to get too close. Distance was a very good thing in our situation. Removal was even better. We could be amiable with each other but had to keep walls up and borders drawn for this to work.

It was a Saturday afternoon, and like the Pacific Northwest was inclined to do in the fall, it was drizzling. Maybe not the best day for an outdoor date, but contrary to what Max thought, I had commitments. Like my day job.

I managed to check the new phone Max had picked up for me and keep hold of five leashes at the same time. I hadn't missed a call or text from him, but he was late. I wondered if this was his way of paying me back for being late last week. Probably. He seemed like the type who believed in payback. Although while I had public transportation to blame for my tardiness, Max was not the public transportation type.

With Kate's help, I'd managed to open one of those silly social media accounts. I had a whopping twelve friends already which, sadly, was more than I thought I would have. When I'd posted the picture of Max and me at dinner—Kate had added the commentary—I'd received a myriad of comments ranging from *Wow!* to *Damn girl.*

When I looked at the picture, I saw a relationship of convenience. A man who was merely enduring the woman beside him. A woman who positively despised the man sitting across from her. I saw it for what it was.

No one else did though. I guessed that was a good thing. If friends were already convinced we were a thing, hopefully, it would be that much easier to convince the federal government.

Taco, the hellfire Chihuahua on the end of one of the leashes, was starting to dance circles around Tank, the Great Dane. If Max didn't show up soon, I was going to have to ditch him on our second date because trying to keep five dogs still when it was time for their walk was like locking a kid in a candy store and telling him not to touch.

That was when I noticed someone moving down the sidewalk toward me. Just from that damn confident stride alone, I knew it was him. Max walked, moved, sat, and looked like he ruled this planet and the next one over.

It was revolting. That was the story I was attempting to sell to myself.

I waited until he was a few steps away before I acknowledged him. It was a Saturday afternoon—raining and cool—yet there he was in his three-piece suit and fancy shoes like he'd just come from an important business meeting.

"Do you sleep in your suits too?" I said, noticing he wasn't wet. That might have been due in part to the umbrella he was clutching, but it was almost like even the rain was too intimidated to get close.

"I would. If I slept." When Max took a good look at me stretched out on the bench, his forehead drew together. "In case you didn't get the weather report, it's raining. Will be all day long." He moved around behind the bench to slide his umbrella over me, which was kind of charming. Except I was already drenched, so it didn't matter.

"You better give that expensive suit the same report before it gets itself good and ruined." I twisted on the bench to look back at him. The shoulders of his jacket were already darkening from the rain. So was his hair, and his face, and . . . I cleared my throat and twisted back around.

That was when Taco leapt into my lap to growl at Max.

Keeping his umbrella above me, he held out his hand for Taco to sniff. Or bite. Who knew with that little beast.

"Your day job," Max said, not flinching when Taco nipped at the air around Max's hand.

"In all its fame and glory."

Max smiled at the menagerie of dogs tangled around me, Taco now licking his hand like it was a meat popsicle. That dog didn't like me that much yet, and I'd spent the last six months walking him thirty minutes three times a week.

"So," I started, pulling my new phone out so he could see the time. "Who isn't respecting whose time today?"

He didn't look at the phone. He was looking at me. "You told me twelve thirty. It's twelve thirty."

"No, I told you twelve fifteen," I argued. I picked up the last dog here at twelve fifteen. Why would I have told him to meet me fifteen minutes later?

Then his phone, which matched mine save for the color, settled in front of me. My text with the time and place was on the screen.

"You told me twelve thirty."

Well, crap. "Oh."

"I respect you, Nina. That's all-inclusive. Your time, your opinions, all of it." When I stood, Max came around the bench, hovering the umbrella back over me.

"You just met me. What have I done to earn your re-spect?"

"Agree to marry me." He shrugged, stating that so mat-ter-of-factly I didn't think anything of it until his words had a chance to settle in and spread.

God, I was marrying him. The reminder made my stomach draw in on itself. The next three years of my life would be shared with Max. We'd exchange vows. Rings. We'd live together.

We'd get divorced.

That's what I focused on. The reality instead of the fan-tasy.

"Nice second date idea." He held out his hand for a leash, so I gave him two.

He was a big guy, but I gave him the smallest dogs, Ta-co and Bruiser, the English bulldog. They were the bloody terrors of the bunch, and I might have been interested to see how he handled himself with two little demons dragging him down the sidewalk in hot pursuit of a skateboarder.

"Yeah, sorry. I don't have a lot of free time this week, so I figured I could multitask our date." I glanced at him as we started down the sidewalk, led by a team of five dogs. His suit was wet, and he was holding the leashes of two dogs that were birthed in hell. His date maybe hadn't been my kind of thing, but it had been more considerate than mine was. "Do you mind?"

He shook his head. "It's nice to get some fresh air. I'm cooped up in my office so much that this is a welcome break."

"Even if you're a walking puddle by the end of this?"

Max's eyes moved to my shoulder farthest away from him. He scooted closer and adjusted the umbrella, so I was totally sheltered. "Even then."

I bit my lip when I inspected him, droplets of water rolling down his hair. "Really, I'm okay. If I was worried about the rain, I would have brought my own umbrella."

"Yeah, but I'm not okay with it." Max turned with me as I rounded the corner. Miraculously, Taco and Bruiser were trotting along like the perfect gentlemen they *never* were. "Besides, what kind of enamored lover would I be if someone we knew saw us and I wasn't holding my umbrella over you?"

Now I understood. I slid out from beneath the umbrella a little. "So you're doing this for the show?"

Max moved with me, the umbrella hovering right above me. "I'm doing this because I want to."

"But you just said—"

When he sighed, it wasn't one of those short, subtle ones. "Are you going to do this all the time? Analyze everything I do and say?"

Probably. This was such an unusual situation, made even stranger by the foreign things I felt for him. Sometimes I wanted to smack him across the face, and sometimes I wanted to do something else. I disliked him as much as I liked him, but that wasn't really the unsettling part—it was how extreme each feeling was. I'd never felt much more than apathy and general disinterest around guys, but I felt neither of those with Max.

Instead of arguing over the umbrella any longer, I glanced at him hovering a foot above me. Whatever they fed boys in Germany, growth hormone must have been sprinkled into everything. "You're kind of a giant, you know that?"

He smiled, shaking his head at my sudden turn in conversation. "You're kind of . . . a *non*-giant." He seemed to edit his answer when I issued a warning look at him.

I wasn't short. I was a perfectly average five four.

We walked the dogs in silence for a few minutes after that. Crossing Main Street put us down by the long stretch of paths that led along the Willamette River. The drizzle had grown into more of a shower and Max was pretty much just dripping water from everywhere now. It didn't seem to faze him any—he still had that level, even expression.

"I went over your biography," he said.

I was wondering how long it would be before he brought that up. "Do you have any questions?" I swallowed, keeping my eyes forward.

"Lots of them. But the beauty of spending a few years together is that we'll have plenty of time to go over them."

I was relieved he wasn't going to pepper me with questions right now, but it sounded like the questions would come. Eventually. I'd almost rather just get them all out of the way now. "Beautiful."

"I should mention there was a section you forgot to—"

"I didn't forget to do it." I blushed internally when I thought about some of the questions I'd left blank. "I *chose* not to."

"Why not?"

"Because it's personal."

Max's socks must have been wet because I could hear them squishing with every step he took. "It's *all* personal."

"*Extra* personal."

Max's hand holding the umbrella dropped to the out-side of my arm and gently shifted me toward the edge of the path. At first, I thought he was trying to get me closer to him, but then I noticed the cyclists whipping down the trail in front of us. "Not when you're sitting in front of the USCIS officer it isn't."

"Not yet." I shook my head adamantly. No way in hell I was answering those questions for him right now. "Eventually, but not yet."

"You don't have anything to be embarrassed about. I won't judge." When Taco yipped at the cyclists streaming past us, Max made a weird hissing sound and Taco shut the hell up. So not only did the humans around him behave like he was a God, the canines did too. "At least I won't unless I find out you have some kind of freaky fetish, and then I'll judge." He nudged me, smiling, but I kept my eyes forward.

He was confusing me. A few days ago at dinner, he'd left in such a cool rush, and now he was saying and doing things that were almost . . . tender. Thoughtful.

"I'll fill it out," I promised, sneaking a little more space between us. "Just not yet."

"But you already know my answers to all of those questions."

My stomach dipped. "No, I don't. I didn't read a single one."

He broke to a stop for a second. I kept moving.

"What? Really?" he asked as he caught up. "It was the first part I went to when I opened yours."

My eyes lifted. "Of course it was. Because you are of the male species." I tried to swallow the heat I could feel rising up in my throat from thinking about him flipping to that section first. Why he'd want to know those answers.

What he'd hoped to read there. What he'd think when he found out the real answers.

"Come on." Max nudged me again, and this one I felt seep inside me a little. How he'd made it past the iron casing I never took off, I didn't know, but I didn't like it . . . at the same time, I did. "I'm a guy who's just agreed to be celibate for three years. Give me something. Anything. One answer."

I caught myself looking at him from the corners of my eyes. His suit was pasted to him, hinting at a body . . . I was not going to waste a goddamn second fantasizing about. "If you're expecting me to feel bad for you and your celibacy, not going to happen. You're the one who signed up for it."

Max's umbrella continued to bob above me as he kept powering down the path. I usually kept a slower pace, but the conversation was firing me up, and I didn't want to have any energy by the end of it to give him any more sideways inspections or think about what his body looked like under the wet layers of his suit.

"What size is your ring finger?" he asked as we reached the turnaround point. "For the ring?"

My pace quickened even more, but he had no trouble keeping up. I could probably break into a jog and he would keep up without breaking his stride. Perks of being the size of someone spawned by Zeus.

"I don't know," I answered.

His hand holding the leashes grabbed my elbow and pulled me to a stop. I didn't realize how out of breath I was until I realized I was almost panting like the dogs were.

Max's hand moved to my left one, his fingers skimming along my ring finger like he was sizing it up. Despite being soaked, Max's skin was warm against mine. Not hot, but warm. The kind of heat that was welcoming instead of consuming.

When his finger curled around my finger, tightening around it, I felt a jolt shoot up my arm. I promptly wrote it off as him using too firm a grip.

"Seven," he said, his finger twisting around mine slowly before letting it go. "Maybe a seven and a quarter. I'd like to get the ring purchased, so it's done. Is there a certain style or cut you prefer?"

When his hand dropped away from mine, I could still feel the warmth of it pulsing in my hand. My head felt a little foggy, like I was just waking up. What in the hell was going on? Why did I feel like this? What was happening?

I'd never felt any of it before and I wasn't sure why I was now, with a man who was paying me to marry him. It must have been the rain, the hard walk, the lack of sleep.

Months of strain and stress had caught up to me finally and this was the way it was manifesting. Max hadn't caused this. His one finger wrapped around one of mine had not made me feel this way.

"I don't know what you mean," I said when I realized he was still waiting for an answer. I couldn't even remember the question.

"Is there a certain stone you like? A certain shape?" Max tipped his head at me, something that resembled concern falling into his expression. "A diamond is the obvious choice—round-cut being the classic—but I'd like you to have something you'd enjoy."

Rings. Engagement rings. Damn. I was reeling from one little touch and now he was throwing the topic of rings at me. I couldn't keep up, and the dogs were starting to get antsy from just standing here.

"Don't get me a diamond," I said, starting down the path again. Max fell in beside me. "Get me one of those fake ones. No need to waste a bunch of money on a real ring for a fake marriage."

Max's jaw popped through his skin, his grip tightening around the leashes. "You'll be my wife." His tone was clipped. "No matter the reason, no matter the duration, you'll be my wife. You'll have my last name. I'm not putting some cheap ring on your finger."

We were clipping right along again. At this pace, my usual thirty-minute route would be done in fifteen. "Actually, I'm a fan of the hyphen."

Max's head turned toward me. "The hyphen?"

"Yeah. That neat little dashy thing that allows me to keep my name and add yours to it." I shrugged. "The hyphen."

His brows came together as he processed that, then his head whipped side to side. "No. No hyphen."

My own eyebrows drew together as my blood heated. "Then no. No wife," I stated right back.

I wasn't thinking about Grandma's house or bills or desperation right then. No, I was only thinking about not wanting to give this man an inch more than he was already asking for. He'd already gotten me to agree to marry him. He wasn't going to get one more damn thing, me donning his last name included.

"You're going to let one little hyphen get in the way of a million dollars?" The arrogance in his voice, the tone that said he knew better, had me ducking out from beneath his umbrella.

The bastard dodged right with me. Every time until I'd worked all five dogs up into a barking, bouncing fit.

I gave up dodging the umbrella with a sigh, but not the reason for me dodging it in the first place. "You're going to let one little hyphen get in the way of your green card?"

Max let that hang between us for a minute, continuing to stride down the path, making wet, slurping sounds with every step. "Fine. A hyphen it is."

My smile slid into place.

"But I'm getting you a diamond. You can fight me on it and throw as many threats as you like, but that's that."

Tank's tail started moving between his legs from Max's tone. I wouldn't be so easily intimidated though.

"It's your money. Waste it however you wish."

"I will," Max snapped. "I'll waste a whole bunch of it on the biggest, most obscene rock I can find."

I rolled my eyes. For being such a man, he could behave like a child. "You wouldn't want anyone to think you were compensating with a giant diamond for something"— my gaze briefly drifted to his belt region—"not so giant?"

A smug smile shadowed his face. "Liebling, if you think the size of a diamond has to do with compensating for a certain piece of the male anatomy . . ." Max's voice dipped a few notes lower as he slid closer. "You'd be getting a fleck of a diamond only visible under a magnifying glass."

It was the first time he'd said anything German to me, and even though I had no idea what it meant, it sounded a little too nice to my ears given it was him saying it.

And of course there was the issue of him alluding to his man region, which made me think about his man region . . . which made me want to knee his man region for making me think about it. "My, someone's confident."

Max's arm brushed my back. When I jolted, his smirk stretched into place. "You would be too."

Letting out a snort of doubt, I continued to march along. His arm stayed behind me, the umbrella above me, the whole time. I didn't think a single drop of rain had fallen on me during this walk.

His arm had to be tired. He had to be freezing from being soaked and having the breeze cutting down the river rolling over him. He had to have preferred a million things to this date I'd "planned" for us. But if he was uncomfortable, he didn't say anything. If he'd rather be somewhere else, doing something else, he didn't complain. He just stayed right beside me, moving with me, as we cut through the gray storm.

It made me wonder what kind of man Maximilian Sturm really was. The arrogant, proud man who lived life like everything had a price tag? Or the gentle, easygoing one I'd caught a glimpse of today? I knew the weeks and months to follow would answer that riddle, but I wanted to know now.

I felt like I needed to know now, so I knew exactly the kind of man I was dealing with, so I could plan exactly how to act around him. So I knew exactly how to counter his advances when they came because I could feel them stirring. He was going to challenge me. Push me. Drive me to a breaking point.

Part of me was looking forward to the ride. Part of me was wondering if I should step out of line now. My situation might have been dire on a good day, but I wondered what would happen if I opened myself up to this man. Would I leave this in worse shape than when I started?

I thought I already knew the answer to that. Our relationship was fake. Conjured into being on false pretenses. It had an expiration date.

It was an absolutely hopeless situation.

So why did I feel something that felt a lot like hope flickering inside me right now?

When my internal musings materialized in the form of a sigh, Max's attention turned on me. "Everything okay?"

No, nothing's okay. Instead, I nodded and kept walking.

We were about to make our way out of the park when Cruz, the labradoodle I was walking with Tank and Penny the mutt, decided this was the ideal time to take care of business. Right there on the sidewalk.

I pulled a plastic sack out of my jacket, already prepared for a situation like this. With five dogs on a rigorous walk, it happened a lot.

"All its fame and glory," I muttered as Cruz panted back at me, smiling like he was proud of himself.

Max took the plastic bag and held out the ends of his leashes. I took them, shooting him a confused look.

"What?" he said, shoving his hand deep in the bag. "I grew up with dogs. I'm used to cleaning up shit on the sidewalk."

I watched him crouch down and clean up Cruz's mess, my forehead's creases of confusion only burying deeper. He was in a suit so expensive I didn't want to know how much it had cost. He was sopping wet. He seemed like the kind of guy who'd pay people to do anything resembling a chore, from brushing his teeth to cleaning up dog shit.

But there he was, throwing my theory in my face.

"That's kind of romantic actually," I said as he turned the bag in on itself and tied it shut. "Wow. I didn't think you had it in you."

Max lifted a brow at me, tossing the bag into the garbage can beside the path. "How is me cleaning up a pile of steaming shit with a plastic baggy romantic?"

Exactly. How is that romantic? Hell if I knew, but it was.

I shrugged. "Because you did it so I didn't have to."

Max took the two leashes back from me "And?"

"And that's romantic. To me."

He was giving me a look that made me shift. Rain dripping down his face, his white dress shirt clinging to his chest, the way his eyes were pinning me to some invisible wall—it all messed with my breathing, making it uneven and rushed.

When his brow lifted higher, I continued. "Save the flowers, save the poetry. Clean up a pile of dog crap for me or fix the whiney hinges on my front door, and I'm a goner."

One corner of his mouth pulled up. "Good to know."

Then, before I knew he was moving closer, his face slid beside mine and I felt his warm lips press into my face, just above my jaw, right below the hollow of my cheek.

Fuck. I felt that ribbon of warmth weave inside me again. It spread down my neck, into my core, settling into a part of my body I wasn't used to feeling ignited.

His face moved back, but it stayed close to mine. I hoped he couldn't tell how I was breathing faster now. I hoped he couldn't hear my heartbeat. I hoped he didn't know I could feel his touch . . . down there.

But something in his eyes—something that lit up in them—told me he might have.

"What was that for?" I said, though it came out as more of a whisper.

"Today was the day."

"For what?"

His gaze dropped to my mouth, his face pulling together like he was fighting some internal battle. Then he pulled back. "Our first kiss."

NINE

Max

Today was move-in day.

Two months had passed since Nina's and my first meeting. In those two months, I'd failed to do what I was presently attempting to do as I loitered in my car outside her house. Get my shit together.

I'd pulled into her driveway five minutes ago, but I couldn't get out. Not yet. Not until I'd managed to pull my head out of my ass and reattach it to my neck. Not until I'd figured out a way to keep her at that careful arm's length distance I seemed incapable of facilitating.

Nina Burton. I hadn't seen her coming. I hadn't expected her. I hadn't known I'd . . . *feel* for her. The girl I was paying to marry me was not the one to go and get my head in a mess over. We'd be spending the next two years and some change together. That wasn't so long where friendship was concerned. That was a fucking eternity for a relationship based on attraction and romance and all that came with that.

I'd find some way to screw things up. Or she would. Or we both would. It was inevitable. So the person I was depending on to get my green card was the one person I could not get involved with.

Friendship was allowed. We could still be civil. Share a laugh. Eat dinner together and talk about our day. Go on walks together. Touch . . . the occasional careful hug here and there, the innocent arm graze.

My growl filled the interior of my car. Innocent and careful were not ways I wanted to be with Nina. At least not all of the time.

There were times she made me feel like she'd found my pin and was pulling, bringing me to self-detonation. There were times when she'd challenge me and dig her heels in so deep I knew better than to keep arguing with her, but it didn't stop me from going another ten rounds.

Nina was my sanctuary as much as she was my war zone. Peace and solace one moment, explosions and massacre the next.

When I caught her sticking her head out one of the windows and giving me a curious look, because I was just sitting in my car, I waved then pointed at my phone propped to my ear. She flashed a thumbs-up then disappeared from the window. She was used to my phone being smashed to my ear, but in this instance, I wasn't talking to anyone.

I just didn't want to look like "that" guy sitting in front of some girl's house, trying to get my shit together before climbing the stairs to her front door.

Because I was "that" guy. The one who'd lost his shit was trying to get it back and was not going to let it get away from him so easily again.

She didn't know that thankfully, and she never would. If Nina ever found out I was wrestling with these kinds of feelings . . . these emotions . . . this inexplicable pull toward her, I knew what would happen.

She would knee my balls into my throat, like she'd already threatened to do no less than a dozen times, and sever our deal. She'd told me she'd never go back on her agreement, but she would if she found out. If she found out I saw something else, something more than a solution to a problem, when I looked at her, she'd be out.

So fast my head would spin. If it wasn't already buried in my ass, which it still was. No thanks to my attempts to pull it out before I went inside her house and spent the next two years sharing the same space as her. Falling asleep every night with her close by. Waking up to the same.

"Fuck it," I growled, shoving the door open and sliding my phone back into my pocket. I could spend the next month sitting in front of her house and not figure it out. Feelings were fine. Attraction was allowed. Acting on any of it was positively not.

I'd already let one woman run a knife across me and gut me—I wouldn't let another. Especially the one I was paying to marry me. Especially the one responsible for me earning something I valued so much.

I didn't want a green card so I didn't have to go. I wanted one so I could stay. In my home. The city where I'd carved out my own life, created my own fate, all on my own.

I'd do anything to hold onto this life—including getting a damn lobotomy if it meant digging out my feelings for this woman. The dangerous ones that might result in jeopardizing everything. The dangerous ones that might manifest in the form of her body tangled around mine . . .

I'd do anything to be rid of these feelings, including making sure she hated me so much that she'd never let herself get close. So it didn't matter how many looks I gave her or words I fed her, all she'd see was a despicable, morally bankrupt person. So she'd never look at me the way I looked at her. Never.

She must have been looking out some window again, because as I started to make my way to the porch, the front door opened.

"Really, Maximilian? A suit on moving day?" She was in a worn-in pair of overalls and a bright blue tank top. Her hair was tied up in a messy bun, and she had smears of paint on her hands and arms. Nina didn't mind getting messy. In fact, it seemed like that was her element.

My smile stayed aimed at the grass as I moved closer. She'd taken to calling me by my full first name in the way a parent might scold a child with their full name—first, middle, and last. She meant it in a scolding way, but damn my soul to hell if I didn't get a rise out of it. The way it rolled off her tongue made me picture her whispering it in my ear while I did things to her body . . .

That were not allowed.

"Were you expecting something else?" I replied, pausing when I got to the edge of the stairs leading up the porch.

"Well . . ." She swept her arms around and did a quick spin. "Welcome. In this instance, mi casa really is tu casa. At least for the next two years and eight-ish months."

She was counting down the days until she was rid of me. That was a good sign.

"And four days," I added, so she thought I was also counting down the days. Which I was, but for a different reason.

"Aren't you supposed to drive one of those German cars?" She tipped her chin at my car in the driveway. "You know, the ones with that blue and white emblem thingy, the one with an acronym for a name. B . . . W . . . M . . . *something.*"

I kept my smile aimed down. "Yeah, I'm supposed to drive a B*MW* because I'm German. I'm also supposed to wear lederhosen and eat bratwurst for dinner every night."

"What is that thing though?" From her voice, I could tell her nose was crinkled up like it did whenever she was working something out.

"A car."

She sighed. I'd gotten lots of those over the past two months. "Not a very nice-looking one."

I couldn't keep staring at the ground. When I glanced at her, looking down at me from the top stair, I felt that familiar tightness in my chest. The one that felt like my muscles were trying to break through my ribcage to get to my heart. What I had yet to determine was if this came from my body's urge to strangle the life out of my heart or to encase it so as to keep it protected.

"It's a Tesla. It's battery-operated," I said when she went back to examining my car like it didn't belong in her driveway.

"Yeah, well, hopefully you didn't spend much on it."

I shrugged like I hadn't and tried not to let another reason to like her pile up. It didn't work. Another grain of sand dropped into the pile that would grow until I had an entire beach of reasons why I liked Nina Burton. I shouldn't have more reasons than I could keep in the palm of my hand. Not so many that I couldn't control them.

"You've never heard of a Tesla?" I asked.

Her eyes darted down to me, narrowing a little. "No. But I have heard of a BWM."

I rested my foot on the first step and kept smiling at her. "Well, that's a start."

Most girls looked at my car and saw dollar signs. Nina looked at it and saw an eye-sore. I looked at it as a mode of transportation and an environmentally friendly one . . . that might have been insanely fast. I'd just purchased it in hopes Nina might eventually let me give her my other car so I could stop worrying about her taking the bus.

"Well? Do you want the tour first or should we get you unpacked first?" She backed up as I climbed the stairs.

When I reached the top, finding her standing in front of me with the front door open behind her, I knew there was no going back. Nina and I were living together from today on.

That knowledge shouldn't have made my blood rush the way it did.

"The tour," I answered.

She nodded and spun around, moving through the door. "Then follow me."

This wasn't the first time I'd seen her house, but I'd only seen the outside when I dropped her off after one of our dates. Our "dates," I clarified for myself because they weren't real ones, they were illusions. A web we were spinning.

This was the first time I'd ever stepped inside though.

Her home was located in Portland's historical district, which seemed to have become where the wealthy of the city congregated. Nina's house was one of the smaller ones in the neighborhood, but even the smallest, most decrepit home in this area sold for nothing short of half a million.

I wondered what was so special to her about this place. Why she'd be more willing to marry a stranger and sacrifice a few years of her life than leave it. She could sell it no problem and make close to as much as I'd offered her. She could stop working the odd jobs and late hours. She could be free.

But something told me she didn't want to be free of this place—that maybe this was where she felt most free.

The house had belonged to her grandmother before it was passed on to Nina after her death, but that was the extent of my knowledge. Of course there was more to the story, but I wouldn't push her. I guessed Nina would tell me when she was ready. Or she wouldn't and I'd have to leave the mystery behind the house a question mark.

"So this is the living room, the dining room." Nina lifted her arm as she indicated at rooms we passed, but it was clear she wanted this tour over quickly. She was apparently uncomfortable with me being there, no matter how much she'd told me otherwise.

She was uncomfortable around me. I'd done my job of driving her away.

I should have been patting myself on the back. Instead, I wanted to punch myself in the face.

"Here's the kitchen, obviously—oh and by the way, feel free to help yourself to whatever you want." She did a quick spin, her eyes landing on mine for a moment before she spun away. "No need to use separate His and Hers cupboards or anything. Just help yourself to whatever of mine you want."

My molars ground when my mind went there—what I wanted to help myself to of hers.

You've got a brain, Max. Use it for Christ's sakes and stop letting your dick do the thinking for you.

"Thank you. And same for me," I said, following her down the hall. "Just feel free to help yourself to whatever of mine you want too."

I watched her for a sign of the same kinds of feelings that had been firing up and down my body when she said the same words to me. There was nothing. No raised skin. No quickened breathing. No nothing.

She heard what I'd said and thought of food. I heard the same thing from her mouth and thought of fucking.

She had no idea what kind of man she'd let into her life.

"This is the guest bathroom right here, the guest bedroom here, and upstairs . . ." She paused at the bottom of a flight of stairs, staring up them with her brows drawn. "There's just more bedrooms and bathrooms. A dusty attic stuffed with junk above that."

I came around behind her and looked up the stairs. The house was probably a hundred years old or more, but still in good shape. There was wear in places, areas hinting at repair in others, but I could already tell from my one-minute tour that this was a well-loved home.

"And where is your bedroom?" I asked before clearing my throat.

She worked her lower lip with her teeth for a second, her eyes pinging from me to the closed door we'd passed in the hall. She'd just moved toward the closed door, her hand moving for the handle, when we both heard something rolling up her driveway. Nina glanced at me with her eyebrows tied together.

"Move-in time," I said, staring at the sealed-up room as we headed for the front door. Closed. Shut. Off-limits.

It wasn't just her room that needed to stay that way.

"A moving truck?" Nina exclaimed when she shot out onto the porch. "I thought you said you were only bringing a few things over from your apartment."

I came up behind her slowly. She was framed in the doorway perfectly, the light from outside highlighting her in such a way that it almost looked like she was glowing.

"I was. Then I picked up a few new things just in case."

"Just in case of what?" Nina's hands went to her hips as she watched the moving guys climb out of the cab and throw open the back door.

"In case I wanted to barbecue." I came up beside her and tipped my chin at the first item the movers were unloading. "In case I needed my own chair."

They heaved out the next thing, set it on the ground, and disappeared back inside the truck.

I rubbed at the back of my head because I wasn't sure how this next part was going to go over. "In case I needed a pool table."

She spun on me. "A pool table?!"

I slid my hands into my slacks' pockets and watched as the movers carried the first piece of it down the ramp. "Just in case."

"Just in case of what? You wanting to piss me off?"

When the movers climbed the stairs with the top part of the pool table, I grabbed Nina and pulled her aside. I'd meant to grab her arms and pull her back, but instead, my hands found her waist.

My fingers sank into her like her body was almost welcoming me. Nina was soft, not all muscled or bony, and something primal inside me wanted to feel that softness pillow mine while I worked her body . . .

Goddamn it, Max. Two fucking minutes. Give me two minutes where you're not thinking about Nina like that.

"Well, I do that no matter what I do. At least this way, I can play pool while you're yelling at me."

When I didn't let go of her waist right away, she wiggled away from me. "Where do you think you're going to put that thing?"

"I don't know. Where would you like me to put it?"

Her face was a little red from being flustered. "How about up your ass?"

Too late. My head's already taken residence up there. "I don't think it would fit. Sorry."

Her green eyes did that melting thing they liked to do when she was pissed at me. Which was pretty much how we spent half of our time together. "I bet I could make it."

I lifted my hands, conceding that because I had no doubt she could. Something about Nina Burton led a person to believe she could do anything she put her mind to.

"You're not planning on sticking up a bunch of posters of bikini-clad girls, are you? Hanging a few neon beer signs?"

I nodded at the movers as they trudged out of the house. I didn't know where they'd set the pool table top, but unless it was in the back alley, I knew Nina wouldn't like it. I guessed I should have run stuff by her before going crazy.

"Of course not," I answered her. "You don't mind the occasional blow-up doll though, do you? Given my social agenda is taking a hiatus for the next few years, I'm going to need the sweet release only a latex doll named Sheena can provide."

She sighed and shoved my chest as she passed me to head down the stairs. "Please. Latex dolls have been your social agenda your whole life. You're not fooling me, Maximilian Sturm."

I chuckled as she bounced down the stairs, but silently I hoped that wasn't the case. If I wasn't fooling her, I was in trouble. If she really knew what I thought when I looked at her, I was fucked.

It wasn't just her body that lured me in—it was everything that made up the whole of Nina. Her sharp wit. Her inclination to compassion, which was especially pronounced when she thought no one was looking. The way she was so honest about some things and so closed off about others. The way she didn't feel the need to apologize for the person she was, and the way she didn't look at me like I was used to women looking at me—like I was something to defeat. Something to conquer. Something to claim.

I'd gotten so lost in my damn thoughts again that at first, I didn't notice Nina trudging down the ramp, carrying a box that was half her size. I leapt down the stairs in two steps and bounded across the yard in her direction.

"Don't even think about it," she warned before my hands got close to the box. "Go grab your own. I've got this."

"Nina—" This was the box marked books, the heaviest damn box I'd packed.

"Don't think just because my arms are occupied I can't still kick your ass if you lay a finger on this box, you hear me?" She kept striding toward the porch, but her breathing was a little strained. "Besides, I wouldn't want you to get a wrinkle in that pretty suit of yours." With that, she started up the stairs.

I followed her, ready to catch her if she tripped or lost her step, but she made it and disappeared inside the house. My jaw ground together, and I growled in frustration. One minute I wanted her to hate me, the next minute I wanted the opposite. Even when I'd tried just being friends, that never lasted for long.

I thought it was impossible to just be friends with the woman you wanted so much more from.

"You must be Max." A guy around my age was crossing into Nina's yard, his eyes roaming from me to the moving van to the Tesla.

"I must be." My voice came out cooler than I'd intended. That might have had something to do with the way he was looking inside Nina's front door.

"Yeah, I recognize you from the pictures." When my brows knitted together, he added, "You know, the ones Nina's been posting online?"

My fingers curled into my palms. "You're a friend."

The guy threw his thumb over his shoulder at the house next door. "Friend and neighbor."

"Nice to meet you," I said when I more meant the opposite. I held out my hand to shake his when I would have rather ripped his arm off and beat him over the head with it.

Whoa, Max. What the hell?

I wasn't sure where the jealous streak cropped up from, but I needed to get it in check before I put my new neighbor in the hospital.

But I could tell this guy had a thing for Nina. It was the way he'd said her name. The way he kept looking at her front door like he couldn't wait to see her. The way he was doing the same arm-ripping-off musing about me.

He liked her. And I didn't like that he liked her. At all.

"I'm Nathan, by the way. I moved in a few years ago and have tried to keep an eye on Nina and her grandma. Well, just Nina now."

Yeah, I fucking bet you've been keeping an eye on her.

"I work at the hospital. I'm an internist," *Nathan* continued.

I wondered how many rounds we'd have to go before whipping out our dicks and comparing sizes.

I'd win.

"You do something with stocks, right?" he said, shifting when I stood a little straighter, making sure he got good and up close with how I towered above him. "What exactly is it you do?"

I folded my hands into my pockets. "Make money."

His eyes dropped to my watch and his brows rose.

"Lots of it," I added.

I thought he was starting to get it—the back-off-or-I'll-kick-your-ass warning—but he clearly had a thing for Nina I'd have to remedy somehow. It would have been helpful to know about Infatuated Neighbor so I could have worked out a plan for getting him to back off. We didn't need someone extra-observant living right next door.

"So what's all this for?" Nathan tipped his chin at the moving van.

My inner demon grinned. "I'm moving in."

Nathan looked like he'd just choked on something. "Whoa, you guys are moving in together? Didn't you, like, just meet?" His eyes fell back on my car, like money was the missing puzzle piece that would explain everything.

I hated that, in a way, he was right. It made me want to grind all five foot eight of his hipster, internist bravado into the grass beneath my Louboutins.

"We met eight weeks ago," I said.

"And Nina's letting some guy who was a stranger eight weeks and one day ago move in with her?" Nathan slid closer to the front door.

"If you've got something to say, why don't you just say it?" I matched his every step with one of my own.

"I'm *saying*, don't you think things are moving a little fast? Maybe?" he added when my eyes narrowed.

"Well, since I hired the moving company that's presently moving me in, I think you can surmise my answer to that question."

Right then, the movers passed us with the new barbecue.

Nathan was proverbially scratching his head, looking at me, backing away from me. "You don't really seem like Nina's type. Like, at all."

"Yeah? And what's her type?" This guy did not know when to back down. Part of me admired that. The other part wanted to make him back down.

"I don't know." Nathan shrugged. "Just not you."

There was no unkindness in his voice. He wasn't trying to piss me off, but to state a fact. I already knew I wasn't Nina's type though, and him bringing it up like it was obvious to the whole world pissed me off that much more.

Nice, Max. Way to make a good first impression with the neighbor. Way to fly under the radar. Why don't you just lose your shit on the neighborly doctor, so everyone watches your every move from now on?

"Well, that's what happens when you fall in love." Nina's voice rolled down toward us from where the top of the stairs. She was looking down at me like I was a child. Which, okay, she had a point—this time.

Before Nathan looked up, she wiped the look off and bounced down the stairs. Her face lit up as she beamed at me. It was an act—mine wasn't. When she came up beside me, her arm went around my back and she lifted up on her toes to kiss my cheek.

My heart fired to life from a simple, fake kiss on the cheek. Damn. I needed to dig this woman out from where she'd taken residence beneath my skin before things got even more complicated.

"You met our neighbor, honey?"

Wow. Pulling out the terms of endearment too? If Nina was touching and kissing and cooing at me, that must have been because Nathan really did have it as bad for her as I'd guessed.

"We met," Nathan and I answered in a clipped tone.

"Nathan was just telling me why I wasn't your type." I returned her smile, sliding my arm around her and letting my hand form around her waist. It was the first time we'd touched like this, and my body was stirring in ways it shouldn't have been. "Liebling."

Her brows came together for one moment before she ironed them out. "Well, I'm glad you've met, but if you boys will excuse me, I've got a moving truck to unload." Her arm fell away and she stepped out of mine. Something seized in my chest when she left.

Nathan was watching her like I was, and technically he shouldn't have been looking at her like that with us "being in love" and me moving in. Given our real situation though,

I guessed he had as much right to admire her as the next guy did.

Telling myself that didn't dim my desire to kick his ass into the next neighborhood though.

"That's why I hired a moving company," I called after Nina. "To help move me in."

"Exactly"—Nina spun around, continuing to back away—"to *help*. Not do it all on their own."

Shaking my head at her with that smile still in place, I slid out of my jacket and hung it over the handrail. I started rolling up my sleeves as I followed her.

"Thank you for looking after her, Nathan," I said, leaving him standing at the bottom of her stairs with his dick in his hands. "But that's my job now."

TEN

Nina

*e*ight weeks and one day down. Two years and eight and a half months to go. Which meant I hadn't even made it to the five-percent-done mark.

That was what I'd spent half the night thinking about. These first eight weeks had been complicated in ways I hadn't expected—and that was before Max moved in. Moving in together always added complications, even if it was just in keeping to some carefully crafted plan.

How could I make it through another two-plus years if the past eight weeks were any indication of what was to come? I didn't have any answers to that question, but I had to conjure up some—fast. I'd made Max a promise and knew he was counting on me. I wouldn't back out on him, especially because I was having a difficult time working out my feelings when it came to him.

There were moments I wanted to kick his feet out from beneath him and spill him over the side of that pillar he stood on. There were moments I wanted to share everything about myself over a cup of coffee and a game of checkers. Those weren't the moments that were messing with me though.

The moments that were screwing with me were the ones when he looked at me a certain way, like he was inviting me closer. Those looks that seemed to have a direct connection to my body and seemed capable of forcing it closer.

He didn't feel anything for me—he'd made that astoundingly clear—but that didn't do anything to dull the occasional times I did feel something for him. What exactly it was, I didn't know. I couldn't put a name to it.

It wasn't infatuation. Not obsession. It wasn't lust either.

It was something that ran deeper. Something that dug in and got comfortable, only reminding me of its presence at the most inconvenient of times.

Like right now, lying in my bed at five in the morning when I should have been asleep. I guessed I'd been lucky to catch the four hours I had with all the tossing and turning and thinking I'd done all night.

After we moved him in and unpacked most of his stuff, we were both too tired to do much more than crash onto the closest soft surface. I'd fallen onto the couch—Max had fallen into Grandma's old recliner—so when I woke up in my bed a couple of hours later, that might have been why I spent most of the rest of the night awake.

I hadn't gotten in here on my own. I hadn't tucked the covers around me and pulled off my sneakers. I hadn't turned off the lights and closed the door.

Thankfully my clothes were still in place because I didn't know what I would have done if I woke up to realize Max had stripped me before putting me to bed. That was just as likely to earn him a punch as it was a different form of passion.

I assured myself that these things I was feeling were normal. Any warm-blooded woman would war with the things I was when it came to a guy like Max. He was attractive . . . intelligent . . . funny even at times. He was pretty much female catnip in a six-foot-three bundle of ego and muscle. Anyone would feel some degree of attraction to him some of the time and given our situation of pretending to be a couple, that made everything that much more complicated.

The guy I was getting paid to pretend to like was the one I shouldn't like at all. He was the first one I ever had liked though.

My life had become one giant cluster of confusion.

Rolling over in bed, I checked the time. I groaned and beat my pillow with my fist. It still wasn't quite five, and if Max was still passed out in the living room, I didn't want to wake him up by going through my morning routine of making coffee and scrambled eggs.

My overalls were in a heap on the floor from where I'd thrown them after sliding out of them around midnight, but Max had neatly positioned my sneakers up against the wall. The laces were even tucked into the foot openings. He was a details person, someone who seemed to take great care in everything he did . . . including putting away the shoes of the woman he was paying to marry him.

Just as I was burying my head deep into my pillow, trying to silence my thoughts about one German sleeping a couple of rooms away, I heard a crash. Some shouts followed right after.

After scrambling out of bed, I sprinted across my room, threw open the bedroom door, and lunged down the hall.

This was a sturdy old house. It didn't shake like I'd just heard it. Not unless there was a big thunderstorm passing overhead or . . .

Two grown men had crashed to the floor.

"What the hell, Max?" I rushed up to the scene of the crime, trying to figure out why Nathan was spread out on the hardwood beneath Max, who was pinning him to the floor, his hand at Nathan's throat.

Max lifted his arms in the air a second later, but he kept himself braced over Nathan so he couldn't move. "I caught him sneaking in."

"Sneaking in? Are you for real?" Nathan looked like a child in comparison to Max. "I used the key."

"What key?" Max snapped.

"The one your girlfriend gave me."

Something in Nathan's tone when he said the girlfriend part pissed Max off. Actually, it kind of pissed me off too. Kind of sounded like he was challenging the title.

Max's head whipped back at me, looking for a confirmation. Before I could answer, his gaze swept down me from neck to toes. The look on his face made my stomach bottom out. His return journey was slower, and when his eyes met mine, there was something dark in them that made me wish I'd taken ten seconds to throw those overalls back on.

"Mind letting me up? I think your dominance has been sufficiently asserted." Nathan glared at Max, trying to wiggle free, but it was a feeble effort. Max had half a foot, fifty pounds, and adrenaline on his side.

"Is that true? He has a key?" Max ignored Nathan, only focused on me.

I nodded. "Yeah, he's got a key."

Max's jaw ground, his eyes flashing with something. His silent disapproval was louder than anything he could have yelled at me.

"Don't worry. I won't use it again, Nina." Nathan lifted himself up, watching Max carefully. "I can see someone feels threatened by my presence."

"I think we both know who's threatened by whose presence," Max fired back.

I shook my head, forgetting I was in a tank and boy shorts, and moved between the two before they took it to the ground again. "Nathan, I'm sorry. I'm sure you just startled Max. He probably thought you were an intruder or something." When I looked at Max to confirm the assumption, he huffed. "I should have told him I'd given you a key. Are you all right?" I smiled at Nathan, giving his arm a light squeeze.

Max shifted closer, practically riding my damn back.

Nathan shot a glare over my shoulder, but his face softened when it returned to me. "It's okay. I should have thought twice before dropping off your breakfast with your new houseguest." Another glare aimed over my shoulder, but this time when Nathan's gaze returned, it roamed the area south of my neck for a couple of moments.

I crossed my arms and stepped back. And this was why those wonderful things known as bras should always be worn by women with obnoxious chests like mine.

Max angled in front of me, squaring himself in front of Nathan. "Now that everything's all cleared up, it's probably time you leave."

Nathan was quiet for a second, then he moved toward the door. He paused when he came to a white paper sack.

"Sorry, Nina. I think your bagel got a little smashed this morning."

When Nathan held it out, Max snatched it out of his hand. "Nina doesn't like bagels."

I sighed behind The Great Wall of Max. I was surprised he'd noticed that I hadn't eaten the bagel last weekend when I'd ordered a breakfast sandwich on one of our dates.

"Since when?" Nathan paused at the door.

I came around behind Max. When he slid back in front of me, I pinched the back of his arm and twisted. Max didn't even flinch.

"Since a little while now?" Why I answered Nathan in the form of a question, I didn't know, but the truth was, I'd never really liked bagels. Nathan had started swinging them by almost every morning after my grandma died, and I didn't have the heart to tell him that most days, those bagels wound up being crumbled into the backyard for the squirrels.

"Bye, Nina." Nathan waved, turning to leave.

I waved back.

Max stuck out his hand. "The key."

I gave his arm another hard pinch. Nothing. It was like the guy didn't have nerve endings or something.

Nathan's gaze shifted from Max to me, but when I stayed quiet, Nathan pulled it out of his pocket with a sigh. "Good luck, Nina," he said, dropping the key into Max's hand. "I'm right next door if you need anything."

After that, Nathan skirted through the front door quickly, like he was afraid Max was going to tackle him again.

Max had barely slammed the door shut and slid the lock over before spinning on me. "What the fuck, Nina?

My blood rolled to an instant boil. "What the fuck, Max?" I flung back at him, waving at the floor. "What were you thinking going Hulk all over our next-door neighbor?"

His forehead creased. "I was thinking someone was breaking in and it was my job to keep you safe. That's 'what the fuck' I was thinking." His voice was so loud, the china rose plates hanging on the wall rattled.

"It was Nathan." I managed to keep my volume under control, but my voice was shaking from emotion.

"It was someone I wasn't expecting sneaking into the house while we were both asleep. I don't care who it is or their reason for being here. I will act first and think later when it comes to protecting what's mine." Max's hand curled around the key, stuffing it deep in his pocket.

"Wouldn't want something to happen to your precious investment, would you?" I hadn't really meant to say that, but with the way he'd just said what he had, looking at me as he'd been . . . it made me feel something I shouldn't. I needed to remind myself I was an investment to him, nothing more.

Whatever Max wanted to say back, he swallowed. Backing away from me a few steps, he looked away like he couldn't stand the sight of me. "What are you even thinking giving some random guy the key to your house he can use at any time he wants? Including when you're running around in your damn underwear?"

My groan filled the living room. He'd been living under my roof for twelve hours and was already acting like he owned the place and was about to draw up a whole set of rules and guidelines.

"Nathan's not 'some guy.' He's my neighbor. A nice one. Or at least he used to be nice before my 'boyfriend' pummeled him to the ground and left a damn indent of his body in the floorboards." My toes tapped the scene of the crime. There wasn't really a Nathan-sized impression, but not for lack of trying.

"Please, that guy's got it so bad for you, he probably had to take a detour to beat off in the bushes since he couldn't make it back to his house first." Max's head whipped toward the door, glaring at it almost like he was daring it to open again.

"Oh my god. Gross. You are so out of line and so, so wrong."

Max grunted. "I know the way a man looks at a woman when he wants to fuck her."

His unabashed word choice kind of hit me like a slap. "Oh yeah? Is that because you have a lot of experience with that look? Giving it to every woman you come in contact with?" Why was I yelling? Why was I even arguing this stupid point with him?

What was happening to me?

"Listen, can we just stop arguing about this already? Nathan does not like me in that way, no how, no way."

"Just because you want to deny it doesn't mean he won't be jacking off again tonight when he watches you through your bedroom window."

Letting out a long groan of frustration, I powered over to the corner of the room where a little trampoline I just couldn't seem to get rid of, old as it was and unused as it went now, was. Grandma used to bounce for five minutes every day when she'd been healthier. She'd read years ago that it was one of the best forms of exercise a person could get, and she'd stayed committed.

Throwing it on the ground from where it had been lean-ing into the wall, I stepped up on it. Max had followed me, but once he saw me step up on the trampoline, he froze.

His arms crossed and his jaw set. "What are you do-ing?"

"Proving my point," I said as I started bouncing. The coils whined with each bounce. "I could be doing this, na-ked, two feet in front of him, and Nathan wouldn't notice." I had to pause to take a breath because I was already getting a little breathless from the bouncing. "Chill out."

Max turned so he wasn't looking at me straight on. Something about his posture seemed wrong, like he was holding himself back. "Thank you, but I won't chill out," he said tightly. "And would you stop bouncing over there al-ready? You've made your point."

I kept bouncing. *Squeak. Whine. Squeak.* My boobs were kind of hurting from all the up and down, but no way was I going to stop when he was ordering me to.

"He saw me on the couch, Nina. There's no way he couldn't have. How does that look? My first night in my girlfriend's house and I'm sleeping on the couch?"

I moved into a side bounce to lessen the impact that was practically making my boobs fly into my face with eve-ry jump. "If he knew you, he wouldn't think twice about you sleeping on the couch. First night here or not."

He was still in his dress shirt and slacks from yester-day, but he was barefoot and wrinkled. His hair was messy from sleep and his voice still raspy from it. It was the most disheveled I'd seen him and, combined with the way he was acting so oddly, I found it kind of a relief. To know he was human. That he wasn't always the pristine suit and com-manding aura he exuded all of the time. Maybe he didn't have every answer to every question and, at times, life threw him a curve just like the rest of us.

"Would you stop with the fucking bouncing already?!" Max paced in front of me, his eyes flickering my way every few steps.

My glare fired into position and I only bounced harder. My heels were almost hitting the floor now. "Yeah, I'll stop bouncing. When I'm damn good and ready to be done." *Squeak, squeak, whine. Squeak, squeak, whine.* "I won't be ordered, commanded, told, or manipulated, Maximilian Sturm. The more you tell me to stop, the longer I'll keep going."

With the next bounce, Max turned into the hall and headed down it. "Do whatever the hell you want. I don't care."

ELEVEN

Nina

We'd been living together for one day and had already managed to get into three small disagreements, one big argument, ostracize a neighbor, and Max had gotten a glimpse of me in my underwear. If that was any indication of what was to come, I needed drugs. An entire pharmacy's worth of them.

Kate wanted to come over and give Max hell for what had happened this morning. It was nice knowing that even though he'd earned the coveted highest screwability rating in the Kate Dixon book of men, she still had my back. After calming her down, I told her I could handle Max on my own and no, I didn't need her to have her friend "tune him up a little with a baseball bat." Whatever that meant. I might have appeased her by promising to pour a splash of Imodium in his coffee in the morning, which I had no plans of actually following through on because I'd finished middle school years ago and never wanted to revisit that time period.

He'd been out of line with the yelling, ordering, tackling thing, but I wasn't innocent on all counts either. I should have mentioned Nathan's key. I should have remembered how he liked to drop a bagel off for me before he left for work in the morning. I should have, knowing Max, realized he would lose it if some guy came through the door unannounced early in the morning while we were both asleep.

So yeah, a whole pile of should have's were stacked in my corner of not-so-blameless.

I'd just agreed to the whole Imodium prank before climbing off the bus, and I was sending Kate a quick good night text when I started up the walkway to my house.

Stuffing my phone in my pocket, I found the driveway empty. Crap. It was almost two in the morning and Max was still working? I knew he worked crazy hours and spent more time in his office than he had at his old apartment, but this went beyond that. He'd left at six-thirty on the dot for his office this morning, which meant he'd put in a cool almost-eighteen-hour day. Or who knew, maybe he was spending the night at his office. He'd told me that he sometimes did that when he'd put in a late night and knew he had an early morning ahead of him.

That would be good. After last night and this morning, we could both use a cool-off period.

As I was pulling out my keys, I heard the screech of tires whipping into the driveway. Spinning around, I found Max's ugly non-German car I couldn't remember the name of screeching to a stop in the driveway, and I could see its driver's face. Fuming would have been underemphasizing his expression.

Shit. I knew what this fight was going to be about. Which was helpful since that gave me the chance to prepare myself.

His door was thrown open, and he was hollering. "Where the hell were you, Nina?" Max slammed the door behind him, powering around the front of the car and across the yard toward me.

I swallowed, a little intimidated by the anger I could feel rolling off of him in waves, but I wasn't going to back away like some creature he could just conquer with an impressive glower.

"If you expect me to answer that, you better rephrase your question." I crossed my arms and stood my ground, letting him get as close and in my face as he wanted.

He came to a sudden stop when we were a couple of body-lengths apart, almost like he'd hit some invisible barrier. "Nina . . ." He blew out a breath, cracking his neck. "Where were you?"

I gave him a look. "At work. Like I told you this morning."

His head shook. "I was just there."

"Let me detail this for you since I can see you're having a tough time with the whole rational thought thing." I lifted my eyes to the night sky. I should have made a wish while I'd been aimed that way. "I went from work, to the bus stop, to the bus, off at the bus stop, to right here." I clicked my heels together.

"I told you I'd pick you up." He threw his arms back toward his car. "It's not safe to ride the bus this late."

The night had been cool earlier, making me think about digging out my winter jacket and gloves for tomorrow, but thanks to Max, I felt like an inferno was burning around us now, blasting us with waves of heat.

"And I told *you* I'd take the bus." My words came out sounding like they'd been dipped in poison. Why he brought out this side of me, I didn't know, but it seemed like every side I had, Max brought to the surface at levels I'd never known existed.

Next door, I heard the screen door slam. If Max heard, he didn't pay it any attention. With Nathan out on his porch now, listening to every word of our heated debate, the front lawn wasn't the place to continue this.

When I turned to head inside, Max's fingers curled around my wrist and he pulled me back to him. "Nina—"

Gaping at his hand on me, holding me in place, I watched my hand curl into a fist. When I tugged away, he let my wrist go, but from the look on his face, he didn't want to.

"I'm still a little tired from our argument this morning, Max." I held my hands up and started for the stairs. "I'm tapping out on this."

"No, you're not. We're talking about this, and we're talking about this now." When I kept climbing the stairs, Max lunged forward, snaking his arm around my stomach and lifting me back down to the ground beside him. "It is not safe for you to be walking around these streets late at night, and it's not safe for you to be riding the bus this late at night, and it's not fucking safe to be working at that dive of a coffee shop this late at night."

This time, he'd let me go as soon as he had me in front of him again, but that had done nothing to mollify me.

"Not safe? I'll show you not safe." I shoved his chest, but he didn't budge. He probably had a hundred pounds on me. The only way I could budge him was if I had a crowbar . . . which right now . . . was not an unappealing notion.

When I shoved him again, he backed up a step. It wasn't thanks to my shove though. It was because he was finally figuring out that he'd just pushed me to a breaking point.

"How do you like that?" I grabbed his wrist, which my small fingers barely curled all the way across, and tugged him with me around the yard. "You like being manhandled like that? You like having someone else control you by force?"

I gave him another spin around the yard. He went, though I knew if he wanted to, he could have snapped out of my hold easily.

When we wound up back at the bottom of the stairs, I gave him one more shove. "Don't you dare put your hands on me again unless I give you permission, you hear me?"

It was clear from Max's face that he'd calmed down. It was also clear that something resembling guilt was starting to affect him. When he wet his lips and rubbed at his forehead like he was searching for the right thing to say, nothing came. I couldn't tell if this was all some act to appease me so he didn't lose his green card prospects or if he really did feel badly.

"Nina?" Nathan called from his porch. "You okay?"

Max's head whipped toward Nathan's house. So much for calming down.

"Yeah, I'm good," I piped up quickly. "Just a lovers' quarrel."

Nathan stood under his porch lights, his gaze shifting between Max and me. "You two seem to have a lot of those."

Max's jaw locked, his fists curling. Just when I thought he was about to make a break for Nathan, he headed up the stairs instead. When Max reached the top, he waited for me.

"What can I say, Nathan?" The way he said it sounded like he'd been thinking asshole instead. "We're real lovers."

With that, Max unlocked the door, opened it, and waited for me to go inside before he followed. The lock turned over into place. I heard his sigh, I felt the apology on his lips, but I just kept moving. Storming down the hall, I fired a glare at the pool table stuffed in the living room after I'd experienced a weak moment and agreed to let it go there. Stupid waste of space.

I rounded into my bedroom and slammed the door. Once inside, I walked circles around the old hardwood, trying not to think about what had happened or why I felt like I was unraveling, one tug at a time.

I'd spun a hundred circles and five minutes hadn't passed, so I decided to work off my nervous energy a different way. Riffling through the big bin of home improvement junk stuffed in the corner of my room, I pulled out the caulking gun and decided two in the morning was the perfect time to get those baseboards caulked, which I'd had on my to-do list for months. The thing about living in a house as old as this one was that there was never an end to the to-do list. Ever.

After changing out of my jeans into a pair of cotton shorts, I tied my hair up into a messy bun and got to work. Even with a caulking gun in my hand and aiming all of my concentration on those baseboards, I couldn't drown out my thoughts of Max. I couldn't even shuffle him to the back of the pile. He wouldn't be shuffled. He wouldn't be set aside. He wouldn't take a backseat.

I'd just finished the first length of baseboard when a soft rap sounded on my door. My chest ached. Not from who I knew was knocking, but because of the way he was. Grandma used to knock like that. A chorus of soft knocks bleeding into one.

"What do you want, Max?"

"We don't have enough time to go over what I want before I have to be at work in the morning."

I ground my jaw. "Then good night."

"I would, however, like to say something to you. If it's okay." What sounded like his forehead thumping into the door sounded next.

"Well, say it. I, unlike others I know, won't try to control what other people do and say." I glared at the line of caulk I'd just drawn. It wasn't very straight.

"Can I open the door and say it? I'd rather say it to your face than this giant mass of wood."

I glanced around my room, making sure I didn't have any underwear hanging out or anything else that would pique Max's attention. All clear.

"Yes," I answered, getting back to my caulking. "Just don't cross the threshold. Or else."

The old doorknob whined as he twisted on it, the door doing the same as he opened it. "Or else what?"

I kept focusing on the baseboards. "Or else. . . stuff will happen."

"What kind of stuff?"

"Stuff, stuff."

"Like the kind of stuff that one guy wanted to do to you the night we first met?"

I bit my cheek. Did he really have to have that good of a memory? "Kind of like that. But the total opposite."

Max chuckled from the doorway, not setting a foot inside. "What are you doing?"

"What does it look like I'm doing?"

"Manual labor."

Sliding down the floor, I kept working. "That's right. It's this thing the rest of the world does on a regular basis. You know, the ones who don't swim in pools of gold coins and wipe our asses with twenties."

When I finally glanced back, I found him looking at me with a contemplative expression, his forehead pinched together, his eyes searching.

"Do you want a hand?"

I shook my head, trying not to give his exposed forearms more than a passing glance. I hardly ever saw him without his suit jacket on or his sleeves rolled up the way they were now, but Max had some serious forearms. The kind that should not be covered up with clothing, no matter how expensive or custom-tailored it was.

"No, thanks," I said when I realized he was still waiting for an answer. "I wouldn't want to give you a callous or something. Ruin those soft hands. You need those for typing on your computer and making trades."

Max smiled, lifting his hands, palms facing me. "I'm good with my hands. I've got references should you need them."

"I'm sure the only reference who'd give your hands a glowing recommendation is the region south of your belt." I turned away when I realized what I'd just said. Why was I bringing up Max's below-the-belt region? Why was I even thinking about it?

"After eight weeks together, they're actually kind of sick of each other." Max's nose crinkled as he inspected his hands. "Might not be the best reference to attest to the skill of my hands."

I'd been just about to draw another line of caulk along the baseboards when his comment totally threw me off. As in, made my body kind of flinch at the same time it made my stomach flutter.

"You made a mess. Sure you don't need my help?" Max stared at the blob of caulk I'd just pumped onto the floor.

"Didn't you come in here to say something?" I set down the caulking gun and got up to grab a wad of paper towels out of the bin.

Max had managed to reach into the room without stepping into it and ripped a wad free and held them out for me. I snatched them from him and went to clean up the caulk mess before I had to add resurfacing the floorboards to the to-do list.

"I'm sorry about all of that. Outside. What I said. What I did." Max's voice carried through the room, but he stayed where he was. "This is all so much harder than I thought it would be. Moving in with you and living together . . . I never imagined this would be so difficult." He watched me clean up the floor with that look on his face again. The brooding one that gave the impression he was being tortured from the inside out. "I had no right to say those things or touch you like that. It won't happen again."

Wiping at the floor, I felt whatever anger I'd had vaporize. Just like that. One heartfelt apology and it was like all was forgiven and forgotten.

"I know. It's harder than I thought it would be too." I stopped swiping at the floor once it was clean, then I glanced at him. It didn't seem like he was blinking with the way he was looking at me. "It's okay. We'll figure it out. This is our first day of living together. It's bound to take some adjustment, especially with our situation being what it is." I paused, almost like I was waiting for him to fill in the details of what our situation was because I felt like I no longer knew how to define it.

"But just in case I wasn't clear outside"—I picked up the caulking gun again and aimed it at his chest—"no more of that grabbing, yelling, chest-pounding stuff, okay? I don't do that shit."

Max took in a breath. "I don't either. Usually," he added with a sheepish grin.

He was smiling at me, and I was smiling back, and I felt the air charging around me. It felt like if I were to put my hand out, I'd be shocked by it.

This man had too much power over me. Too much sway. I couldn't risk letting him get any closer. I couldn't risk letting him take any more of me than I'd already agreed to. I wasn't sure I had much left to give anyway—I'd already sold him three years of my life for a million dollars.

The reminder of our arrangement flamed across my cheek like a slap.

"Good night, Max," I said, twisting around so my back was to him as I leaned over the spot where I'd left off on the baseboard.

I heard the door whine closed behind him. "Good night, Nina."

When I glanced back, I saw he'd left the door open a crack. He'd left it open just enough.

TWELVE

Max

What the hell was wrong with me? What. The hell. Was wrong. With me?

That was what had been playing on repeat in my mind since I'd apologized to Nina and crashed on the couch, trying to get my shit straight. That was an hour ago, and if anything, I'd only managed to get my shit even less straight.

When I heard her door squeak open, I sat up and listened to her pad down the hall. This was one hell of a house, but it wasn't exactly quiet. It made more noises than the ones blasting into my office from the busy streets of downtown Portland below.

"Nina?" I sat up higher when I saw her.

"Are you still awake?"

I guessed that was a rhetorical question since, you know, I was sitting up, looking at her.

"What's up?" I focused on keeping my eyes lifted because she was wearing the same kind of "pajamas" she'd been wearing this morning after that clusterfuck with Nathan. A paper-thin tank top, boy shorts—which were really just underwear that rode a little lower down the hip—and knee-high socks were not pajamas. That was like some sporty-girl role-play outfit.

"We need to do something about the Nathan situation." She held up her new phone, her shoulders falling a little. "He keeps texting me, checking in to make sure I'm okay."

My teeth ground together. That doctor was going to need a doctor if he didn't back off. "So? Just text him back that you're fine and tell him you're going to bed and to leave you alone." That was when I realized what time it was. "And why is he texting you at three a.m. anyway?"

She waved that off like it wasn't important. Like hell it wasn't. "I already did that. It's the last text I'm worried about." She licked her lips, her gaze dropping to her phone. "He basically said he knows something's up and that he wants me to tell him tomorrow. He said he won't leave me alone until I tell him what's really going on between you and me."

A laugh rolled past my lips. Yeah, he'd leave. When I made him.

My hands were quivering at the thought of this asshole next door texting Nina late at night with his accusations and suspicions. I wanted to leap off the couch, pound down his front door, and show him what happened to guys who messed with other guys' girls.

And then I reminded myself Nina wasn't really mine. Not where it counted at least. She might have agreed to the whole thing, but her heart wasn't in it. The most important part of the whole thing was the heart, and if anything, hers was stone where I was concerned.

"What do you want me to do about it?" I asked, guessing she hadn't come here just to inform me.

"Nothing," she said instantly, her eyes drifting to the spot where she'd found me towering over Nathan earlier. "But I think I have an idea for something *we* can do."

It wasn't so much what she said, but the way she looked away when she said it. I was instantly intrigued. "What did you have in mind?"

When she shifted her weight, licking those damn perfect lips again, I felt an issue starting to come up. In that below-the-belt region she had referenced earlier. The way she was dressed—or scantily dressed—the way she seemed unsure—which I didn't think was possible when it came to Nina Burton—the way she kept working her lips to death . . . I'd follow her through the doors of hell if she crooked her finger.

"Follow me. I think it would be easier to show you than try explaining it."

She didn't wait for me to stand before she scurried back down the hall. And I might have taken that opportunity to check out her ass because I was starting to accept that I was already damned where Nina Burton was concerned, so I might as well embrace the journey to hell.

I slid off the couch, adjusted myself so I didn't further embody the pounding chest beast she was already under the impression I was, and headed for her room.

The house was dark and her room was the same. I'd been too busy watching Nina wielding her caulking gun earlier to really check it out, but I took that opportunity now. It was simple, understated . . . without trying to fall into that category. Her bed was propped in the middle of a wall where a couple of windows hung above it. Her bedding was all white, and the rest of the room kept in the same spirit of functionality and shades of ivory.

"Nice room." I paused in the doorway. "Is it okay for me to cross the threshold now? Or should I still be quivering in fear of 'stuff'?"

"You can enter." She checked her phone when it buzzed in her hand again. Fucking hell. That guy was not going to let up. "Though do so at your own risk."

"Consider me warned." I moved inside the big room, and thankfully she was still focused on her phone, typing in whatever was her reply. Because I wasn't just checking her out. I was staring.

The moon was full tonight and glowing through the window she was standing in front of. The silver light seemed to shimmer when it touched her fair skin. It highlighted her curves, shadowing her frame, lighting up her hair so it almost looked like it was burning.

My throat tightened when I made myself stay where I was, not daring to move any closer for fear of how my body would respond to her being so close. I considered myself a strong man, a civilized one most of the time, but she brought every weakness to the surface at the same time she freed the savage within.

She brought out the best in me. She brought out the worst. She brought it all out, and I was her willing victim. Her eager student. Her obedient apprentice.

When she set her phone on the round table beside her bed, she turned around before I could tame my stare.

"So what's this great idea?" I glanced away and meandered deeper into the room, keeping my distance. Hopefully without looking like I was trying to. "Because I've got some very compelling ones when it comes to putting Nathan in his place."

Nina was quiet for a minute. "We make noises." She cleared her throat, her voice higher than normal. "Loud noises."

"Noises?" My forehead creased. "Like you want to get in another fight?"

She worked her tongue into her cheek. Now she was the one unable to look at me. This must have been one crazy-ass idea if Nina couldn't make eye contact.

"No. Like the noises you make *after* a fight." A pause. "When you're making up." Another pause. "Loudly." During this pause, she stepped up onto her bed and started fighting with the windows. "With the windows open."

When she waved her hands at the open windows that were facing Nathan's house, not even ten feet from his front porch, I thought I was starting to get it.

"Oh," I said, still processing.

Then she glanced at her bed before lifting her eyebrows at me.

"*Oh.*" I felt a smirk form as I realized what she was suggesting. Fully understood it. "Ooohh."

"The gloat, rein it in. It's getting messy."

I slid my hands into the pockets of my pajama bottoms to hopefully disguise the hard-on I'd just managed to get back under control before she told me about her solution to the Nathan problem. "I like your idea. I'm so on board with your idea."

She rolled her eyes. "Yeah, I figured you'd be obliging."

"So this idea . . . is it only the noises we'll be making? Not the rest of it?"

Another eye roll, but this one had to be forced. It didn't come quite as naturally as the first one. "Not unless you want to figure out what 'stuff' happens to a guy who fucks with me." A smile plastered into place. "In all ways, fucks with me."

"Figuratively?" I crept closer.

She nodded.

"Metaphorically?" Closer still.

Another nod.

My head tipped up at her when my shins bumped into the side of her bed. "Literally?"

Nina backed up a couple of steps, crossing her arms. "*Especially* that way."

She was close enough I could have pulled her to me. She was close enough I could have laid her down, climbed over her, and felt her body form around mine as I pressed my weight into her. She was close enough . . .

And yet a fucking galaxy away.

"So how do you want to do this?" I gave myself an imaginary sucker punch to get a grip. "I've done a lot, I've seen even more . . . but this is a first."

She blew out a breath as she dropped onto the mattress, her legs curled beneath her. "I don't know. I've kind of been putting this together on the fly." She studied me hovering beside her bed, then she patted the mattress like she wasn't quite sure but was going with it.

I wasn't quite sure about it either, but I took a seat, the mattress springs groaning from my presence.

"I just thought that if Nathan heard that we were a couple, you know, *that* way, he'd leave us alone. Or at least give us a little space."

I nodded through the fog. Being on her bed, feeling her sheets against me, smelling the faint scent of whatever she washed them in, it was messing with my head. Making me feel like I was stuck in some dream I couldn't wake up from. "I think you're right. And it's better than my top idea of hiring a hit man to ensure Nathan 'gives us some space.'"

She looked at her hands spread open, palms up, in her lap. "Okay. So how should we start?"

"The way make-up sex usually starts. Hard and loud."

She wet her lips, and my fingers twitched with the urge to grab her face and pull her to mine so I could feel her lips against mine. So I could wet them with my tongue. So I could taste them.

My eyes squeezed together, clearing the image.

"I can't do this looking at you like this." Nina collapsed back onto the mattress, her head burying into her pillow as she stared at the ceiling.

"Okay. So we'll just scream and grunt and make fucking noises while staring at the ceiling." I laid back into the other pillow beside her. "I could make that work."

There was another minute of silence. Then I looked at her from the corners of my eyes to find . . . she was already looking at me from the corners of her eyes.

We both started to laugh. Which was great and eased the tension. Right up until I noticed the way her chest was moving with her laugh, bouncing because, shit, she wasn't wearing a bra. Because why would she when it tortured me that much more?

"Some time tonight, Maximilian," she said, her laugh rolling to an end.

"It was your suggestion. No way I'm taking lead on this." I was still laughing, concentrating on the ceiling instead of her chest a foot away.

"Why not?"

I lifted my arms. "Because what if I set the tone at hard porn levels when you meant something more along the lines of NC-17? No way I'm running point on this. Your idea. You start."

She rolled onto her side and rested her head on her hand. "The difference between hard porn and NC-17 make-up sex noises being?"

I kept looking at the ceiling. "The fact that you have to ask that tells me you've clearly not been watching porn."

"You have?" She slugged my arm.

I rubbed at the spot she'd just nailed. "I'm European. We're different about that kind of stuff."

"A European willing to pay a million dollars to become a *US* citizen," she mumbled.

"And I was a teenage boy once who spent half of the day with his dick in his hand. I had to give my mind a break. Fresh material, you know?"

Why was I admitting this to her? Why was I telling her about my prolific masturbation habits as a teenager and my familiarity with porn?

Because I was an idiot. That's why.

So much for wanting to dismiss the beast beating its chest and speaking in grunts and snorts theory.

"So?"

Her voice was like a magnet, pulling me closer against my will. I couldn't fight it. I moved closer to her because it was in my nature. Rolling onto my side, I found her eyebrow raised, her breaths a little shallow, her green eyes that liquid hue.

"So?" I said back.

She fought a smile, then she squeezed her eyes closed and opened her mouth. It was sexy as hell watching that pretty mouth of hers fall open . . . and then some noise fell out of it . . .

That was not sexy as hell. At all.

"What in the hell was that?" I asked right as she was opening her mouth to let out something else. Hopefully, this wouldn't sound like a cat was being humped by a grizzly bear.

When her eyes flashed open and caught me fighting a smile, they narrowed. "That was NC-17 make-up sex. In case you never got around to something so 'clean.'"

I choked on the laugh rising. "So you haven't been watching anything sexy. Ever."

"So? Who says a person needs to watch sex on a screen to know what sounds to make when they're pretending to have it?" She slugged my arm again.

"No one. But, FYI, Nina, that is not the way people sound when they're having make-up sex."

She rolled onto her back and punched the mattress. "Give me a break. I've never done this before."

My brows came together. "Make-up sex?" Who hadn't had make-up sex? It was the best kind. It was like the anger was like some damn aphrodisiac.

"*Pretend* make-up sex," she clarified.

"Oh," I said. "Well, this is my first time too. We can pop each other's cherry."

Her eyes squeezed shut again. "Not helping."

She was right. I wasn't, and we were only wasting time.

"Well, pretty sure the pretend kind should sound like the real kind."

She nodded, a shake running down her body like she was psyching herself up. When she opened her mouth again, I never would have believed that horrendous of a noise could have passed through that beautiful of a mouth.

She groaned, glancing at me, already knowing. I managed to keep a straight face and not wonder what kind of pathetic lovers she'd let into her bed that she'd learned those kinds of sounds.

"Here. I've got an idea." Lifting up, I grabbed her hands and pulled her up with me.

"What are you doing?"

I held onto her hands because I couldn't let them go once I had them. Then I started moving. "Bouncing." I jacked my brows a few times as the mattress springs whined in protest.

She smiled like we were doing something obscene, then she started to bounce with me. Just a few little ones at first, and then she was really going. Higher than she'd gone on the trampoline earlier.

And fuck. The trampoline.

Watching her jump on that from half a room back had made my balls ache. I felt like someone had just kicked them into my ribs having her a foot in front of me. Bouncing. Braless. Boobs.

I gave my head a shake and kept my eyes above the neck. As much as I could.

The springs were really singing now, the headboard joining in as it smacked against the wall like someone was

getting seriously drilled. Nina was beaming, leaping into the
air with me and kicking her feet back each time.

God, she was beautiful. Too beautiful. I should have
turned and walked out of the bar that night I first saw her. I
should have known. But I hadn't. And now I'd already fall-
en. There was no going back.

Throwing her head back, she let out a sound that made
the hairs on the back of my neck stand on end. That same
sound made my dick feel about to split.

"Oh god, Max!" She moaned, making that damn hot as
hell sigh-scream again. "Right there!" The last part she paid
special attention to shout out the window. She winked at me,
still bouncing.

"You like that?! You want more of that?!" I hollered
out the window, hoping that Nathan-fuck was getting an
earful.

We both grunted and moaned, bouncing so hard the
headboard sounded close to splitting in half. She was trying
not to laugh, and I was trying not to throw her down on the
mattress and fuck her until I had her making the exact same
sounds.

"Fuck me, Max! Fuck me hard!"

Fuck me. I stopped bouncing for a moment, totally falling out of character. Watching her, holding her hands, hearing her say that . . . it was a testament to my strength of will
that she wasn't pinned below me.

I got back to bouncing when she gave me a look that
implied *get to it*. "Yeah, baby, I'll fuck you all night long!
I'll fuck the shit out of this tight pussy!"

Her mouth dropped open, and she hissed my name.

"What?" I hissed back.

"You just referred to my . . ." Her eyes dipped to the very spot I was having far too vivid of fantasies about. "As a . . ."

"Pussy? That's what you call it when you're having make-up sex, Liebling."

Her eyes narrowed, but she didn't take her hands out of mine. "Fuck me with your cock, Max! Pound me hard, baby! Give it to me good!" She was screaming out the window so there was no way she could see the look on my face. "Pump me full of your cum with that huge, throbbing cock!"

I tugged on her arms, hissing her name this time.

"What?" she mouthed.

"Too far. Too damn far," I hissed.

When she shrugged like she didn't know what I was talking about, I felt a smile that had been gifted straight from the devil form. "Look who's been watching their fill of hard porn now?"

She rolled her eyes. "Oh, shut up and come already."

Hearing her say it, watching her get back to bouncing, almost really did make me come. In my shorts. Because that wouldn't have been awkward or anything.

"Okay, so when I start to go off, you have to scream harder and louder than I do," I whispered to her as we kept leaping into the air. "If Nathan hears that I can do to you what you're going to lead him to believe based on the way you're screaming, he is going to bow out and bow out hard. No guy named Nathan who wears khakis could ever make a girl make the kind of sounds you're going to make for me."

Nina's eyes were kind of wide and her bouncing was slowing down, so I pulled her up and down with me until the mattress was starting to fold around us each time we bounced back down.

"Ready?" I lowered my head toward the window with her.

"I'm coming, baby! Yes! Yes! YES!!!!" Nina panted out the window, waving me closer. "Harder! Harder!! HARRRRDER!!!"

I wasn't much of a talker when it came to the orgasm part, so I just grunted and moaned my pretend release.

Our bouncing came to a gradual end, and we were quiet for a moment. Both of us were panting hard from the effort, and I saw beads of sweat forming along Nina's neck and chest. I felt my own trickling down the seam of my back. Damn, for all the effort, we might as well have done it.

Nina stayed close to the open window, lifting her finger to her lips when I opened my mouth. I listened with her. Not even a minute later, we heard his front door slam closed, followed by the screen door right after.

She lifted her hand and gave me a high-five, beaming, before we both crashed down onto her bed. It took us a few minutes before our breathing returned to normal. Then Nina rolled onto her side toward me. I was still hard and fighting a pull I'd never felt before. A desire that ran deeper than I'd ever experienced. I was fighting it every step of the way.

It was a futile fight, but I wouldn't stop. I'd made Nina a promise. She'd made me one and was determined to hold up her end of it. I'd return the favor.

What had happened to me before—who I was now as a result—I wanted to protect her from, because I knew I couldn't give her what she needed. I couldn't love her the way she deserved to be loved. Someone else had stolen that from me years ago, and I'd made sure it never grew back.

"Max?" She didn't wait for my answer. "That was the best fake make-up sex I've ever had."

I wrestled with the smile tugging at my mouth. "Me too."

I wanted to give her a quick kiss on the forehead before leaving, but I couldn't. One touch, innocent as it might have been, wouldn't have been enough. I couldn't let myself do it or else I might as well finish the process of selling my soul.

Some girls I might have been content to just share a touch with, a night with, but not Nina. Never her. One touch, and I'd want it all. Forever.

When I started to crawl out of her bed, her hand found my wrist. "You don't have to go. We just had pretend sex in my bed." Her tired eyes opened on me. A sleepy smile moved into place. "I think it's okay for you to sleep in it now. So long as it's pretend."

I knew I shouldn't. I knew I should go back to the couch and try and fail to fall asleep. I knew I should keep whatever distance I could between us before I ruined everything.

I knew, but I didn't heed my knowledge. Like a river rushing toward a waterfall, I couldn't stop it. I couldn't pull back or slow down or stop. I knew I was going to fall. Hard.

When I slid back into bed beside her, she lifted the blankets for me to slip under. She didn't say anything else. She didn't move closer or farther away. She just drifted off to sleep, her hand still around my hand like she was as incapable of letting me go as I was her.

I stayed up the rest of the night, watching her. She never let me go. Once, when I tried to pull away, her grip tightened. Even in her sleep, she wouldn't let me go.

And that was when I started to wonder if maybe it would be okay if I fell in love with Nina Burton. So long as it was pretend.

THIRTEEN

Nina

Starving. That was what I woke up feeling like. I would have thought I had been up half the night having voracious sex—the real kind, not the pretend.

Max wasn't in my bed when I crawled out of it, but that was probably for the best. Too much temptation to roll over and stare at him while he slept, which was creepy. Too much temptation to touch him, which was also creepy.

I could still smell him on my sheets though, and before I crawled out of bed, I burrowed my face in the pillow he'd slept on last night and breathed in that scent. Which was also creepy.

After grabbing a big hoodie from my dresser, I threw it on and moved out of my room. The windows were closed now—Max must have done that sometime last night—but too much cool fall air had seeped in while they were open.

Last night had been unexpected, fitting most of the theme of Max's and my relationship. It had been fun as well, getting to see that lighter side of him that seemed to get suffocated whenever he slid into a suit.

It had been crazy sexy too. Having him in my bed, making those sounds, saying those things while he held my hands. There had been a few moments when I thought I saw something in his eyes—desire, maybe—but it passed with the next blink. I guessed that would have been normal for any two people doing what we had last night, no matter the extent of their relationship.

I moved lightly down the hall, trying to keep the house from waking up in case Max had come out and crashed on the couch. We'd only fallen asleep a couple of hours ago, but we both had places to be this morning.

When I rounded into the kitchen, I probably shouldn't have been surprised to find him sitting at the little round table, working on his laptop, phone resting beside it, newspaper on the other side. His suit this morning was a lighter blue, and his expression was drawn back up into those serious lines he wore the majority of the time.

"You're up early," I greeted with a wave.

His gaze lifted from his laptop to me for half a second. "Not the only one."

"My grandma was an early riser. Can't seem to break the habit." I checked the clock on the stove. It was a few minutes past five, which was just all kinds of awful since neither of us had fallen asleep until three-ish.

"Yeah, the New York Stock Exchange is an early riser too." Max's eyes flickered on me again, a smile working into position.

"Coffee?"

He nodded. "Love some."

I grabbed the coffeepot and filled it with water all the way to the top. Usually I only made half a pot, but now there were two of us in the house. Two of us who'd gotten a nap last night.

"Working from home today?" I glanced at his screen. It looked like he had multiple screens open and was working on them all simultaneously.

"At least until I make sure Nathan doesn't come knocking on your door again this morning." His fingers flew across the keyboard. "I don't want him upsetting you. He needs to learn the new boundaries now that I'm here. What he can say and can't say. Who he can covet and who he can't." He glanced back at me, his brow raised. "You being on that list of can't covet now."

As I twisted the coffee canister open, I gave him the raised eyebrow look right back. "You're kind of possessive, you know that?"

His attention was back on his laptop again, but his head shook. "Not possessive. Protective."

I made a face. "There's a difference?"

Max's phone chimed, but he ignored it. "Possessive's for my benefit. Protective's for *yours.*"

"Oh," I said brilliantly, scooping grinds into a filter. That kind of made sense, but I wasn't giving him a verbal confirmation because whatever Max was—protective or possessive—it trended toward the overbearing end of the spectrum. "So? How's work going?"

I rolled my eyes at my question. I sounded clueless. Which I kind of was. The stock market and currency trading and all of that made a whole lot of no sense to me, but it seemed second nature to Max. Obviously. The expensive suits and million dollars to pay a woman to marry him hadn't cropped up out of nowhere.

"Good. And bad," he said. "That's the tone of every work day."

"What are you planning on doing with all of that money you're squeezing out of those stocks and . . . other things?" I flipped the coffeemaker button over.

"Fill a pool with gold coins, of course." He tipped his head back a little.

"I knew it," I teased back, pulling a couple of mugs from the cabinet.

"No, my plan is to make what I need to in the markets, so I have enough assets to get into commercial development." Max leaned closer to his screen.

"Commercial development?"

"I want to build skyscrapers."

I sighed. "Of course you do."

He shrugged and kept typing.

"How much longer before you'll be able to start building these skyscrapers?" I wandered to the fridge and pulled the door open.

"If everything continues going according to plan, a couple more years."

If everything went according to plan, he'd be getting another wish in a couple of years too. "That's why you want your green card so badly, isn't it? So you can stay and build skyscrapers?" I doubted investors and zoning committees would look favorably on a man who was in the country illegally.

"No, I want my green card because this is my home."

I pulled some eggs and creamer out of the fridge then slammed it closed with my hip. "Your home you want to build skyscrapers in."

"Precisely." Max had a pen in his mouth, which made his accent more pronounced for some reason.

"With those kinds of big plans, it's a good thing you found yourself such a great girl to marry under false pretenses."

Max chuckled, the pen still clutched between his teeth. "I thank my lucky stars."

"One who gives you wild pretend make-up sex." I smiled at the frying pan I was melting a pat of butter in.

"She *is* a freak of nature in the sack. Says the filthiest things. Drives me wild." He'd stopped chewing on his pen and was looking back at me at the stove

"I hope you're paying her a lot. Like, a lot a lot."

"Oh, I am. Plus, I give her mind-blowing pretend orgasms." Max's wicked smile slid into place, but I kept my attention on spreading that pat of butter around.

He had no idea how close I'd come to a not-so-pretend orgasm last night. He was never going to get an idea either.

"Do you ever think one day, after all of this, you'll marry again? For real love?" Max twisted in his chair, so he was more facing me than his laptop.

I shook my head and pulled a couple of pieces of bread from the bag on the counter. "Nope. No way in hell." I shook my head again. "I'll never marry for love."

Max's head tipped as he continued to study me. "Why not?"

"Because it doesn't work." I found my grandma's old biscuit cutter in the drawer and cut a couple of circles out of the center of the bread. "Marriage and commitment don't work together. Marriage and love don't go together. I've seen it again and again. It's a sham."

Max watched me for another minute before getting back to his computer. I focused on the sound of the coffee percolating to calm me down after that topic.

"Have you never been with someone you've thought that yeah, maybe?"

When the first piece of bread dropped into the pan, the butter sizzled and spit around it. "Not once." I threw the second one down beside it. "I've never let anyone get close enough."

The only sound for a minute was the butter sizzling and Max typing.

"So you're against marriage because you've never let anyone in, and I'm against it because I've let too many people in."

I cracked the first egg into the hole of one piece of bread. "I guess so," I said, cracking the second egg into the other piece. "How many people have you let get too close?"

When Max didn't answer at first, I glanced over. His back was tense, his shoulders stiff.

"From my experience," he said slowly, "one's too many."

I kept watching him, spatula in hand, wanting to ask so much more. I'd read about there being one woman in Max's past. One he'd been in love with. One he'd almost married. He hadn't gone into much detail other than to write that it had ended. Some of me wanted to know everything about her and what had happened—most of me didn't want to know anything more than I already did.

"So it was just you and your grandma in this house when you were growing up?" he asked as I flipped the bread-and-egg combo.

"Pretty much, yeah." I went along with his agenda to change the topic. God knew if I've had my heart drawn and quartered by someone who'd turned me off to the whole idea of marriage, I wouldn't want to talk about it either.

That was why I'd never let anyone get close enough to do that.

"My mom came and went until I was seven. Then she just . . . went." I swallowed, forbidding myself to feel anything for that woman. I'd felt enough for her as a child without getting anything in return.

"What happened to her?" Max's fingers stilled over his keyboard.

"Don't know. Don't care." I checked the underside of the bread. Still needed another minute. "She followed Loser Number Thirteen out that front door seventeen years ago, and that's the last I saw or heard of her." I inhaled when I felt my throat tighten from remembering the wave she'd given me before rushing out the door. I'd known it was a good-bye wave—I just hadn't known it was a good-bye forever wave. "Her lucky number thirteen."

"You never heard from her again?" Max asked.

"Oh, you know, the occasional postcard from Reno here, collect phone call from Tampa there. After a few years, even those stopped coming." I pulled a couple of plates from the cupboard. "We were better off without her. Better off without all of the guys coming and going, seeing the things they'd done to her face the next morning at the breakfast table. Seeing the things she'd done to herself from the bruises and damaged veins." I slid the first piece of bread onto a plate. "We were better off without her. She was better off without us too."

When Max's phone chimed, he silenced it. "You never knew your dad?"

"Nope. They were good and divorced, and he'd good and bailed before my third birthday. Not much to remember." Setting a couple of forks on the plates, I carried them to the table.

"And your grandpa left your grandma after your mom was born, right?" When I slid his plate next to his spot, he added, "Thank you."

"Yeah, I never met him, and Grandma never said much." I headed for the coffee because I needed some caffeine in me to have this kind of conversation. "But look at what she did all on her own. This house. She worked, supported herself in an era that was not particular fond of or used to women in the workplace. She raised my mom and me. She was better off without him, my mom would have been better off without all of the hims, and I'll be better off without any him."

Max had twisted around in his chair and was watching me. The skin between his brows was drawn in a hard line, his eyes clouded. "I'm sorry, Nina. I don't understand how anyone could do that to you."

My weight shifted. "Human nature. Commitment isn't part of it." I poured some creamer into my cup and left Max's black.

"But what about your grandma? Seems like she knew a little something about commitment." He peaked his brows at me as I carried our coffees to the table.

"My grandma was special. One in a million."

"And no one else could be special in your life? No one else could be that one in a million?" He scooted his paper and laptop over when I slid into the seat beside him, setting our coffees down.

"Everyone's left me, Max. Even Grandma now." I chewed on the inside of my cheek for a second, wondering why I was even telling him all of this. He wasn't my best friend or my closest confidant. He was some guy paying me to marry him. So why did I feel like I could tell him anything? Like I could tell him everything and he wouldn't blink an eye? "I'd be a fool to expect anything different from a relationship. I'd be setting myself up for failure."

He took a drink of his coffee, watching me over the side of the cup. He drained half of it in one long drink. "If you look at the odds, sure. Statistically speaking, you're right. But haven't you ever heard that love defies the odds?"

My head shook as I huffed. "Yeah, I think I have heard that. In those fairy tale book things."

Max laughed and cut into his breakfast with the side of his fork. He stabbed a chunk and stuffed it into his mouth, somehow managing to not get runny yolk all over his suit. He kind of moaned as he chewed. "What is this?"

"Eggy in a basket." I tried not to stare when he shoved another big bite into his mouth. In his suit, with his laptop flashing with the markets changing, he looked so dignified. At least until he started to eat.

"It's . . . it's . . ." He searched for the right word, continuing to chew.

"Good?" I suggested.

Max shook his head and finished chewing. "It's the breakfast equivalent of what we did last night. That's what it is."

Thinking about last night made my legs squeeze together. I was just taking a sip of my coffee when we heard the sound of a garage door opening. Max leapt out of his chair and powered toward the window by the door.

"Mission fucking accomplished," he crowed from the door as I came up behind him.

I caught a glimpse of Nathan's hybrid whipping out of the driveway. He usually drove slow and defensively, like he was expecting some kid to come cruising past his driveway on a bike at any second. This morning, he was driving like he was in training for NASCAR.

"I didn't know Priuses had so much get up and go." Max whistled as Nathan's wheels screeched as he accelerated down the road.

"Think he heard anything last night?" I teased, nudging Max.

"Liebling, that is the way a man drives when he realizes all of that sexual frustration that's been building up is getting worked out in his hand instead of the hot neighbor." Max fired a wink at me.

"Well, one problem solved. We've probably only got a thousand more to make it through before this is all said and done, right?"

Max's smile started to drift away. "Probably."

Exhaling, I walked back to the table. I had six dogs to walk at seven. "Something to look forward to."

"Nina?" His voice stopped me. When I turned around, I found him facing me, his forehead lined. "Is there anything I can do for you?"

My lungs strained from the way he was looking at me. My heart ached from his question. There was sincerity in his tone, concern in his expression. How could someone who'd sought me out for the purpose of using me be so convincing? How could he make me feel like I was special to him when really, I was only a means to an end?

I knew better though. I'd learned from experience. It didn't matter what he said. It didn't matter how he looked at me. Eventually, he'd leave just like the rest of them.

"Yeah," I answered, walking away. "You can keep your promise to not fall in love with me."

FOURTEEN

Nina

Max was home. Or Max was *here.*

Him moving in was still weird, and thinking of him and home in the same thought was a stretch.

As I clomped up the porch steps, I noticed the front door was open slightly. Then Max's head popped into view. His eyes softened when he saw me, then he pulled the door open.

"What are you doing?" I asked as I appraised the scene just inside the door. There was a toolbox and Max was in . . . *jeans.* And a T-shirt. I hadn't thought he owned such pedestrian clothing.

"Romance," he said with a shrug.

I felt my forehead crease.

He motioned at the door. "Fixing your whiney hinges. Romance, right?"

That was when I noticed the can of WD-40 on the porch at his feet. "I can't believe you remembered that."

"Why not?" Max pulled the screwdriver out of the back of his jeans and got back to work.

"'Cause you're a guy. In one ear, out the other." I was staring at him as he worked, pretty much stupefied. "Especially if it's romance related."

"I'm not just any guy though." He lifted his screwdriver for a moment before putting it back to work. "I'm the one who's spending the next couple of years with you. The guy who'd like to stay in your good graces. Besides, look who's talking?" He glanced at the armful I was wrestling with.

"I picked up your dry-cleaning. Looks like it was just in time too." I waved at his jeans, letting my gaze linger maybe a bit longer than I should have. Thanks to Max's suit jackets, his backside was almost always hidden from view. I supposed that was a good thing since I couldn't seem to stop staring at it.

So what? He had a nice butt. And a nice face. And a nice everything else in between. So he was fun to look at.

It wasn't like he . . . waited to take a shower in the morning so I could have the hot water. It wasn't like he . . . had my coffee ready when I emerged from that hot shower. It wasn't like he . . . took time to fix my damn whiney door hinges.

Ugh. My mission of hating Maximilian Sturm was getting harder and harder by the minute.

"How did you know what shop I use?" Max asked as I laid his stack of suits over the back of his chair he'd moved into the living room.

"I noticed one of your receipts sitting out last week." I wouldn't mention I'd "noticed" it in the trash. "Not a big deal. Besides, you've been so busy with work I didn't want you to run out of suits."

Max crouched down to work on the bottom hinge. "I'm always busy with work."

"Yet you're fixing my whiney hinges."

One of his shoulders raised, stretching the fabric of his shirt across his back. "I had a little free time."

"And you picked home improvement to fill it with?"

Max looked back over his shoulder at me. His eyes held mine in such a way I couldn't escape them. "I picked doing something to take care of you to fill it."

My chest ached when he said that. It kept aching as he continued to look at me with that same expression. It wasn't until Max went back to focusing on the door that I was able to think again.

"That's why you went this route, right? Paying for marriage?" I swallowed and leaned into the back of the couch. "You're too busy to invest anything into making a relationship work."

"Yes"—Max nodded—"that's part of the reason."

"And the other part has to do with?"

He stopped working on the hinge. "I don't believe in commitment. In marriage. We've talked about that. It just doesn't work."

Yeah, we had talked about that. Funny that he was the one reminding me of our shared opinion on the topic.

"Yeah, because it's so realistic to expect two people to not only be best friends forever but to also be the only person they could ever imagine having sex with until they die. Talk about a fairy tale," I said, kicking out of my sneakers. "With an unhappy ending."

Max snorted his approval. "Go figure two people who don't believe in marriage are getting married. How's that for irony?"

"I believe in fake marriage," I called back as I headed to the kitchen to grab a water. "Just not the real kind." After rummaging around in the fridge for a bottle of water, I pulled it out, twisted the cap off, and headed back to the front door. "Could maybe another part of your reason for not believing in marriage and commitment have anything to do with a certain someone from your past?"

When I paused behind Max, holding out the bottle of water for him, he didn't move. "It could."

His voice was distant. Almost cold.

"What happened?"

The muscles banding down his neck popped through his skin. "It didn't work."

When he didn't seem to notice the water I was holding out for him, I tapped him on the shoulder with it. "Why didn't it work?"

Max took the water, smiled his thanks, and drained half of it in one drink. "Because you can't make love work when the person on the other end doesn't love you back."

Leaning into the wall beside me, I stared at him. "But you loved her?"

"At the time, yes, I thought so, but we were young and I was stupid." Max's knuckles started to turn white from gripping the screwdriver. "What I learned from that experience wasn't love. It was a lesson in what love was not."

I wasn't used to these flashes of vulnerability from Max. I wasn't sure if what he needed most was a hug or just to not talk about it anymore. I went with something that fell in the middle. "How did you find out that she didn't love you?"

He exhaled sharply. "When a friend back in Germany called to tell me that she'd been being unfaithful. For years.

With multiple partners." Max glared at the shiny brass hinge like he was seeing something reflected on it. "That was the day before I was set to fly back to Germany for good. The day after I'd dropped out of my last year of doctorate classes. The day I was ready to give up everything for a woman who was willing to give nothing in return."

"My god, Max . . ." I exhaled, not sure where to go from here. I'd never guessed he bore this kind of a story—that he wore this deep of a scar. "What did you do?"

He was contemplative for another moment before he got back to work. "I pleaded and begged with my professors to let me back into the classes I'd formally dropped, ripped my one-way ticket in half, and adopted a personal manifesto to never let another woman do that to me again. That I'd never let myself wind up in a position where I'd give up everything for what I thought was love."

Watching Max work, it was hard for me to imagine what kind of woman could do that to him. What type of person could betray him like that. Max had his shortcomings, like the rest of us, but his strengths more than made up for any perceived downside. At that moment, I kind of wanted to kick her cheating German ass, whoever she was.

"Your parents? How long have they been married?" I asked, changing the subject since I could see how it upset him.

"Thirty-five unmagical years." Max's voice was dripping sarcasm.

"That shows commitment, right?" I argued, not sure why I was arguing this. I was as big a skeptic of marriage and commitment as he was.

"No, it shows a high tolerance to pain. They both would be happier apart, but they're too stubborn to admit it." He reached for the WD-40 can and sprayed one of the screw holes. "I love them, but they have their faults."

"Just like the rest of us," I added.

"The rest of us"—Max tipped his head back and forth—"plus a few more. Listen, I appreciate my family, but they drive me insane. Just like I drive them insane. There's a reason I put that big, huge ocean known as the Atlantic between us, you know?"

Yeah, because if moving out of state wasn't far enough, there was always the other side of the globe. But it was clear from Max's posture that was time to move on. Before the vein in his forehead burst or the muscles spanning his back tore through his shirt.

"Hey, I just found out I sold a few photographs. Awesome, right?" I patted the little shoulder purse still wrapped across me. "We'll be eating good tonight."

"Nina." Max sighed, twisting around so he was facing me. "I wish you'd just let me take care of all the household expenses."

My head shook. Adamantly. "No way. This is a Dutch fake union all the way. Thanks though."

He opened his mouth to argue. When my eyebrow peaked, his mouth closed. We were both learning. How far we could push the other. What buttons not to push. What to say and what to leave unsaid.

"Since you've got this door covered, I think I'll get on the back one." I shoved off the wall, snagging an extra screwdriver from the toolbox.

Before I'd made it into the hall, Max called after me. "Nina? How has it been? Me being here? Us?" He was standing again, appraising me in a way I was becoming more and more used to. Like I was both an enigma and familiar. "Easier than you thought it would be? Or harder?"

I only needed a moment to consider my answer. "Both."

Max nodded, seeming to consider that. "Is there anything I can do to make it easier?"

Understanding the undercurrent of his question, I gave him a reassuring smile. "Don't worry, Max. I'm not going anywhere."

His chest fell from his exhale. "Neither am I."

Before continuing down the hall, I waved the screwdriver at the door behind him. "Thanks for the romance."

His reply came a moment later. "Anytime."

FIFTEEN

Max

E ngagement day. I would have thought I was getting engaged for real with how nervous I'd been all morning.

Another month had passed and Nina and I had fallen into a sort of routine, our schedules merging together, our lives melding into one. Living with her, sharing the few stolen moments we rarely had at the same time, having her presence near me, had made it the best month of my life.

If sharing one month with a woman I was paying to marry me constituted the best, that didn't say a lot about the life I'd been living up to now. But Nina wasn't just special to me because of our arrangement—she was special because of who she was.

She was like no woman I'd ever met and no woman I ever would. She was everything I wanted in a partner and everything I couldn't have. She was, at the end of the day, *everything*.

That was why I wanted tonight to be so special. I couldn't admit my feelings went past the bounds of friendship, but that didn't mean I couldn't do something to show her just how much she meant to me. Let her believe it stemmed from friendship, I didn't care. I just had to show her, in my own way, how much I cared for her.

I was just finishing tying my black bow tie in the hall mirror when I heard Nina's bedroom door open.

She thought we were getting dressed up to take pictures to post about our "engagement." She had no idea I'd planned anything else for the rest of the night.

"I was certain dresses like this didn't come in my size, but lo and behold, designers do make clothes that fit people who actually eat."

I never would have guessed that people were serious when they described the feeling of a wrecking ball hitting them. But when she stepped into the hall, that was exactly what I felt. Like something big and powerful had sacked me in the chest. I couldn't breathe. I could barely keep upright.

"What do mean?" My voice sounded like I'd just been smashed by a two-ton ball of metal too. "Dresses like those were made to be worn by woman like you."

She glanced down at herself as she kept moving down the hall, smoothing her hands down the dress. "Not so sure about that, but thanks."

God. She wasn't real. She couldn't be.

"What's the point of curve hugging if you've got no curves to hug?" I tore my eyes away from her when she caught me staring. She'd caught me checking her out enough lately.

"Well, I've got no shortage of those."

"No." My eyes moved back to her. The hell with it. "You don't."

"Thank you for the dress. Even though I kept the tags on and plan on returning it tomorrow."

"I bought it for you. Not for you to return it." My eyes roamed over her. The dress was perfect. The same color of her eyes, it made her skin almost glow, the color of her hair flame, and it made her body look like the sum total of every fantasy every man had ever dared to conceive.

"I'm only going to wear it for five minutes, Max. It cost—"

"I know how much it cost. I bought it for you. As a gift."

When she took a deep breath, her chest lifted, sending even more of it spilling out of the top. My teeth gritted together.

"So enough about me. Look at you." She threw her arms at me. "It's not fair how good you look in a tux, Max. Pretty sure there are laws against it. You know, the ones meant to protect the hearts of young women everywhere."

I slid a step closer, sliding my hand in my pocket when I caught it reaching for her. "I only see one young woman around."

"Yeah, and she had her heart removed years ago, so you don't have to worry about me dropping dead from that smile and penguin suit you're sporting."

A laugh rose up from my chest. I couldn't help it. Nina kept me on my toes in every damn way a woman could. I loved every second of it, as miserable as it made me at times.

"So? Photo-shoot time?" She nodded at my phone sitting on the coffee table and put on a big smile.

"In a hurry?" I backed up to grab my phone, unable to turn my back on her.

"Actually, yeah." She checked the clock hanging on the wall. "Devon called in sick tonight at the coffee shop, so I volunteered to cover for her."

I froze, my fingertips brushing my phone. "What? To-night we're supposed to be getting engaged."

Nina gave me a look. "And look at us . . ." She waved between her and me. "We are! Congratulations. Now let's hurry up and take the picture so all of our family and friends can celebrate with us."

When she checked the clock again, she bit her lip and hustled toward me. Her dress swished and swayed around her legs while I worked to recover from what she'd just said.

When she came up beside me, her face fell. "Oh god, you didn't have anything planned, did you? I thought we were just getting dressed up to document it. I didn't think to ask if you were planning on something else . . ."

I swallowed, shaking my head. "No, no. Nothing like that." Unthawing myself, I grabbed my phone and got it ready to snap a photo. "All we need to do is document it. We just need to look like we did something amazing."

"Oh, well, in that case." Nina slid up beside me, wind-ing her arm around me and burying herself into my chest as she swung her other arm around me. Her hands tied together at my side. "Document the best night of my life."

Working my jaw loose, I wound my arm around her too. My hand curled into her waist and a hole opened up in my chest when I realized that when I touched her like this, I felt everything, while when she touched me like this, she felt nothing.

As I lifted my phone so it was looking down at us, she flinched. "Wait. Should I like have the ring on already? You know, stick my hand out like girls do when they're showing off their engagement ring?"

The little box in the inside pocket of my jacket burned against me. "No, I haven't picked it up yet. So just keep your hand tucked behind me. No one will notice." My voice was wrong. Too cool. Too removed.

Nina didn't miss it. "Max?"

"Let's just take the picture, Nina." I focused on the camera while she kept focusing on me. "Three . . . two . . ."

At the last moment, I forced a smile into submission and Nina glanced away from me long enough to beam at the camera.

When I checked the photo, I was surprised by how convincing we looked. How genuine my smile seemed. How honest her excitement looked. It just proved that the lie was as real as the truth.

The camera wasn't facing us any longer, but Nina's arms tightened around me. She slid in front of me. "What's the matter?"

My arm slid away from her, but my hand still burned with her heat. "Nothing. Everything's fine. Going exactly according to plan."

Nina's brows lifted. "Something's wrong."

Yeah, I know. All I asked from you was your hand in marriage, and now I want the rest.

"I'm just tired. Long nights. Early mornings." I pulled at the bow tie, undoing it. "It's catching up to me."

"That happens when a person goes on three hours of sleep for weeks on end." One of her hands formed around my cheek. It was gentle and comforting and everything I needed right then. "You can't keep doing this to yourself, Max. You're going to kill yourself."

I know.

"I'll get some rest tonight. I promise," I added when she raised a brow like she knew better. "Now why don't you go get changed and I'll drive you to work."

Her fingers curled into my cheek, and when her lips parted as she looked into my eyes, I had to brace my hands on the counter behind me. I couldn't touch her. If I did, she'd know. She'd feel it. She'd feel everything if I touched her.

So I just kept clinging to the edge of the counter like it was all that was keeping me from drowning.

When she dropped her eyes, her hand followed, then she stepped back. She exhaled, shaking her head like she was clearing something from it. "No, that's okay." Her voice sounded different now. "Kate's heading to work a night shift at the hospital, so she's swinging by."

I rolled my head to stretch my neck. "Pick you up after then?"

She backed away, heading down the hall. She took the ground out from under me by walking away just as she had by walking toward me. "Kate's getting off at the same time. I'm good. But thanks." She paused when she made it to her room, smiling at me as she kicked off her heels. "And thank you for the fake proposal. It was everything I always dreamt of."

"You're welcome," I whispered after she'd closed the door.

I stood there for a moment, staring at the empty hall, clinging to the image of her walking toward me. Then I set a match to it. It was nothing more than a mirage. A sleight of hand. It wasn't real. None of it.

As I headed to the guest room I'd moved into across from Nina's room, I fired off a few texts. One canceling the gallery I'd managed to convince to stay open extra late tonight. The same one I'd managed to get some of Nina's photographs displayed in.

The next text canceled the boat I'd reserved to take us down the river while we had dinner.

Once that was done, I marched into the kitchen, threw the fridge door open, and pulled out that damn pie I'd spent half the night making without her finding out. I'd found her grandma's peanut butter pie recipe tucked in the little recipe box above the fridge. There was a note that said it was Nina's favorite.

I kicked open the cupboard door below the sink and tossed the pie in the garbage. Nina didn't want homemade peanut butter pie. She didn't want a sunset dinner on the Willamette. She didn't want the real date that came before the fake engagement. She didn't want *me*.

I was an idiot on a fool's errand who'd signed a contract with my own damn blood.

As soon as I was in my room, I slammed the door shut, locked it, and charged into the adjoining bathroom. I needed to get her out of my head. I needed to stop clinging to this hope that she'd ever want me, because she never would.

I needed to be free of her. Get her out of my system so I could survive the next few years.

After closing the bathroom door, I lowered my zipper and freed myself. My hand moved against me instantly in hard, punishing strokes. If I could just fuck her out of my system, this would be easier. I could be around her without feeling like she was draining me of every last drop of my lifeblood. I could be close to her without feeling like it was breaking off a piece of my heart every time she pulled away.

Bracing my other hand on the sink, I clamped my eyes closed and pictured Nina right in front of me, her ass balanced on the edge of the sink, her dress bunched up around her waist while I drove into her again and again . . . and again.

I pictured the sounds she'd make, the way her face would look, the way she'd feel inside. It didn't take long before I felt on the cusp of my orgasm, but I needed to hold out. A little longer. A little harder. I needed to be free of Nina Burton, and no quick fuck was going to do that.

My body quivered from holding back, right before it flinched when I pictured Nina's nails digging into my back as her body came undone around mine. The image was so vivid, so real, I could feel her pulsing around me as she screamed the same filthy things she'd shouted that night out the open bedroom windows.

"Fuck," I grunted, unable to hold off any longer.

My hand tightened around me, pumping faster as I shot my release into the bathroom sink. It didn't end quickly, it wasn't disappointing—it was the single best orgasm of my life, and I'd had it while jerking off picturing a woman I could never have.

My hand was still braced against the sink while my chest rose and fell. I kept my eyes closed. I had to dig her out. No more of this.

I pictured pulling out of Nina, zipping my pants, whispering a quick thank you in her ear, and turning my back on her and walking away. I pictured the look on her face, the look on mine as I left her behind once I'd gotten what I wanted.

I imagined crawling into my car, speeding back to my apartment, sufficiently fucked for one night, and crawling into my own bed.

My breathing was starting to get back to normal, but that was when I rolled over in my imaginary bed to find I wasn't alone at all. Nina was in my bed, lying on her side and smiling at me like she had that one night. Her hand molded around my cheek like it had earlier. I melted into it, ringing my arm around her waist and pulling her to me.

"No," I growled, shaking my head. I tried erasing the image, but it refused to leave.

Dammit, this was a scene of my own conjuring. I should be able to control it, but I couldn't. Nina had wound her way deep into my subconscious.

SIXTEEN

Nina

"By the way, congrats on your engagement. I'm so thrilled for you guys," Kate said in a flat tone when she pulled into my driveway.

"Your sincerity is staggering." I shot her a look before grabbing my bag from the backseat of her Honda.

"Did he at least get you flowers or something?" She held her phone in front of her, shaking her head at my post about the big engagement, complete with the photo Max and I'd snapped together.

"No flowers." I set my bag in my lap when I twisted back around.

"Man, that guy really is all business, isn't he?" Kate shook her head as she glanced at the house. Max's car was still in the driveway, but it wouldn't be for long. It was just past four in the morning, and lately, he'd been heading into the office earlier than usual.

"I don't know." I wondered if I should tell Kate. She wasn't Max's biggest fan, but she liked him more than she had at the start. "I think he had something nice planned for last night. I could tell he was disappointed when I had to go to work."

Kate turned in her seat, hanging her arm over the steering wheel. "Something like . . .?"

"I don't know. He played it off like he didn't, but he probably had dinner reservations or something." I pictured his face when I'd told him I had to work last night. "I feel bad."

"Why? He's paying you to marry him. That's the beauty of this kind of relationship. You don't have to feel bad for ditching him, and he doesn't have to feel bad for being a total and utter disappointment in the romance category."

My forehead crinkled. Kate was recently single after she'd found her latest boyfriend in bed with someone else. A man someone else. She'd taken to parading the flag of Men Are Pigs, but I knew it wouldn't stay up for long. Only as long as it took a good body and a pair of dimples to smile her way.

"Please, you know what I'm talking about." Kate tsked. "The male species' height of romance includes grunting his approval after crawling off of a woman in bed."

"I don't know . . . Max can be pretty romantic. When he wants to be." I knew better to argue with Kate when she was on one of her man-hating quests. I should have kept my mouth shut.

Kate's mouth fell open. "Please don't say it's true."

"Don't say what's true?"

"That you've become all twitterpatted with your husband-to-be."

Looking away, I reached for the door handle.

Kate hit the lock button. "Please don't say the first man my best friend's gone and fallen for is the same one who's paying her an obscene amount of money to commit a felony because, damn, that's just plain tragic if that's the truth."

"Kate—"

"It's okay. You've caught a case of German Fever. I get it. He's sex in a suit." She locked the doors again when I hit my door's unlock button. "Get him out of your system. Have him make you moan, then move on. Don't, and I repeat, do not, fall in love with him. If you take one relationship piece of advice from me, take that gem."

"There's so many," I said sarcastically. "Why this one?"

Kate's hand formed around my arm as she leaned closer. "Because that man will ruin you if you let him in."

Our eyes locked like she was waiting for me to agree with her. Part of me knew she was right. The other part knew Max would never do anything to hurt me.

Clearing my throat, I winked at her. "Well, thank you for the relationship advice, as always, but I'm afraid it's unnecessary. I have no intention of falling in love with Max. We're friends. I respect him. I find his company enjoyable. That's all."

This time when I unlocked my door, she let me go. "I bet you'd find his company a lot more enjoyable if you let him bang your brains out. That kind of man . . ." She shivered, her gaze tracing back to the house. "You know he's good in bed."

"How do you know that?"

She cocked an eyebrow. "The way he walks. The way he holds himself. He knows what to do with his body. That translates into the bedroom too, you know?" Now she was wiggling her eyebrows. "Let me know if and when you find that out on your own."

"Thanks for the ride, Kate." I sighed, climbing out of her car.

"And for the advice?"

"Not so much for that." I waved as I backed toward the house. "See ya."

She honked her horn as she reversed out of the driveway like she was trying to set some record.

As I climbed the porch, I glanced at Nathan's house. Ever since that night Max and I'd had pretend make-up sex, I hadn't heard a word from him. I guessed the message had been effective.

After unlocking the door and slipping inside, I tried not to make a noise, which was pretty much impossible in a house this old. Hopefully, Max was still asleep and had gone to bed early, as he'd promised. He was wearing himself out, expecting too much of himself, and I didn't want to see him keep driving himself into an early grave.

The thought of my warm bed sounded so good after being awake for close to twenty hours, but my gaze drifted to the spot where I'd seen Max in the hall earlier. In his tuxedo, grinning at me as I paraded down the hall in that ungodly expensive dress that had made breathing a chore.

Damn, that man looked good all dressed up.

I'd gone from hating the guy to liking him to *liking* him. Not that it mattered because I couldn't act on it, but I was aware of it at least. The more aware I was of my feelings for him, the more I could be on the lookout to keep them from manifesting.

Something was on the kitchen table we usually sat at every morning for breakfast. A little square box covered in black velvet and lined with gold metal.

My heart jumped into my throat as I moved toward it. I already knew what it was. I was surprised, with how rigid he was about all of this, he hadn't had it last night, but I supposed even a person like Max Sturm erred every once in a while.

When I opened the tiny box, a folded white note popped out. After unfolding it, I found nothing more than a question mark scratched down.

It made me smile. So Max.

Then I saw the ring.

Wowza. It was huge. I was going to have to turn it around when I worked at the coffee stand. At least if it did get ripped off, Max wouldn't be out a lot. I'd finally managed to convince him to get me one of those cubic zirconia stones instead of the real deal. It had taken a while and a few heated arguments, but I'd gotten my way.

I thought it was crazy that people would spend thousands on a diamond when they could get something that cost a fraction of that and looked the same. This stone was every bit as sparkly and shiny as its diamond counterparts.

I pulled the ring out of the box, wondering if the darn box had cost as much as the ring. Apparently Max adhered to "the bigger, the better" when it came to engagement rings, because yeah, it took up a quarter of my finger when I slipped it on. Other than the size, the ring was simple. Round solitaire, gold band, that was it.

Max had asked a few times what kind of ring I wanted, but I'd never given him any clues. I just told him to surprise me. He had. With the same exact ring I probably would have picked out on my own. Save for the size.

I was still admiring the ring on my finger, letting it catch whatever light it could find and throw prisms across the room, when I heard the door at the end of the hall whine open. So much for him catching up on his sleep.

His footsteps echoed down the hall, the sharp tap of his dress shoes telling he was in a hurry.

"Coffee?" I asked when he came into view, before I lifted my left hand. "Thank you for the ring. It's perfect."

All it took was one look at his face to tell me something was wrong. Really wrong. His jaw was already set before he glanced at my hand. It set a little more when he did though.

"What's the matter?" Setting down the black velvet box, I approached him. As soon as I did, he started backing away, so I stopped. The hollows beneath his eyes were dark, his eyes were bloodshot, and his tie was a little crooked. "Max? What the hell's wrong?"

My heart stalled for a moment while I waited for his answer.

Finally, he moved, glaring at the front door. "My parents. They're coming."

SEVENTEEN

Nina

I was tired, so my head was running at half speed. It was taking a minute to catch up to what Max was saying and why he was acting like this was the end of the world.

"What?" was the first brilliant thing to spill out of my mouth. "When?"

"Tonight." Max's gaze lowered to my hand, where the ring was in place. His forehead creased.

"Why the sudden rush?" I asked, catching up to why he was stressed.

"Apparently the news about our engagement spread quickly. They're concerned." His hand curled tighter around the briefcase he was holding. "And they might be under the impression I'm not exactly marrying you for love."

My mouth fell open. "Shit."

"Exactly."

I didn't know a lot about Max's parents, other than what I'd read in his biography. He didn't talk about them much, and I didn't ask. I felt like there was some silent agreement between us that we left each other's pasts alone.

"What are we going to do?" I asked, feeling his panic spread.

"I don't know." He shook his head and started for the door. "I don't have time for this right now. I've got to get to the office. I have a few big trades going through today and I just can't deal with this right now."

When I heard the front door open, I rushed to the freezer. "Wait!"

"Nina, I'm in a hurry." He sighed, but he stayed where he was.

After grabbing the Ziploc baggy, I jogged toward the front door he was hovering just inside of.

"Breakfast. You need to eat." I held out the packaged breakfast burrito and waited for him to take it. "I'll stuff it in your pocket if you don't take it. You can't not sleep and not eat. I won't allow it." I let a smile form when he reached for the bag. "Not under my roof."

"When did you do this?" he asked, looking at the homemade frozen burrito like he didn't know what to make of it.

"Yesterday morning. I made a bunch, for these types of situations."

"There types of situations?" he echoed.

"The ones where I have to take care of you because you won't take care of yourself."

When a certain expression fell over his face, I felt heat spill down my spine. I didn't know what to make of those kinds of looks. They seemed like they were intended to invite me closer, but it was Max behind those looks, the very man who couldn't possibly think of me the way I did of him. He'd said he wouldn't let feelings get in the way. He'd promised.

"Thank you, Nina," he said softly as his fingers curled around the baggie. Then he turned and walked down the front porch stairs.

"What do you need, Max?" I asked, following him to the top of the stairs. "What do you need from me?"

He paused with his hand on the handrail. He glanced back at me over his shoulder. Whatever he saw made him look away. "Just hold up your end of our agreement. That's it, Nina. Nothing more."

I watched him walk away. I watched him climb into that ugly car of his. I watched him drive away. I watched the spot where he'd disappeared minutes after he had.

I watched.

He never glanced my way once.

EIGHTEEN

Max

This was wrong. All of it.

My parents being here in Nina's living room. This wasn't the way it was supposed to be. They were supposed to find out about the engagement, send their conventional congrats, then possibly fly in for the wedding. They weren't supposed to show up twenty-four hours after Nina and I'd gotten engaged.

Maybe I should have been expecting this though. Maybe I'd been a fool to think they wouldn't try something when they found out about my sudden engagement to some girl they'd never met.

Of course it was about money. That was what it always came down to in the end. I had some. A lot of it. And they did not.

The Sturms had done well for themselves for generations, growing that wealth with shrewd investment deals and commercial developments. That trend changed when my dad came along. He sold next to everything to put together enough money to start his own automobile company.

It couldn't have come at a worse time during the inter-national economic downturn, and what had once been a family fortune was squandered in a foolish business venture that bankrupted my parents.

Of course they'd never mentioned any of that when we talked on the phone every few months, but it had made the news. It didn't take long for word to get to me. Millions of dollars that had taken generations to make had been wasted by one man's selfish desire to see his last name on the back of a sporty car.

It was part of the reason I'd moved to the States. The main reason I'd gotten into investments and, one day soon, commercial development. I was going to do right by the Sturm name and get back to what my ancestors had excelled at. It might have been in a different country during different times, but I was giving something, instead of just taking it all.

My family didn't know how much I'd made in my years of investing, but I guessed if they knew what half of that total was, they'd tie me up and swim me back home if that was what it took to keep that wealth in the family.

That was why they were here now. In Nina's living room. Glancing around it like they were almost afraid to touch anything. They didn't want this American girl to get half of what they deemed rightly theirs.

"Wann wird sie zu Hause sein?"

I shook my head firmly at my dad. "This is Nina's house. You'll speak English in it, so she doesn't feel left out."

My dad was a big man. Tall as me, but wider thanks to years of overindulgence. He spilled out of the chair Nina liked to sit in at night, sipping her tea as she swung her legs over the side and seemed lost in her thoughts.

I wished he wouldn't have sat there.

"But she's not here right now, Max. What does it matter if we speak German when she isn't around?" Mom was sitting as far away from Dad as she could and still be in the same room.

It appeared their marriage was just as strong as ever. Kind of what happened when Dad had a reputation for screwing anything female that fluttered her lashes in his direction.

"Because I'm here. And it matters to me." I was pacing in front of the big window looking out over the front yard, on edge and waiting for Kate to bring Nina home.

She had been scheduled to work the afternoon and had offered to see if she could get it covered, but I'd told her to continue on like nothing had changed. It was just after eight, so she should be here any minute.

"So how long have you two been together, Max?" Mom asked, stroking the clasp of one of her gold bracelets.

"Almost three months." My tie had long ago been loosened, but I pulled at it again.

"And engaged already? Isn't that moving a little fast?" Mom pressed.

My teeth ground together. "Not with the way we feel about each other." *Not with the way I feel about her*, I corrected myself.

"If this girl's already managed to get you to put a ring on her finger, there's only two possible explanations." Dad shot me a wink. "You got her pregnant or she gives better —"

I broke to a stop and leveled him with a lethal look, cutting him off. "Nina is my fiancée. The woman I care deeply about. Please treat her accordingly."

Mom was glaring at him too, and with the two of us on him, he raised his hands and backed down. "Or you could just be madly in love with the girl."

I turned to look out the window again. There were headlights in the driveway. I could just make out Nina as she crawled out of Kate's car.

"I am," I answered. "I *am* madly in love with her."

She must have seen me in the window because she waved as she jogged across the yard. She looked so at ease, so unconcerned about what was waiting for her inside. I loved that when she was about to jump into a tank full of sharks, Nina's response was a smile and a wave.

"She's coming," I said, moving toward the door. "Be nice."

"Please, Max. We only wanted to meet the girl. To celebrate with the two of you," Mom said in her tsk-tsk tone.

Restraining my grunt of doubt, I met Nina at the door, pulling it open before she could get her key in the lock.

She was still smiling. "Hi, handsome."

She popped up on her toes and planted her lips on mine right when I was in the middle of saying hi back. The suddenness of it made me fall back a few steps. The feel of it made me want to keep falling, until I landed wherever she was taking me.

My hands found their way around her waist and my mouth found her rhythm, until I felt every nerve in my body surge in response.

When she leaned back from the kiss, her eyes opened on mine. They were wide, like she was surprised by something. Her lips were parted from the shallow breaths she was taking, then her body shivered.

"Get inside. It's freezing out there." I waved at Kate when she blasted the horn before peeling out of the driveway. "Where's your coat?"

"I kind of forgot it because I was busy with other things." Her brows lifted at me before she stepped inside the living room.

My lungs collapsed in on themselves for a second. I didn't want her around them. I didn't want them around her. But it was too late. I'd dragged her into it, and I'd make sure she came out on the other side.

"Nina, how wonderful to finally meet you." Mom's voice filtered from the living room.

"I'm sorry I couldn't be here sooner, but I'm so happy to finally meet you both."

When I stepped back inside, I found Nina coming around the couch and wrapping my mom up in a hug. Mom looked like she was being attacked, her face frozen in shock, her arms stiff at her sides.

"Max has told me so much about you." Nina gave her one final squeeze before bouncing over to my dad, who was checking her out in a way that made my fists curl.

He didn't have much of a moral code when it came to getting what he wanted. He'd cheated on his wife; I was sure he'd have no qualms getting into bed with his son's fiancée.

"Mr. Sturm, so nice to meet you." Nina held out her hand for my dad instead. Probably had something to do with the way he was eyeing her. "You must be so proud of Max. He's such a wonderful man."

"Yes, I am. He's done very well for himself." Dad shook Nina's hand, his eyes dropping to her engagement ring. "As I'm sure you're well aware."

"Can I get you anything to drink?" Nina pulled her hand out of Dad's hold.

My parents shook their heads.

Nina's eyes landed on me. "Max?"

I shot her a soft smile. "I'm good."

"Where are you staying?" Nina asked. "Somewhere close by hopefully?"

I groaned internally. Somewhere far away hopefully. After picking them up from the airport a couple of hours ago and bringing them here so they could see the house and meet Nina, we'd spent the day in relative silence. I was still trying to catch up with the sudden turn in events.

Mom exhaled, shooting Dad a look. "We don't know yet. Hans failed to make hotel reservations when he booked the airfare yesterday."

"My firstborn son had just gotten engaged. I wasn't thinking straight. I just couldn't wait to get here." Dad's half-smile went into place. It was one I was familiar with. It might have been a half-smile on the surface, but beneath it was all disappointment.

"You don't have a hotel booked?" Nina looked between my parents.

Again, I kept my sigh to myself. Of course they didn't. They'd been too busy getting here and making sure we didn't exchange *I Do's* before they'd managed to talk me out of it. Or at least talked me into a watertight prenup.

Tired of pacing, I moved toward the chair I usually sat in at night, watching Nina swing her legs and chew life out on her lip. I loved the view from this chair normally. Not so much tonight.

I'd barely gotten comfortable before Nina collapsed into my lap.

When I sat there, kind of frozen, she pulled my hands off of the chair arms, one by one, and wound them around her waist. I had to adjust beneath her so she wouldn't feel something that was *not* so frozen in surprise.

"Well, you can stay with us, of course." When I gave Nina a little pinch on her side, she backpedaled. "At least until you're able to find a hotel. There's plenty of room."

Mom's smile almost looked convincing while Dad looked like the only thing on his mind was securing his son's fortune.

"Thank you, Nina. That's very kind of you," Mom said. "Isn't that a lovely gesture, Hans?"

Dad took a moment before answering. "Yes, very generous. Are you okay with this, Max?"

My arms tightened around Nina. When I stayed quiet, she gave my hands a squeeze.

"I'm okay with it," I said.

"Then it's settled." Dad clapped and leaned forward. "Besides, this house seems as nice as any hotel we're likely to find around here."

Nina forced a smile, but she didn't miss the undercurrent of the insult.

"So, Nina, Max hasn't told us much yet." Dad leaned forward a little farther. "Does your family live around here too?"

Her pinkie tangled between my fingers. "They used to."

"But not anymore? Did they move?"

I opened my mouth to change the subject, but Nina cut me off. "My grandma died last year. This was her house." She wet her lips. "And my mom ran off when I was seven. I haven't seen her since."

Dad and Mom exchanged a look. I knew what they were saying to each other.

"And your dad?" he pressed.

Another finger of Nina's dug between my fingers. She shrugged in answer.

Another shared look between my parents.

"It's late—" I started.

Dad cut me off. "What do you do, Nina?"

"What do I do?" she repeated the question like she didn't understand.

"For work."

"Oh." She exhaled like she was relieved this wasn't a loaded question. Even though it really was. "For my day job, I walk dogs."

Dad's face flattened. "You walk dogs?"

"Yep." The rest of her fingers tangled through mine, and she seemed to nestle a little deeper into my lap.

"And am I to infer that you have a night job as well?" Dad's silver brow peaked.

"You are." Nina nodded.

Dad's hand circled. "Doing?"

"I work at a coffee stand. An all-night one."

I swore to god, if my parents exchanged one more look, I was putting a wall between them.

"A coffee stand," Dad stated.

Nina and I nodded.

"A coffee stand." Mom smiled, this one the contrived kind I was used to. "How nice."

"It's not what I plan on doing forever—I'd like to go to school eventually—but it pays the bills for now," Nina added.

An awkward moment of silence passed, and if it hadn't been for Nina on my lap, I would have been gone. They might have been my parents and raised me, but I hadn't invited them here and they were basically insulting my fiancée in front of both of us.

"Have you set a date for the wedding yet?" Mom folded her hands in her lap, that smile still perfectly in place.

"Not really," Nina said, glancing back at me like she wasn't sure how much to say.

"Soon," I added. We already had a date, but they didn't need to know that.

"How soon?" Dad's forehead creased.

"Soon, soon."

Nina twisted on my lap to face me, picking up where I was going with this. "Really?"

I shrugged. "Why wait. I want to marry you. You want to marry me. I don't see the point in waiting just so we can take our time picking out the 'perfect' party favors."

Dad sounded like he was choking on something, but I was too busy staring at Nina. Her smile had stretched into a beam.

"*Really?*" she repeated.

"I want you to be my wife, Nina Burton. Now."

"*Now?*" Dad was really choking on something now. Probably the imaginary dollar signs he felt slipping away.

"Well, yeah. We might have a few things to sort out, but I don't want to wait. I want to marry this woman. The sooner, the better."

I'd barely finished my sentence before Nina's lips landed on mine again. Pressing deep into me, she held her mouth against mine, one of her hands dropping to my cheek. Just like the last time she'd touched me there, I felt myself melting into her.

When she pulled back, her green eyes were swimming in some emotion I didn't have a name for. "I want to marry you now too."

When she shifted on my lap so she was almost facing me, her face flattened because yeah . . . pretty sure she'd just felt my predicament behind my zipper. She shifted back to her original spot.

"No need to rush into things." Dad's voice was loud enough it echoed into the next room over. "You're both riding the engagement high. Give it a few days to settle in, then decide on a date. Make sure this is what you want."

Nina met Dad's stare. "He is," she stated matter-of-factly. "Max is who I want."

I knew she was just playing a role, giving the performance of her life trying to convince my suspicious parents that we were the real deal, but my chest seized when I heard her say that.

"We had dinner with Elena last week," Mom said, changing the subject. This subject made every muscle in my body tense. "Just as beautiful as always. Sweet girl."

My parents exchanged a nod of agreement while my jaw locked.

"The sweetest," I growled.

Nina blinked back at me. "Who's Elena?"

I waited a second too long to give Nina my explanation.

Dad gave his. "Max's old fiancée. Hasn't he mentioned anything about her?"

Nina stiffened in my lap, but I was probably the only one who noticed. A slow breath escaped her lips, then she hid her surprise behind a smile. "Well, yeah, I just forgot her name."

"Elena and Max grew up together." Mom crossed her ankles and turned, so she was facing us. "We thought they were going to grow old together too, but then Max went and let her get away."

Anger was pumping in my veins from them bringing her up. Something that went beyond anger started to surge when I thought about what had happened between Elena and me. My parents didn't know the real story, and that was fine. If they wanted to believe I was the one who'd broken her heart, fine, I didn't give a shit. So long as they just stopped talking about her.

"To find you, my dear," Mom suddenly added when she noticed Nina's face. "He let her go to find you."

Nina managed a smile, but I could tell she was jarred. I'd brought up that I'd been burned, but never that I'd been engaged. I guessed I didn't think it was that big of a deal since Nina wasn't really in love with me the way a fiancée should be. I didn't think she'd care who I'd fucked or got on bended knee for.

With that shell-shocked look on her face though . . . damn, she almost had me convinced she was in love with me.

"She's got a great family. We go way back," Dad added.

Mom nodded. "And she's a fashion designer. One of the top ones in Germany."

I shifted on the chair, knowing what they were doing. They were trying to intimidate Nina. They were hoping to scare her away. Too bad they didn't know the kind of woman Nina was, and she was not one who'd be intimidated by another woman, one of Elena's brand especially.

"Wow. She sounds great." This smile of Nina's looked almost real.

"She isn't," I added.

"Max," Mom half-snapped. "How can you say that with you two's history?"

I exhaled. It was this very policy of believing what they wanted to that had been behind them wasting the Sturm family fortune. "Believe me, Mom, if you knew our history, you'd know why."

Nina glanced back at me, concern on her face.

What in the hell was happening? Yesterday, everything had been good and going according to plan, and tonight, someone had tossed a damn grenade into my life. I loved my parents in the most conventional of ways and I knew they loved me in their own way, but I couldn't deal with them right now. I wouldn't tolerate them hurting Nina the way they were planning to, driving her away the way I knew they were determined to.

"What are you two doing here?"

My mom shifted on the couch, but Dad stayed solid in his chair, unflinching. "What do you think we're doing here, Max? We wanted to meet our future daughter-in-law. See our son."

Nina managed another one of those smiles that would convince a Supreme Court Justice, while my face went with something of the opposite variety.

"Why are you *really* here?" I looked between the both of them. "I want to hear you say it. I want to hear you admit it."

Mom's hands were fidgeting in her lap when she looked to Dad for an answer.

"What are you talking about, son? We're here for you," he said.

"No, you're not. You're here for you." My head whipped as it shook. "You've always been about you, and that hasn't changed."

Mom looked close to tears, but Dad's face stayed as stoic as ever. I was trembling in my seat from the anger surging through me. It was unlike any other I'd experienced, and I guessed that had to do with Nina. I was used to my parents' backhanded compliments, their veiled insults, their personal agenda. But I was not used to them bringing those I cared about into that sick web of malcontent.

It was something I wouldn't tolerate either.

"Would you excuse us for a minute?" Nina leapt off my lap, grabbing my hand. "I need to talk to Max alone."

She didn't wait for my parents' response; she just tugged me out of the chair and pulled me down the hallway until we were rounding into her room.

When she closed the door and turned on me, I was bracing for a fight. Nina and I'd had no shortage of those over the past couple months, and I knew I deserved this one. They were my parents and I was the one totally failing to play the right part. Nina had given a flawless performance that could have convinced the most skeptical, and I'd let emotions get in the way.

Fuck. This was one of the worst nights of my life.

But her face wasn't drawn up like she was prepping for a battle. Her eyes weren't blazing the way I was used to seeing them as we battled out whatever topic of the day we'd latched onto.

"Are you okay?" she asked gently, moving toward me.

My brows drew a hard line. "What?"

Nina's hands formed on my chest, the length of her forearms running down my body. "Are. You. Okay?"

Her touch. It was messing with my head like it always did. Instead of working at its typical pace, my brain was moving at quarter speed. "I'm fine."

She gave me a look that implied she knew better. "No, you're not."

I sighed, irritated that I could rarely get a thing past her these days. Well, other than the fact that I'd fallen for her for real.

"It doesn't matter if I'm fine or not. Right now, we just need to get through tonight without me strangling my father."

She looked up at me, her hands pressing deeper into me. "It matters to *me*. You matter to me."

Before I could work out my reply to that, her hands tied around the back of my neck as her body fitted against mine. Her head pressed into my breastplate, and she held me tightly.

Was she hugging me?

God, I thought she was. As innocent as a hug might have been, I was not having innocent thoughts with her body pressed into mine. She might have been the woman I was paying to marry me, but right then, I wanted her to be the woman I spent the rest of my life with.

Squeezing my eyes together, I backed away, searching for the place where reality had left off.

"They can't see us anymore. You can cut the act, Nina." My voice was off, sounding like someone was squeezing my vocal cords.

She looked at the space keeping us apart, indecision heavy on her face. "This isn't an act. Maybe it was in the beginning. Maybe I wish it still were. But this"—she motioned between her and me—"it's not an act."

Okay, so now my brain was working on back-up power. The way she was looking at me, the way she'd just been touching me, what she'd just said. What the hell? I couldn't tell up from down right now.

"What are you saying?"

Her gaze lifted to meet mine. "You know what I'm saying."

My lungs were laboring, and my head was swimming. I could comprehend the words she was saying, just not the meaning behind them.

I didn't know how long I stood there in that dark room, staring at her, working out what she'd just said, trying to make sense of it. However long it was, it was a moment too long.

"Just forget it, okay, Max?" Nina shook her head and turned away. "I shouldn't have said anything."

"Nina," I called, finally able to put my thoughts together enough to manage her name.

"No, forget it." She kept walking away, pulling the door open. "We've got enough to deal with tonight without having to work out what I just said."

I stood there, dumbfounded. Had Nina just said what I thought she had?

Smiling at the spot where she'd disappeared in such a hurry, I replayed her words in my head. Again and again until I had my answer.

Fuck. This was one of the best nights of my life.

NINETEEN

Nina

*A*nd that just happened. The guy I'd promised to marry, the guy I'd sworn to myself to hate, was the one I'd confessed to having feelings for.

I'd been replaying the scene from last night in my head all day. When I'd pulled him into my room, I hadn't planned on dropping that FYI on him. That was a secret I had been planning on taking with me to the hereafter. Why I'd told him, I didn't know, but I would have given a limb or two to travel back in time and get a redo.

Had Max responded differently, then it wouldn't be such a big deal. But he'd stood there, silent, in shock, not having a clue what to say. Just thinking about the way he'd looked at me made my stomach churn for the five hundredth time today.

It wasn't a face of outright disgust and betrayal, but more one of shock. Surprise. Like he hadn't expected it, wasn't ever expecting it, and didn't have a clue what to do or say knowing I felt something more for him. Shit, I'd promised him nothing more than a farce. I'd promised myself that. So why had I gone and gotten feelings tangled up between us? How had I let myself get to this point, where thinking about him made something ache inside me? Where being around him made that ache subside?

So much for vows and promises. I couldn't seem to keep to one.

My thoughts had fueled my day so far. The dogs had gotten in an extra mile thanks to my furious pace, and the handful of potatoes I'd planned on peeling had turned into the whole bag.

Max was at work, and his parents had gone out sight-seeing this afternoon but were back now. They'd come through the front door arguing, paused long enough to throw a couple of conventional smiles at me, then picked up their argument as they marched upstairs to the room we'd put them in last night. A half hour later, they were still at it. I'd turned on the radio a while ago to drown out the noise, but it wasn't that effective.

Max's parent clearly weren't thrilled about our engagement, and I got that. Any parent would probably be skeptical of this rushed engagement, especially when it was between two people as different as Max and I were. That wasn't my issue with them. My issue stemmed from the way they clearly set Max on edge.

Last night, he had been a different man in that living room with them. Tense, terse, cold. Max had enough going on without adding this kind of tension to his life, and I would do everything I could to make this easier on him.

That was why I was making a big dinner tonight and had already set a few board games on the dining table. So we could all be together without having to actually talk about any of the stuff that had made Max nuclear last night. Hopefully.

We couldn't avoid his parents, but I was determined to make this as easy as I could for him.

After getting the potatoes into a pot to boil, I went to work dicing up the strawberries for dessert. Max loved strawberry shortcake—which I found all kinds of amusing since he was such a sophisticated, powerful man—and I was making it as a kind of peace offering for what I'd dropped on him last night.

Because what said, "I'm sorry for confessing I dig you" more than a slab of strawberry shortcake?

When the shouts from upstairs dialed up a few decibels, I turned the radio's volume dial up with my elbow. My hands were red and sticky from the strawberry juice and I still had a whole extra basket to slice.

The sound of the front door opening made my eyebrows come together. It wasn't even six. That couldn't be Max. The earliest I'd ever seen him get home was eight, but I didn't know who else would be shoving through my front door unannounced

"Hello?" I called.

Then I heard familiar heel-strikes moving down the hall. It was him. What could have happened to make him leave work when everyone else did?

"Nina."

I flinched when he appeared in the entry of the kitchen. His voice was back to normal and so was the rest of him. At least as far as I could tell. I hadn't seen him since late last night when he'd left, saying he had an early morning and would be staying at his office for the night. Part of me was relieved I wouldn't have to crawl into the same bed as him after what I'd admitted. Part of me was kind of disappointed too.

It was supposed to be our first night sharing my room. He couldn't exactly sleep in the guest room now that his parents were here. I'd figured him leaving last night to stay at his office was his way of putting off us sharing a bed and giving him some time to process what I'd said and formulate his response. It was his way of keeping his distance.

The noise upstairs dialed up again.

My eyes lifted to the ceiling. "They've been at it for a while now. Should I go check on them?"

From the corner of my eyes, I watched Max shake his head. "This is how they spend most of their days. It's normal for them."

"Oh. Okay." I plucked the next strawberry from the colander, not sure what to say or where to look. Max didn't seem to have a problem looking at me, but he wasn't the one who'd confessed his feelings for me last night.

Nope, that was this girl. The idiot slicing strawberries, totally tongue-tied.

"We have to talk."

My knife wobbled as I sliced off the stem cap. "Just, please, forget it." I wetted my lips. "I shouldn't have said that. Forget it, okay?"

Max moved into the kitchen, his steps echoing through the room. "You couldn't plead, beg, or pay me enough to forget what you said."

My hand was trembling now, but I kept slicing. So what if I chopped my finger off—I'd already exposed my heart for the chopping. "Why not?"

He moved closer. He didn't stop until he was beside me. His hand reached out for mine, stalling it before he slid the knife away and set it on the counter. Then his hand returned to mine, his fingers tying through my sticky ones.

He was waiting for me to look at him, but I couldn't. I was having a tough enough time breathing and remaining upright. If I looked at him, I wouldn't be able to manage that either.

He leaned in like he was about to tell me a secret. "Because maybe I feel the exact same way."

More of my body was trembling. I couldn't tell if it was from his touch or from what he'd said. "You don't have to say that."

"I know." His other hand slid my hair over my shoulder. "I wouldn't unless I meant it." Then his head lowered to my neck, his lips grazing it.

My body shivered in response. "Max."

He sucked at the skin gently. "Nina."

Tipping my head to the side to allow him better access, my hand pressed into him like I was bracing myself. "I don't know what this is anymore."

His mouth continued to work my neck. "Then let me show you," he whispered against me.

I managed a nod.

Taking that as a green light, his body suddenly pinned mine up against the counter. A gasp slipped past my mouth. His chest was pressing into my back, holding me captive. His hand tied around mine released it and traveled up to my neck. His fingers formed around my cheek as he turned my head to the side.

"I'm going to kiss you, Nina." His eyes dropped to my mouth, which I was wetting with nervous anticipation, and his forehead creased. Then his hips pressed into me so I could feel him hard against me. "I'm going to do more."

When he ground into me from behind again, another gasp seeped out of me.

"If this isn't what you want, if I'm not who you want, walk away. Walk away now." Max's eyes traveled back to mine. "I won't stop you. I'll let you go. But if you stay. If you let me kiss you. If you let me take your body, I won't be able to let you go after that. It won't be possible, so make sure this is what you want before I start."

His words were priming my body almost as much as his actual body smashing into mine was. My heart was beating out of control and my lungs were straining. The rest of my body was malfunctioning too. I'd never felt this way. No one had ever drawn this kind of want out of me—pulled this kind of need from where it was hidden.

Max could have been asking me to leap off the edge of the earth and I wouldn't have walked away.

Tipping my hips back, I angled my face so it was better in line with his. "Then kiss me."

His eyes darkened with want. "No going back." His thumb slid higher, so it was touching the corner of my mouth.

When his lips touched mine, I felt a jolt burst down my spine. When his mouth moved against mine, I felt jolts bursting in other places. His other arm wound around my waist, clinging to me like I was clinging to him as we shared our first real kiss. It was different from the fake ones we'd done for show. Entirely different.

The others had given my butterflies, but this one was making me feel things that I couldn't ascribe a word to. When my tongue passed his lips, Max's fingers dug deeper into me. His hand wound around my waist traveled up my body. It didn't stop until he was kneading my chest with hungry, urgent touches.

The sensations were too much. My mouth fell away from his as my head fell back into the cradle of his shoulder.

"Your mouth on mine, Nina." Max's hand tipped my head back toward his. "I'm not done kissing you."

His mouth captured mine again, and his tongue wound past my lips. I moaned against his mouth, my tongue tangling with his as he kissed me with a passion I hadn't known existed.

Feeling him touching me, feeling the way I was touching him, I got it now. Why women and men made such stupid decisions in the name of love. It was a drug. A dangerous one. Something a person would do anything to keep, give up anything to feel.

That was the exact way I felt as Max continued to consume me with his lips and body. He was igniting something inside me I couldn't tame. He was drawing something out that scared me because I had no control over it. At that moment, pinned against the kitchen counter with Max wrapped around me, I was controlled by it.

Max's hand slipped over to my other breast, his fingers capturing my nipple pushing through my cotton dress.

My mouth broke free of his again, unable to breathe when he touched me like this. Seeking refuge against his shoulder, I draped an arm around his neck and held on while he stroked my nipple. Each time he pulled on it, I felt it all the way down between my legs.

"You're having a difficult time listening tonight." Max nuzzled into my neck, sucking at it again.

Fuck. It was stimulation overload. His mouth sucking on me, his hand teasing my chest. I'd never been so turned on in my whole life.

"I'm sorry," I panted, my arm tying harder around his neck when he gave the spot above my collarbone a hard suck. "I can barely breathe right now."

His hips pitched against mine, fitting himself hard against my ass. Breathing just got that much harder to regulate.

"I told you I wanted to kiss you," he said slowly against my neck. "But I suppose it doesn't have to be on your mouth."

My body went limp against his for a moment when I realized he wasn't referring to my neck. Not with the direction his hand was traveling down my body. His fingers stopped when they reached their destination, his thumb stroking me through my clothes.

Without his mouth to muffle it, my gasp filled the kitchen.

Twisting me around, his hands cupped my backside before he lifted me onto the counter. His body pressed into mine again as he scooted my hips to the very edge.

"What are you doing?" I looked down at him, my body already spent from what he'd done to it. Having him touch me in the way I knew he had in mind would be the end of me. I knew it.

"I want to kiss you." His mouth covered mine for a moment, sucking on my lower lip. Then he released it with a wet pop. "Remember that more part I mentioned?" His hands slid up my thighs, bunching the material of my dress up with them.

My head bobbed.

His eyes lowered to the spot between my legs. "This is part of that."

When his fingers trailed up to my panties, his thumbs curled beneath the sides and pulled. "Lift up. I want to see you," he ordered then kissed my neck.

I didn't even give it a second thought. I just lifted up so he could pull off my underwear. He slid them down my thighs, over my knees, then pulled my feet out of them, one at a time. They landed on the floor at his feet.

Christ. What is happening?

His eyes held mine for a moment before they trailed down to my exposed body. Something vibrated deep in his chest as he appraised me.

"You're perfect," he rasped.

Something that resembled a laugh came from me. "Yeah, that's what I hear from all the guys."

Max's eyes cut to mine, something dark sweeping through them. "No one will be seeing this but me from now on, you understand?" The sharpness in his voice made me flinch, but like before, he tamed his words with a tender kiss. "Do you understand?"

I nodded.

"Good. I don't share. I won't share you, Nina," he whispered against my mouth. "I want to show you why you won't have any reason to ever want to share your body with someone else." His face nuzzled into my neck again. "Because when I'm done getting you off, you'll be seeing stars."

"God, Max," I breathed, actually feeling myself get wetter.

Leaning back, he lowered onto the kitchen floor in front of me. His hands formed around my knees, spreading my legs apart. "Lift your dress, Nina. Show me you want me."

I stared at him on his knees in front of me. How did we get here? How did we wind up in this place?

An arrangement. An agreement. A business transaction. How had that led to this?

Right then, something sounded like it was shattering a floor above us.

When my eyes lifted, Max shook his head. "Don't worry. They're just warming up. They won't be down anytime soon."

Holding his stare, I curled my fingers around the hem of my dress and lifted it for him. Max's hands slid up my thighs, his eyes dropping to me as his head moved closer.

"Then show me the stars," I whispered, right before his mouth settled between my legs. My whole body tensed up. I felt like I was flying at the same time I was falling.

"Relax, Nina." Max's tongue tasted me, and fire shot up my spine. "Let me make you feel good."

Exhaling, I tried relaxing. It was impossible. Max's head was between my legs, doing things to my body with his tongue that were already making me see stars. When his fingers spread me apart, his mouth sucking on me, my head fell back into the cabinet behind me.

My gasp was more of a moan this time, and it was loud enough I reached over to crank the volume up on the radio.

I felt my orgasm surging closer. But I fought it. If I did this, let Max draw an orgasm from my body, our relationship would forever be changed. There'd be no going back to the comfortable friendship. No going back to even the distant congeniality.

Gritting my teeth together, I clamped my legs around him tightly, holding myself off. I couldn't think straight. All I knew was that I didn't want to lose Max, and I wasn't sure if I let him force this from my body, if that would hasten his loss or lessen the likelihood.

"Don't fight it, Nina." Max leaned back just enough to look up at me. His eyes were untamed, dark with need. "Let go. Let me make you come."

When my legs tightened this time, Max threw them over his shoulders and pulled me farther down the edge of the counter, so half of my butt was hanging off of it.

"Fine"—his tongue drew a line down me—"I'll just have to force you to come."

When his mouth covered me then, I knew fighting it would be impossible.

"Max," I breathed, curling forward so I could bury my hands in his hair. My fingers made a mess of his hair in no time at all as I pulled, pitching my hips in time to his tongue's punishing rhythm.

When I started to work with him, my body responding to his, Max growled against me, which was my undoing. My body went rigid, letting my orgasm surge to the surface, then Max's finger just barely slipped inside me.

His mouth barely dropped back over me and my orgasm ripped through my body. My cries filled the kitchen as I moved Max's head against me while he kept sucking me off.

He didn't stop until he'd pulled every spasm from me. Not until the last aftershock had spilled through my body.

His mouth left me first, then his finger. Staring up at me, a tilted smile moved into place. "Stars?"

I smoothed down some of his hair I'd mussed. There were streaks of red from the strawberry juice coating my fingers. "The whole fucking universe."

My body was still shaking, my lungs were still straining, and my heart . . . I didn't know where the hell it was, but I couldn't think about anything but making him feel the same way.

When he stood in front of me, he helped me off the counter. His arms came around me to keep me from crumbling to the floor. But the floor was exactly where I wanted to go. On my knees. In front of him.

When my fingers moved to his zipper, feeling his hard-on pressing through it, he sucked in a sharp breath.

"I want to feel you in my mouth," I whispered. "I want to make you come the same way."

His fingers dug deeper into me, but before I could lower to my knees, his hands cupped around my backside and lifted me off of the floor. My legs tangled around his waist as he carried me out of the kitchen.

"As much as I've been fanaticizing about that pretty little mouth of yours wrapped around me, I want that part of me buried inside a different part of you right now." My thighs squeezed around him. "But first, let's get you into your bedroom."

My hands cinched around the back of his neck. "So you can give me head on the kitchen counter, but sex requires a bedroom?"

"For what I have planned? Yes. A door that locks is a good idea." His fingers gripped deeper into my backside. "You remember that night we were pretending to have sex? The sounds we were making?"

He waited for me to nod.

"You'll be making those same sounds, but this time, it will be because of what my body's doing to yours. This time, you're going to cry out those filthy things because I'm taking your body. Again. And again." His teeth grazed the skin along my collarbone. "And again."

I shuddered against him, feeling another orgasm building just from his words. "Your parents might hear."

"So?"

I lowered my mouth outside his ear as he stopped in front of my bedroom door. "I'm not sure they want to hear about the size of their son's package and what it's doing to my body."

He pressed me up against the door, digging that part of himself against me. "So don't scream it at the top of your lungs. Or do. I don't care. That won't change that my 'package' will be making you come as many times and ways as I can take you."

He ground against me again before opening the door.

"I never knew you had such a dirty mouth," I breathed, desperate for the friction of him on me again.

Max carried me into the bedroom and kicked the door closed. He had me on my bed, hovering above me instantly. "You're going to be learning a lot about me you didn't know before." He slid out of his jacket. "Your dress. Take it off," he said, unbuttoning his shirt.

Sitting up, I pulled the dress up over my head and tossed it onto the growing pile of his clothes. Mesmerized, I watched him slide his undershirt over his head.

"I want you naked, Nina. The rest of it comes off."

My arms whipped behind my back, making quick work of unlatching my bra. When it slid down my arms and fell on my knees, Max's breath caught.

His eyes roamed my chest while I did the same to him. I'd never seen him shirtless, but I hadn't guessed he'd look half as good as he did standing before me now, fragments of twilight spilling across him. He had the kind of body that didn't just hint at power, it embodied it. It was evident he could do whatever he wanted to me and I'd be powerless to stop it. He could take me however he wanted, whenever he wanted, wherever he wanted with that kind of body, and that made my inner animal whimper. When Max worked his belt free, I swallowed.

"Eyes on mine, Nina. You'll be feeling him soon enough, but I want your eyes on mine right now."

I did as he asked, somehow managing to keep them on him when he slid out of his pants. When he stepped out of them, his hand lowered and he gave himself a few slow strokes.

My eyes dropped, because damn, how was a girl supposed to keep staring at a guy's eyes when he was touching himself that way?

Air rushed in through my parted lips when I saw him. *Shit. Kate was totally right.*

"I thought I told you to keep your eyes on me." There was a smirk in Max's voice. I could hear it. He stroked himself again, slower. "You're having a hard time listening tonight."

My hand lowered down my body so I could touch myself as I watched him do the same. "Yeah, well, you didn't listen to me about the no-sex part of our agreement, so consider us even."

Max peaked a brow. "We haven't had sex yet."

I lay back as he moved closer. "Then what in the hell are you waiting for?"

Max stared at me for a moment, worshipping my body with his eyes, before lowering himself over me. As his body settled over mine, the mattress whined. I moaned when I felt his length slide against me, his head pressing into my stomach.

His mouth covered mine again, his kisses slow and teasing, while his hands roamed my body. One settled into the slope of my backside as the other pressed into my chest. His hips ground against me, about to drive me to another orgasm just from his shaft sliding up and down me.

When I started to pant again, my body tensing below his, his hips tipped back, sliding lower.

"No, Liebling." His tongue touched mine. "I'm afraid your next orgasm belongs to my dic=\k."

Nodding, I angled my hips against him.

His hand moved between us, aligning himself into position, then something seemed to hit him. "Are you taking anything?"

At first, I didn't know what he was talking about. Then I felt him flex against me just enough he barely moved inside me.

"Oh, yeah. We're good," I said quickly, remembering something else this might be a good time to mention. "On that topic at least."

Max's whole face relaxed. "Are you okay with us doing it this way?" He gripped his bare shaft between my legs, waiting. "I'm clean."

My eyebrows came together, then I got what he was asking. What he'd just said.

"Oh, yeah. I'm good. On both. Really good." I was rambling, but Max was starting to push deeper inside me. "But I should mention one little thing first. You know, before you go any farther." Because he was about to find out on his own if I didn't bring it up.

He was breathing hard, his forehead creased from our connection. "Fantastic. After."

I wiggled back a little bit, but he didn't let me get far. "You remember that part of the biography I didn't fill out?"

"Yeah." His mouth lowered to my body, then he sucked my nipple into his mouth. He was trying to distract me. I'd probably be doing the same if this was the other way around, but this was important. Or it would be for a whole two minutes before it became a non-issue.

"It's about that." I tried pulling his face back, but no sooner had I done that then his mouth latched onto my other nipple. I cried out, my muscles clenching so hard they pushed him out.

We both groaned in anguish.

"Great," he said around my nipple. "After."

My back was arching against him, trying to get more of me into his mouth. "Coincidentally, it has something to do with what we're about to do."

"It can wait. I can't." He leaned back, pressing his length back against me.

When I felt him start to slide inside me at the same time his finger circled higher, all warnings drifted away with the promise of my looming orgasm.

"Yeah, me neither," I panted as he took more of me. "After."

Max's hands were just moving to my hips, bracing around them to claim the rest of me, when a pounding at the door stopped us both.

Sitting up, I was waiting for the bedroom door to explode open.

"It came from the front door." Max kissed my fore-head, pulling back as he crawled off the bed, reaching for his pants.

"Are we expecting anyone?" I frowned as he zipped his pants.

"No. But I wasn't expecting my parents to show up yesterday, so Christ knows who it could be tonight." Max pulled me off the bed, reaching for my dress. When he slid it over my head and tugged it into place, he looked as crest-fallen as I felt.

"Later." His hand moved around my head and pulled it to him, kissing my forehead. "I promise."

"You didn't get yours though."

He grinned as he shrugged into his undershirt. "Don't worry. I'll be taking mine." His hand grabbed mine as he pulled me toward the door. "I hope you weren't planning on actually sleeping tonight."

He winked at me, pulling the door open when we heard another pounding coming from the front door.

"Someone's impatient," I grumbled, irritated we'd been interrupted right when things were about to get really, really good.

"Yeah, that someone being me." Max motioned at his crotch where his hard-on was pressing against his zipper.

Swallowing the flames licking up my throat, I let him lead me out of the bedroom.

His parents' voices were coming from the front door, joined by other voices. They must have taken a break from their arguing long enough to answer the door. It sounded like they knew whoever was outside and like they were hap-py to see them.

We'd barely reached the end of the hall when Max broke to a stop. His hand tightened around mine while the rest of him went rigid.

A young man stood inside the front door—he looked a lot like Max, just a little rougher and younger. There was a woman too. A woman who looked like she was used to getting what she wanted whenever she wanted and, from the way her eyes had just latched onto Max, I knew exactly what she wanted.

"Get out of this house." Max's voice thundered around us, his finger pointing at the door. "Now."

The woman didn't look fazed. Instead, she finished taking off her leather gloves, one at a time, a smile making its appearance. "Is that any way to greet your first love?"

Max's jaw went rigid. When she walked toward us, her eyes landing on me, he backed us away from her.

"You must be Nina," she said, closing in. Max kept backing me away from her. "I'm Elena. I've been looking forward to meeting you."

TWENTY

Max

"Are you planning on eating dinner? Or are you going to spend the rest of the night pacing circles around the living room?"

My eyes flickered over to Nina leaning into the wall, her eyebrow peaked as I circled the room like a caged lion. That was what I felt like. A man-eating animal just waiting to get loose.

"Will they be there?" I asked, doing another circle. I was still barefoot, in my slacks and undershirt, but I didn't care.

"'They' being your family and former flame? Yes, they will be eating dinner as well."

I shot her a warning over the former flame part, but Nina rolled her eyes. She didn't seem threatened by Elena, which was good because she had nothing to be threatened by. However, I'd known my share of women who cowered in Elena's presence.

"Then no. I'll carry on with the pacing."

"You know"—Nina's thumb jabbed into her chest—"I will also be there. Your fiancée. The one whose dress you just had your head under."

My mouth twitched as my eyes skimmed the hem of her dress. I wanted to do it again. I wanted to have Nina in every way I could have her. Now. Maybe if I could just fuck some of the anger out of me, I could sit at the same dinner table as the rest of them.

My eyes drifted down the hall, lifting my brow at her.

"After dinner. It will be your reward for behaving yourself."

Throwing my head back, I groaned. So much was coming at me. Nina. My family. Nina. Elena. Nina.

"Come on, they don't seem that bad, Max. We can make it through a few dinners."

"Not so bad?" I waved in the direction of the dining room, where they were gathered. I didn't care what any of them heard. "You know why my parents invited her, don't you?"

Nina lifted a shoulder. "Because you guys grew up together."

I huffed. "Because they're hoping she'll drive a wedge between you and me. Because they're hoping Elena will do what Elena does best and destroy everything in her path."

Looking calm, Nina continued to watch me pace the room. "She won't come between us, Max. That wouldn't have happened before, and it definitely won't happen now."

When she peaked her eyebrow at me, I caught her meaning. She was right. We were getting married no matter what, but after what had just happened, so much more than promises and arrangements bound us together now.

"She needs to leave. Now." I'd wanted to force her out the moment I saw her standing in the entryway.

"Max, it's late. I'm not just going to kick someone out. Especially a friend of your family and an old friend of yours." She emphasized the old part, but hearing her refer to Elena as any kind of friend of mine made me wince. "Besides, she doesn't seem so bad. Maybe kind of self-absorbed, but she's been helping me out in the kitchen, and I really think she just wants the best for you." When I didn't say anything, she shoved off the wall and came toward me. "Please come to dinner. For me?"

I let her block my path. I let her hands settle onto my chest as she looked up at me with those innocent, trusting eyes of hers.

"All of your family is here, your ex-fiancée is sitting at my dining room table, and you just got me off on the kitchen counter I used to frost Christmas cookies with my grandma at." Her mouth lifted on one side. "I'm kind of reeling here. Could use a little help."

I didn't want to sit at the table. I didn't want to be surrounded by the people I knew were plotting to take this woman away from me.

But I wanted to make her happy more than any of that.

"Fine. But don't expect me to be civil."

She let me take her hand as we headed for the dining room. "Not civil seems to be a trend for you tonight." She eyed the kitchen counter as we passed it.

"It's going to be the trend for the rest of the night too." My hand drifted around her to squeeze her ass right before we emerged into the dining room.

Nina cleared her throat, pulling at the hem of her dress. The four of them had been talking and laughing, but when we showed up, the table went quiet.

"Look who decided to show up for dinner?" My brother, Magnus, twisted around in his chair and tipped his chin at me. His accent was the strongest of all of us, but that probably had a lot to do with him being under the impression that the degree of his accent had a direct correlation to the number of American women he could screw.

"Look who decided to show up to our house unannounced?" I smiled tightly.

"God, Max, nice of you to get all dressed up for dinner. Don't mind us." Elena searched me, her gaze lingering around my belt region. When her eyes narrowed, I guessed she'd figured out what Nina and I had been busy doing before she and Magnus showed up.

"I haven't minded you for a long time now, Elena."

Nina gave my hand a squeeze before guiding me to an empty chair that was as far away from Elena as I could get. Nina winked at me, sliding into the empty seat beside it.

"So what brings you two here?" I asked, guessing Magnus's and Elena's answer to that question would be as dishonest as my parents'.

"I had a show in New York. When I heard the good news and found out Magnus's flight would be stopping over in La Guardia, I just couldn't help myself." Elena didn't blink as she answered. She was used to lying. More of a first nature than a second nature with her.

"Yeah, I bet you couldn't."

"I wanted to congratulate my good friend. I wanted to meet his future wife." Elena shrugged, like that was that.

"So now that you're here and have met her and con-gratulated me, when are you leaving?"

When the roast came around to Nina, she served a piece on my plate first. Maybe she was hoping I would keep my mouth shut if I was chewing.

"Dude, I love the West Coast. The women here are freaks." Magnus bobbed his head at me like we shared some kind of secret. "I'm staying until I wear out my welcome."

"Consider it worn out."

Nina had to bite her lip to keep her smile hidden.

"And I've got a few vendors I'll be meeting with while I'm over here," Elena said.

When the potatoes came around, Nina mounded a heap onto my plate.

"And those vendors are where? On the other side of the country?" I sighed when Nina scooped another heap of pota-toes onto my plate. Her message was silent but effective—*shut up and eat.*

She laughed silently.

Elena was looking between us. "A few in LA, a couple here, a couple more up in Seattle. I'm planning on making Portland my home base for the next few weeks while I get it all taken care of. There's a chance for relocation too. The company I'm working for is looking to open a branch on the West Coast, so I'm scoping out the area, seeing if America would be a good fit for me."

Nina glanced at me, looking like she was bracing for whatever I was going to say next.

"What a great idea, Elena. Hans and I were just saying how nice it would be to extend our stay, see some of the sights, while we help Max and Nina with their wedding plans." Mom smiled across the table at Elena, the daughter she never had. The daughter-in-law she'd always planned on.

When Nina looked about to say something, probably along the lines of offering her place to Magnus and Elena, I shook my head at her. I loved how generous she was, how trusting and good and kind. It was everything the woman on the other end of the table had fooled me into believing she was, but I would not survive the four of them sharing the same living quarters as Nina and me.

She drew an invisible zipper across her lips and stayed quiet.

"Where are you staying, Elena?" Dad asked.

"I think the company put me up in a nice hotel downtown. I haven't checked in yet. Magnus and I just couldn't wait to get here and see everyone." Elena glanced down the table at Nina, but Nina didn't notice. She was looking at me. "I couldn't wait to meet you, Nina, and now having done so, I can say you do not disappoint." Elena lifted her glass of hemlock or water or whatever it was. "Max is lucky to have you. You're lucky to have Max. To luck." She tipped her head and smiled a little wider. "To those who have it and those of us in search of it."

"I'll cheers to that." Dad lifted his glass and clinked glasses with Elena and Mom.

Magnus was too busy tearing into his roast to be disturbed, and Nina and I were too busy reeling from the past twenty-four hours to keep up with anything else.

"Dude, this roast is like trying to chew through a piece of leather." Magnus gnashed his teeth, working the hunk of meat he'd stuffed in his mouth.

I loved my kid brother, but he was clueless when it came to things like manners and women's feelings.

"Magnus." I shook my head at him.

He stopped sawing at the meat with his teeth instantly.

"Yeah, I'm sorry about that. I think I overcooked it." Nina stabbed at her own piece of roast. "I got a little distracted."

When her hand found my knee beneath the table, sliding up the inside of my leg, I went hard instantly.

"Well, I think it tastes divine, Nina." At the end of the table, Elena's plate remained untouched. "You know, I bought a special bottle of champagne to celebrate. Let me run and grab it." After scooting out of her chair, Elena left the dining room, her heels echoing through the house.

"So. Nina." Magnus swallowed his chunk of meat. "You're marrying my brother."

Nina shrugged a shoulder. "I guess that's what this ring means." She threw me a sideways glance.

"Why?" Magnus waved at me like it was unfathomable that anyone would want to marry me.

Nina picked up her fork and stabbed at her green beans. "He's really good in the kitchen." Her hand crept higher, curling around my package.

I flinched, making the whole table shake. Everyone gaped at me while Nina grinned at her lap, her shoulders shaking from her contained laughter.

"Do you guys have a little girl living with you too?" Elena reappeared in the dining room with a bottle of champagne in one hand and a pair of underwear in the other. A familiar pair of underwear.

"Nope." Nina clucked her tongue. "Those are mine."

Elena looked at the underwear dangling from her finger, her nose wrinkling. "Really? I haven't seen cotton underwear since I was ten."

Magnus was grinning, his gaze going from Nina to the pair of underwear . . . which reminded me. She didn't have any on. Was in a dress. A short-ish one.

Because my dick was not already aching from restraint tonight.

"Yeah, well, I'm a big fan. Comfort. Cost. Breathability." Nina shrugged then looked around the table. My parents were kind of gaping at the dinner table scene. "And moving on . . . sorry, they must have fallen out of the laundry when I was folding it."

I nudged her foot with mine. "Must have."

She sighed, giving me a look that led me to believe she thought me quite immature.

"Here, I'll hang on to those." Snagging them off Elena's fingertips, I stuffed them in my front pocket. When Nina looked at me, I licked my lips slowly and she shifted on her chair. "For safekeeping."

"Champagne anyone?" Elena waved the chilled bottle.

Three glasses went in the air. Nina's and mine stayed on the table. As Elena tore off the foil, a look crossed her face. It was one I knew well. I was already bracing myself before she opened her mouth.

"So I just checked with the hotel to make sure my reservation was still set, and it seems they've overbooked."

Mom made a sad face. Dad threw his arms in the air. Magnus kept eating. Nina looked at me. I glared at Elena. I knew her games. I knew them all too well.

"But don't worry, you two. I'm sure I can get a reservation somewhere else. This is a big city. Lots of hotels, right?" Elena tossed her smile our direction. "I won't impose, I promise."

"And yet you're here. Unannounced. Imposing."

Nina kicked my foot as Elena shot me a semi-wounded look.

"I'm here for work, to congratulate you, and have a fresh start with my old friend and his lovely fiancée." Elena worked the cork until it burst free with a loud pop.

"Forgive my skepticism. I'm a little biased where you're concerned, Elena."

Magnus tuned back in, giving his head a shake. "Dude. You're acting like she was fucking your best friend behind your back, Max. Chill. You guys didn't work out. Not a big deal. It happens all the time."

The taste in my mouth turned bitter. Elena glanced away, something that almost looked like guilt settling into her expression.

When Nina's hand moved under the table this time, it found mine. Her fingers wove through mine, giving them a gentle squeeze.

"Just stay here for the night, sweetheart. It's too late to be worrying about finding a hotel at this hour," Mom said before taking a sip of her champagne. "I'm sure Max and Nina won't mind. There's plenty of room."

When Nina glanced at me, searching for what to say, I stayed quiet. This was her house. Her place to decide who could be here. I might have been a dominant son of a bitch in the bedroom, but I knew better than to take that into the kitchen. At least, I knew better now. Nina was her own woman and I wasn't going to stifle that by calling all of the shots.

"Nina? What do you think? Elena could stay in the room next to Hans's and mine tonight, and tomorrow, we'll find her a hotel." Mom waited for Nina's reply, sipping on her champagne, which was almost gone.

Nina swallowed.

"Really? That would be wonderful." Elena covered her chest with her hand. "I mean, is that okay with you, Nina?"

Nina shifted on her chair. "Um . . ." She shifted again. "Maybe?"

Mom clapped. "It's settled. You'll stay here tonight."

Elena beamed, pouring more champagne in Mom's glass. "Perfect."

Nina was working her lip, glancing around the table like she had no idea what was happening. Her hand stayed in mine the entire time.

I shoved back from the table then headed out of the room. "I just remembered something that needs my attention at the office."

As I left, I realized their plan was already working—they were already driving Nina and me apart.

TWENTY-ONE

Nina

I'd done it. Fallen for him.

The question mark that came after that was gone. The dot, dot, dot was gone as well. I'd fallen for Max Sturm, the last man on the planet I probably should have.

That was what I was thinking as I took what felt like the world's longest elevator ride. How I'd been so sure he'd be easy to despise. How easy I'd thought it would be to treat him with a kind of cool removal. Maybe it was my confidence in my lack of attraction to him that had ultimately led to the opposite happening. I'd been so sure of one thing that I hadn't guarded myself against the opposite happening.

It was too late to go back. With any of it. I was marrying Max Sturm in a couple of short months according to his meticulously laid-out schedule. Of course us confessing our attraction to one another made things more complicated. Would the marriage still be one of convenience? Would there be benefits other than money and a green card? Would marriage complicate what we already had? Would it last? Would we still divorce at the end of that two-year period?

Everything felt so up-in-the-air and undecided. I felt like a hundred glass balls were floating above me, just waiting to fall out of the sky and shatter at my feet.

After Max had escaped dinner, I'd stayed with the rest of his family, finishing a meal I didn't really taste, taking part in conversations I didn't really hear, making nice. I wasn't usually one for making nice, but this was Max's family and old friend/fiancée/enemy, and whatever his feelings toward them, they were in my house and owed a margin of respect.

Elena and Anya helped me clean up after, while Hans and Magnus decided a game of pool and bourbon were in order. Elena even offered to mop the kitchen floor since, somehow, strawberry juice had kind of wound up smeared along the linoleum. And the cupboards. And the counter. And Max's hair if we were keeping track.

I told her not to worry about it and showed her to the old bedroom beside Max's parents' room upstairs. She was gracious and almost pleasant. Not that I could share that with Max because it was clear that Elena could find a cure for childhood cancer and that still wouldn't elevate her in his esteem.

Magnus took the room Max had been in before four unexpected houseguests arrived, and after making sure everyone seemed to be tucked in for the night, I sneaked out of the house.

The bus ran all hours, much to Max's horror, and even though he or Kate gave me a lot of rides, I still depended on trusty public transportation for lots of things.

Like showing up at my fake fiancé's-slash-love-interest's office in the middle of the night.

I'd been to Max's office in downtown Portland a couple of times, but never at night and certainly never for anything close to the reason I was showing up now. When the elevator doors chimed open, I stepped into a large, dark lobby. A reception desk, where Ezra could sometimes be found helping out, was parked in front of the elevator. There were a handful of offices running along the wall of windows, a large expanse of cubicles down the hall, a break room, a conference room, all of it.

Only a person or two might work there now, but Max had big plans for the future. His commercial development company was almost fully funded, but he'd need people to work it. He was ready for when that day came.

It seemed to me like an obscene waste of money for him to pay for this large of a space when he was the only employee of Sturm Industries, but I thought seeing this place and its potential motivated him.

Moving through the dark space, I headed for Max's office in the corner. I wasn't sure if he'd be happy to see me or not-so-much, since he'd left in such a hurry earlier, but I was planning on swaying his opinion in my favor.

The door to his office was closed even though he was alone, almost like he was trying to close out the world. I didn't know, but I didn't pause to rethink what I was doing. I just opened the door and stepped inside.

Like the rest of the offices, this room was dark too. The screens of his computer cast a glow across his face as he studied them, his forehead pinched in concentration.

"Nina?" His chair rolled back from his desk as he blinked to adjust his eyes to the dark I was shadowed in.

"Max."

His screens dimmed some so I could just make him out. "What are you doing here?"

"Checking on you. You kind of left in one giant rush."

He scrubbed his face before his head fell back against his chair. "I'm sorry. I just can't be around Elena. I don't trust myself not to say or do something that I would regret later."

My brow peaked. "Because it's not like you were saying anything tonight you might regret tomorrow?"

"Nothing I said to her I'll regret tomorrow. Nothing."

Leaving the door open, I moved inside his office. "Well, you'll be happy to know I found a hotel for her to stay at tomorrow night and we made her an open-ended reservation until she can find more permanent housing."

It was dark, but I didn't miss the way his jaw clamped down. "You know this is all some big scheme she or my parents or all three of them are in on, right? The job, the hotel falling through, the nice act—it's all meant to make us lower our defenses."

I had to bite my tongue. Max had known Elena far longer than I had, but I considered myself a decent judge of character, and she didn't seem like the plague incarnate. Maybe she had been, maybe part of that was still there, but I liked to judge a person based on who they were now instead of holding them to who they'd been before. She might have done some terrible things and hurt Max in a way that made my stomach curdle, but I wouldn't give her as much credit and headspace as Max did.

I didn't want to talk about Elena tonight. Or his family. Or their intentions.

I wanted something else.

I wanted him.

"I'm not here to talk about them, Max. Tonight, I just don't give two fucks about any of those people camped out in my house right now." I slid out of my jacket and dropped it on the floor. I still had on the same dress from earlier, and as I moved closer to his desk, I worked it up my body and over my head. It landed on the floor with my jacket. "I'm here to be with you."

Max's lips parted, his breathing accelerating as I moved closer, naked and unrepentant.

"You and me, we have unfinished business." I came around the side of his desk, and he swiveled in his chair toward me. "And I'm not leaving here until we finish it."

Pausing at the end of his desk, I slid up onto the edge of it, crossed my legs, and swung my feet from it. When he started shoving out of his chair, I raised my finger. "But first, I need to tell you something."

Max was dressed in his suit again, but he was loosening his tie. "After."

I stifled the smile forming. "Nice try. But now."

Rising from his chair, he slid out of his jacket, pulling his tie out from beneath his collar. I had to look away to say what I needed to because watching the Max striptease was a little distracting.

"You remember that biography we each filled out?" I stopped. Maybe I should have waited to take my clothes off until after I'd said this. Especially now that he was half naked already. "Of course you do. You're the one who put them together." Clearing my throat, I stared out the window to keep my thoughts from getting away from me. "There was a reason I didn't fill out that last section on our . . . sexual affairs."

"Because you make it your job to make my life difficult?" Max was working his belt free, his voice low.

"Keeping to the point . . ." I shifted just a little farther down the desk from him. "You thought I didn't answer those questions by leaving them blank when, in fact, those were my answers."

Max's zipper lowered. The sound of it sent chills down my back. "What, so you used invisible ink to write your answers? I'm not following, Nina. Let's discuss this later."

When his pants dropped, I swallowed and continued to stare out the window. If I looked at him, I would have no problem putting a pin in this conversation and getting to the whole reason I was here.

"No." I gnawed at my lower lip. "My answers were left blank because I don't have anything to fill in."

Max was quiet for a moment. "Still not following."

I sighed. How could someone who was able to forecast the stock market not be able to make sense of what I was spelling out?

"I left the answers blank because I don't have any answers."

He still wasn't talking.

"Because I haven't . . . *done* anything. With anyone." My forehead creased as I waited for him to say something.

Max stood there, naked, silent. It was driving me mad trying to tell him what I was and him not getting it. Standing an arm's length away from me, clothing free.

"Not following—"

"God, Max," I roared, throwing my head back. "I'm a virgin."

Silent again.

And more silence.

"Max?" My head turned hesitantly toward him.

He was staring at me, trying to hide his surprise, but it was still swimming in his eyes. "You've never?" His brow lifted. "With anyone?"

"Pretty sure that's the definition of virgin."

Max's hand covered mine as he moved in front of me. He uncrossed my legs then pulled me to the edge of his desk. A breath escaped me as he settled into the space between my legs. "Then we'd better see to getting those blanks filled in."

He slid me closer to the edge of the table, until I could feel him hard against me. My heart took off.

"But I thought you had something urgent that needed taken care of." My gaze fell to his computer screens, where he'd clearly been busy with something. Like making buckets of money.

"I do." His fingers moved up my legs. He smirked down at me when he felt the wetness on my inner thighs. "I'm taking care of it right now."

His fingers kept moving up until they landed on their destination. My eyes closed as his thumb stroked me. "So that whole storming out and leaving for your office act earlier was just to get me alone, spread out on your desk, beneath you?"

Like I'd reminded him of something, he leaned into me until I was laid out beneath him. My chest spilled out beneath his, my body cushioning all of his muscle and mass.

"I can't get much by you." He sank his teeth into my earlobe, keeping his thumb circling me.

My breaths were quick, raspy. "You leaving had nothing to do with your family camping out at the house?"

His fingers moved, circling lower. "What family?" His mouth moved lower, sucking down my neck.

"It had nothing to do with Elena?"

He nipped me when I said her name. "Elena who?"

My back arched into him, my hips tipping in welcome. "Max . . ."

"This has nothing to do with them, Nina." His face lifted above where he'd been nuzzling my chest, his eyes on fire. "When I'm with you, like this, nothing else matters. I don't care what my family's scheming and I don't care about what Elena did. I care about you."

I couldn't forget the way he'd looked earlier tonight. How undone he'd seemed. How lost. "There's a lot coming at you all at once." I bit back the moan rising in my throat when his finger slipped a little inside me. I wanted him so damn badly, but I had to make sure this was right. For him too. "Are you sure this is what you want?"

Max's mouth found mine, teasing me with his tongue between sucking at my lips. "Instead of telling you how much this is what I want, how about I show you instead?"

My head bobbed when I felt his finger slide away, making room for him.

"I don't want to hurt you." His eyes were squeezed shut, like he was fighting some invisible battle, as more of him moved inside me.

"You won't," I breathed, my hips angling to meet him.

Then, at the last minute, I changed my mind. About the position at least.

Pivoting against him, I managed to get him on his back with my body above him on his desk.

"What are you doing?" He glanced up at me, not seeming to mind the change as his gaze dipped to my chest hanging above him.

"This is my first time." I crawled farther up the desk with him. "Therefore I'm in charge."

Once he was laid out below me, I scooted down his body until I was straddling his lap. Rocking my hips against him, I felt my wetness sliding along his shaft.

"No argument from me." He groaned, his head falling back when I increased the friction of my pumps.

Reaching between us, I took him in my hand and fisted up and down a few times.

"God, Nina. Keep that up and I'll be going off before I get inside you."

I stroked him once more. "Well, we wouldn't want that." Lowering my hips, I stopped when I felt him at my opening. I circled him, teasing us both.

"Nina, I'm serious. Stop fucking around."

I lifted my hips up and away, hearing his heavy steel slap against him. "*Stop* fucking around?"

The muscles of his neck shot to the surface. "No, don't stop. Definitely, do not stop."

Grinning at him, I rolled my hips until I could feel him in place again, then I drove down hard.

It was hard to tell who cried out louder—Max or me—but it was a good thing we were in this big office all alone and free to make as much noise as we wanted. I never realized I'd be such a noisy lover, but there was no way to stay quiet with a man buried deep inside me. Not when said man was Max Sturm, and he was gripping my hips, holding onto me like I was both his salvation and his demise.

"Are you okay?" His large hands braced tighter around my hips as I slowly pumped my hips above him.

"Yes," I breathed, more in animal instinct than conditioned response.

"Do you hurt?"

My hands pressed into his stomach, using it to propel my movements. "So much it feels good."

"Nina?" Max's usual voice started to resurface.

I just shook my head and kept moving in a steady rhythm above him. "Don't even think about it, Max. I've waited twenty-three years for this."

His muscles were popping through his skin everywhere, his jaw tight and the veins running down his forearms looking ready to burst.

"Have you ever been with a virgin before?" I asked.

His hands were slowing my pace, controlling the motion of my hips. "I've never been with you. To me, that's worth a million virgins."

When I came down on him, I stayed there. I loved this feeling—having Max so deep inside me he felt like a part of me. "But not a million and one?"

A crooked smile moved into place. "I'll let you know after."

"Then I'd better give you something good to sway your vote." Reaching behind me, I cupped his balls and gently squeezed them as I started to ride him again.

He made sounds I'd never heard come from him before. Sounds I'd never heard come from anyone before.

From the feel of him, he was ready. I wondered if he was fighting it off, wanting to wait for me. Not that he'd have long to wait because with the way he was pitching his hips into me, he was rubbing some place inside that was driving me up a wall each time he plunged back in.

"Fuck, that's beautiful, Nina. Let's see you come, baby. I want to watch it."

Max shoved back on the desk again, trying to get his feet up so he could really thrust into me. In the process, his arms and head kind of sent a couple of his computer screens falling over the edge of his desk. They landed loudly, making a shattering noise as glass scattered across the floor.

"Shit," I cursed, leaning over. I didn't realize how dangerous sex could be. And damaging.

"Don't worry about them." Max pulled me back down, picking up right where we'd left off. "They're computer screens. I don't care. Just don't stop." When I started moving again, his head rolled back. "For fuck's sake, don't stop."

In only a few more moments, he was tensing beneath me, so close I could feel his orgasm building up into his shaft.

"Where do you want me, Nina? Where do you want me to come?"

I stared at him, riding him closer to his orgasm. "Inside me," I breathed. "Always inside me."

"Fuck," he growled, like my words were his undoing.

Feeling his orgasm spreading was my ruin. His thumb drifted back to my clit, stroking it until I was cursing my release with him, filling the silence with our passion. He didn't stop pumping inside me until the last shudder of my orgasm had been pulled from my body, and even after that, he stayed buried deep inside.

I fell over him, my body blanketing his as we gave ourselves a moment to catch our breaths.

"I like that way." I kissed his chest then tipped my chin, so I was looking up at him. He was already looking down at me, his hairline damp with sweat and his face flushed from his orgasm. "A lot. I think we can list that as my favorite position under that blank." When I drew my thumb across his lips, he kissed it. "I guess we can also fill in a few more of those blanks. First lover: Max Sturm. Age lost virginity: An embarrassing twenty-three."

His brows came together as he leaned up on his elbows. "There is nothing embarrassing about that." He paused, looking like he was thinking. "I . . . nope, I can't even try to sum up how I feel about being your first. That's not embarrassing, Nina. That's the damn best gift you could give a man like me. It's priceless." His lips pressed into my forehead as he combed my damp hair away from my face. "Just like you are."

I let his words find their way into my heart, then I kissed him full on the mouth, climbing up his body until I felt him harden inside me again.

"So?" I whispered against his mouth. "What was your favorite position?" I paused long enough to circle my hips over him. His head fell back, thumping against the desk. "That one? It's pretty great, right?"

When I rotated my hips again, Max's hands gripped my hips as he sat up. "I'm more of a show than tell type of guy."

He shoved off the desk, holding me to him, before twisting around and letting my feet fall to the floor. His light eyes were burning, his need hard against my stomach. Kissing my forehead, he swiftly spun me around, pressed my chest onto his desk, and kicked my legs apart. His fingers were already spreading me open, as he fitted himself to me, before the surprised gasp escaped from my throat.

"Let's see what you think of my favorite position." His hands settled on my hips again, his fingers curling deep into my flesh. Then his hips moved against me, sliding inside inch by agonizing inch. When he could go no deeper, he held himself there, leaning over me and breathing outside of my ear. His hands came around below me, cupping my heavy breasts.

"God, Max," I moaned, clenching around him.

A primitive growl echoed up from his chest. Then he took his stance behind me, holding my hips in place as he kept himself buried inside me. "My turn to be in charge now."

As he slid out, my moan filled his office. It was consumed by a cry when he slammed back into me.

"And you will be shrieking *Mister* Sturm by the end of this."

TWENTY-TWO

Max

Something was wrong. Nina had been avoiding me all day and I'd be a fool not to know why. It was about last night. What happened between us. Multiple times.

She hadn't seemed conflicted about any of it last night, but something was clearly upsetting her today. I guessed it had to do with the way we'd both come into this arrangement with the understanding it would be one way, and now, it had gone the opposite.

I guessed it also had something to do with what had happened to her as a child. Being left behind. First by her dad, then by her mom. Commitment was a touchy topic for Nina, and after the things we'd said and shared with each other, we'd both put ourselves in a place to get hurt.

This wasn't just a business transaction we'd agreed to with a handshake—this had become a matter of the heart now too. Neither of us had planned on that.

Planned or not, I wanted this. Her. Us. The risk of being hurt was worth the reward that came from being with her.

"Will Nina be here for dinner?" Dad was manning the BBQ stationed on the porch, turning over enough bratwursts to feed the entire neighborhood.

"Yeah. I think." I checked the street again. No signs of Kate's car or Nina walking home from the bus stop.

"Good. I want to thank her for being so generous, letting us stay here. And what says thank you better than a big juicy bratwurst?" Dad clinked his beer bottle against mine I had yet to take a sip from. "Elena dropped off a Black Forest cake she found at a bakery in town, so your wife-to-be will get the full German cuisine experience."

Hearing Elena's name made my back tense. "She dropped it off? As in she won't be here for dinner?"

"She had to work." Dad drained the last half of his beer. "You seem surprised."

"I am." I hadn't seen Elena since I stormed out of the house last night, but I'd made good and sure she was out of the house before I came back. According to Mom, she was all set in a hotel near the Lloyd Center and would be so busy with work, we'd be lucky to see her.

I was of an opposing point of view.

"I know Elena and you have some bad blood, but you have to allow a person to change." Dad popped the cap off his next beer. "Whatever happened, she really just wants the best for you, Max."

"Of course she does," I snarled. "Because Elena's just that big of a person."

Dad pointed his tongs at me, like he was about to scold me, when Kate's silver Honda raced around the corner. I stood up from the porch swing, straightening my tie. Nina had been gone when I woke up this morning in my office. No note. No explanation. No nothing.

It had taken every ounce of willpower in my possession not to track her down to find out why she'd slipped out like I was the one-night stand she was ashamed of. I'd stayed at the office, worked, did what needed doing, and occasionally called her. Ten times.

Kate didn't pull in the driveway. Instead, she screeched to a stop at the curb, firing a glare at me that had my brows pulling together.

"Fan of yours?" Dad nudged me.

A sigh slipped out. "Not today."

Kate was shaking her head all animated-like, throwing her arm back at me. Whatever she was saying, I got the distinct impression she was advising Nina to turn and run.

A minute later, Nina crawled out of the car, shaking her head at Kate.

Throwing her arms in the air, Kate's reply was loud enough for me and the next block over to hear. "Fine!" Then she aimed another glare at me before stabbing her middle digit in the air in my direction. She drove away like that, waving a fuck you good-bye at me.

"Here comes the blushing bride now." Dad pinched his tongs a few times in Nina's direction.

She wouldn't look at me. She was moving slowly, like each step closer became harder and harder to take. She was in her overalls, which meant she'd managed to get back here to change before disappearing wherever she had. Seeing her today, remembering last night, all I wanted to do was wrap her in my arms and hold her tightly. I wanted to kiss her and touch her and love her body the way I had last night.

What Nina appeared to want was the exact opposite.

Dad scooted closer, leaning into me. "What did you do?"

"Something I probably shouldn't have."

Moving closer to the top of the stairs when she reached the bottom, I cleared my throat, willing her to look at me. To acknowledge my presence and, like it or not, what I'd shared with her last night.

"Hello, Nina."

Her shoulders stiffened as she climbed the steps. "Max."

"How was your day?" I asked. She still wouldn't look at me. "I missed you this morning."

A sharp exhale lashed past her lips as she kept moving past me.

"Nina—" I spun after her as she headed for the door.

"Oh, yeah, sorry, that's right." She broke to a stop, snapping her fingers. "I'm your fiancée."

Twisting around, she marched back toward me, not stopping until her body smashed into mine and she lifted up to kiss me. Then she tugged me over to the swing, shoved me down, collapsed beside me, and stole the beer in my hand.

She lifted it to her lips and started to chug, which was just fantastic. Nina couldn't be around me now without getting herself good and drunk. Fuck. I thought we'd been okay last night.

"So the big day's just a couple of months away." Dad was back at the grill, giving us peculiar looks as he tended to the bratwursts.

Nina nodded, smacking her lips. "March thirty-first. The day before April Fool's day." Then she finished the rest of my beer.

"You still want to marry me?" I kept my voice playful for my dad, but my face said something else to Nina.

She barely gave me a cursory glance. "Pretty sure that's what this means." Lifting her left hand, she rolled her fingers in front of my face.

"But do you want to?" Still the playful tone in my voice, the serious tone in my expression.

Nina thanked my dad with a nod when he exchanged her empty beer for a new one. "I want to keep my promise."

"What does that mean?"

Nina slid a bit away from me. "It means I'm marrying you on March thirty-first."

"Nina—"

"The girl wants to marry you, Max. Sounds like she can barely wait to seal the deal. Can't wait to become Mrs. Max Sturm." The skepticism in his voice was so heavy, I was surprised Nina wasn't glaring at my dad the way I was.

"Mrs. Nina Burton-Sturm." She pointed her beer at Dad before practically upending this one too.

"Nina—"

"What, Max? I, unlike others, like to keep my promises when I make them. So when I told you I was going to marry you, I meant it. Just because other people's promises might stand for shit doesn't mean mine do."

My molars gnashed together. She wasn't saying anything that wasn't true—I hadn't kept my promise regarding not having sex with her.

"So, Nina?" Dad piped up, totally oblivious to the storm culminating on the porch swing a few feet away. "What are your thoughts on starting a family?"

She was quiet, probably as surprised by his question as I was. She let the rest of her beer help her fill in the answer. "I guess I haven't given it much thought." She aimed a lethal glare at me from the side of her eyes. "Max kind of snuck up on me out of nowhere and took me by surprise."

"Do you want kids?" Dad asked.

"I think that's a little early to say," I answered him, hoping he'd read the shut-up-already in between the lines. "We just got engaged."

"I don't know." Dad shrugged, swirling his beer in the bottle. "It seems normal for most couples to talk about family planning before getting engaged. So if one doesn't want kids and the other wants a dozen, that can be worked out before the vows get exchanged. Forever is kind of a long time."

Nina crossed her arms, staring into the yard with something unreadable on her face. "I don't know. What do you want, Max?"

Was she asking to appease my dad or because she genuinely wanted to know? I'd guess, given the sideways glare fired my way again, I had my answer.

"I'd like to have children." I shifted on the swing. "One day."

"Well, there you go." Nina flourished her hand in front of her. "Max wants kids. Max gets kids."

My body twisted toward her. "What does that mean?"

"Oh come on, sweetie, you're the kind of man who gets what he wants." Her voice was overly sweet, her expression overly tart. "Right?"

For a moment, she locked eyes with me and I thought I saw it—the fire. Not the one born from anger but from the kind we'd surrendered to last night. It was extinguished before she looked away.

"I can understand your hesitation though, Nina." Dad pointed those damn tongs at us again. "After watching your dad leave. Your mom after. Surely that must have an effect on a person when they think about starting their own family."

Nina's head twisted in his direction. "What do you mean?"

Dad's shoulders lifted. "The worry of wondering how can you be a good parent when you didn't have one to model from?"

My eyes closed at his words. I'd been right about them going after Nina instead of me in their plans of breaking us up. He'd found her weak spot and had just driven a damn dagger into it.

The swing whined when Nina stood. She didn't say a word. She just shoved through the door and disappeared inside.

"Christ"—I burst up from the swing to follow her—"if that's the bar for parenthood, I'm in the same boat as Nina." I threw him a look before pushing through the door. "*Dad.*"

Slamming the door behind me, I powered down the hall, knowing where she was. It was where she always went whenever we'd gotten into an argument or she needed to be alone. The only place in the house that she could lock me out of—her bedroom.

I rapped on her closed door. "Nina."

"Leave me alone, Max." Her voice was quiet from the other side.

My chest tightened. "No."

"Go. Away."

My hand dropped to the doorknob and I twisted, expecting to find it locked. It wasn't. I didn't ask, I didn't knock again—I threw the door open and stepped inside. It was already closed before she'd had a chance to whip her head in my direction.

"I guess I shouldn't be surprised." She eyed me standing inside her room. "You don't seem to care about or respect what I want. You care about what you want. When you want it. Whatever the cost."

I slid my hands in my pockets to keep me from doing something stupid like rushing across the room and pulling her to me. With the screwdriver she was clutching like an icepick, she'd probably drive it straight through my heart if I got within swinging distance.

She was hurt. Because of me. She felt betrayed. Because of me. She was scared. Because of me.

Maybe I did deserve that screwdriver in the heart.

"Are you okay?"

She snorted, getting back to tightening the glass knob on the bathroom door. "Yeah, I'm fucking awesome. Can't you tell?"

"What's wrong?" I asked gently.

"What makes you think something's wrong?" She started beating at the doorknob with the screwdriver because, I guessed, it doubled as a hammer.

I fought the urge to go help before she drove the screwdriver through her thumb. But she didn't want my help. That was obvious. "The fact that you've been avoiding me, ignoring my calls, and using my face as target practice for your lethal looks." I cocked a brow at her, but she wasn't looking. She was too busy beating at the doorknob. "Plus, you do home improvement when something's wrong."

My answer made her glare at the doorknob. "I do home improvement no matter how I'm feeling because if I didn't, this place would have collapsed by now."

She kept whacking at the handle until it popped off. It rolled across the wood floor of her bedroom and disappeared under her bed. I couldn't stand to look at her bed. Not now. Not with the way she was acting like I was everything bad and painful in the world.

"What do you want, Nina?" I rubbed at my forehead, ready to give her whatever it was if it was anywhere in my ability to give it to her. Anything.

She was quiet, staring at the spot where the doorknob had disappeared, seeming to collect her breath. When she took a deep inhale, most of the anger seemed to wash away from her face. The apathy that took its place was worse than any loathing.

"I just think we need to slow things down." Her eyebrows drew together. "Two days ago, everything was going according to your finely tuned plan, and last night, we were in your office doing . . . stuff."

Her choice of word made me almost smile. "Lots of stuff."

She exhaled through her nose. "Three different times."

"Four," I corrected automatically because I'd been counting. It had been the damn best night of my life—I practically had the entire thing committed to memory. When she shifted and crossed her arms, I fought the question on the end of my tongue. I lost the battle. "Do you regret it?"

She only took a few seconds to answer, but I felt like I'd died a hundred different deaths in that short span of time, waiting for her answer.

"No." Her head shook once, her eyes narrowing on the floor. "I just wish I would have stopped to think, you know? Everything happened so fast . . . maybe we should slow things down to make sure this is what we want."

She was talking, communicating, not trying to kill me with her eyes anymore. This should have been measured as progress, but instead, it felt like failure because she was saying the exact opposite of what I hoped she'd feel. The complete contrast to the way I felt.

"You keep using the word *we*, but I'm not conflicted about any of this. You are. So let's get that straightened out." For the first time since closing the door, I took a step further into her room. Closer to her. "What do *you* want?"

Her answer came instantly. "To slow things down. To get back to the way things were." She was tapping the end of the screwdriver into her palm, a dozen emotions playing on her face.

"Okay," I answered, because what else was there to say? I'd give her anything she needed—even if that meant backing off.

Her eyebrows squeezed together. "I think."

My shoulders fell. "Nina . . ."

"You and me." She flailed the screwdriver between us. "This wasn't supposed to happen."

"I know." I nodded once, stepping closer. "And I don't care."

"How can you say that?"

My stomach hurt from watching her. She was so scared. So unsure. I'd never seen Nina like this—never expected her scars ran so deep—but watching her now made me feel like everything inside me was twisting in on itself. I didn't want her to feel this way. I didn't want to be the cause of it.

"Because it's true," I said slowly. "I care about you. I want to be with you. I don't care about what was supposed to happen and what wasn't."

She leaned into the wall behind her, shaking her head. "You, the man burned to ashes, as against commitment as I am, how can you look at me, say that, and mean it?"

The ice in her voice was meant to send me back. Instead, I drew closer. "Because it's the truest thing I've ever known."

A sharp laugh spilled from her. "Said every human being to another who made them feel a few butterflies."

I felt something bubble up inside me, and I couldn't find the lid to trap it before it exploded out of me. "Dammit, Nina, you want to pretend things are back to the way they used to be between us? Fine, go ahead. You are free to make your own choices, but don't for a minute expect me to do the same."

My body was trembling from adrenaline, and at the same time I wanted to drive my fist through the drywall, I wanted to tuck her close and kiss her gently. I was a mess. A fucking wreck and it was my fault the woman in front of me was in the same position.

"There is no going back for me. And if you want to pretend there is for you, fine. Let me know how this is going to play out." I paused to let her speak, but she didn't, so I kept going. "You want to fuck then go to separate bedrooms after? Fine. You want to never touch again? Fine. You want to hate me? Love me? Despise me? Fine. I don't give a fuck.

I want you. However I can have you." My eyes locked on hers. "Whatever piece of yourself you're willing to share."

She slid down the wall until she hit the floor. Her head fell into her hands, the screwdriver tumbling from them. "Max. I'm confused." She rubbed her forehead. "So damn confused."

Something settled in my throat that made it hard to talk, so I moved toward her. I'd barely made it two steps before her head lifted enough to give me a warning look. She didn't want to be comforted. Not by me.

The realization made me feel like someone had just swung a bat into my stomach. "Yeah, well, I'm feeling knocked on my ass too." I moved toward her again, warning glares be damned. I knew why she was pushing me away, because it was the same reason I wanted to push her away. Fear was a powerful thing. "But I know what I want and who I want. Instead of letting all of the reasons why I shouldn't want you get in the way, I'm hanging on to the reasons I should."

Nina kept rubbing at her head, her red hair spilling around her face. "Why should you want me?

My shoulders lifted. "Because every part of me wants every part of you." They lowered as I cleared my throat. "That's why."

Nina's body shook like she could have been crying, but she wasn't making any noise and I couldn't see her face. When I moved closer, her body tensed instead. Then she shoved off the floor, leveling me with a look.

"I believe one part of you wants me." Her narrowed eyes dipped to my crotch before she pushed inside the bathroom. "Again. And again. And again." She continued to repeat the same thing even after she'd slammed the door. Even when the shower cranked on a few seconds later.

Her words echoed in my head, making me wonder if that was really what she believed. That the only part of me that wanted her was my dick. That that was all I needed from her. That the rest that resided above and below and within me didn't long for her in the same way.

She didn't want to see me. She didn't want to talk. She'd made that clear.

I should have accepted that, walked out of her bedroom, and let her come to me to dictate how we should proceed with the rest of our arrangement, whatever was left of it. I should have given her the space and time she needed. I should have let her go like she'd clearly let me go.

I was incapable of any of that.

When I shoved through the bathroom door, a cloud of steam rolled over me. Nina's bathroom was small, but she must have had the water boiling-hot to create that much steam so fast.

"I'm not letting you do this." I pushed the door closed and leaned into it, staring at the shower curtain she was behind. Her clothes were scattered across the bathroom floor, her smell filling the air.

"Get the hell out." She didn't sound angry. She sounded tired. Worn out.

"No."

"You can leave on your own, or I'll make you leave."

I crossed my arms and continued staring at the shower curtain, willing her to try. "You will have to shove and push and pry me out of your life for the rest of your life because I'm not leaving. Ever. I'm not going anywhere, so why don't you get that through your head now so we can talk about what comes next?"

Nina was silent, nothing but the sound of the shower filling the room. My shoes echoed across the tile as I moved toward the shower.

"You and me. Last night . . . it wasn't supposed to happen. The guy I agreed to marry for a sum of money is the first guy I've slept with and the only one I've ever had feelings for. That's messed up. That wasn't supposed to happen, and now I don't know what to do."

Her words hit me like a balm, soothing every burn and wound. I'd done it. Cut through the disguise. Gotten to the root of her removal.

"We'll do what everyone else does." I moved closer, until I could have touched the shower curtain if I wanted. "We'll take it one day at a time."

Nina's sigh rolled through the room. "It's never that simple. And people who think it is never make it."

"I'm not going to leave you. I'm not going to walk away." My words were loud, bouncing off the walls of the small room. I wasn't sure where my family was or if they were hearing any of this, and I just didn't care. Somewhere in my months of being with Nina, she'd become more important than anything else. My green card included.

It seemed so insignificant now that I'd met her. I'd started our relationship wanting one thing and was standing here now, wanting something else entirely.

"You're not going to walk away?" Nina repeated slowly. "You have the date for our divorce down in a contract."

My eye squeezed shut. The damn contract. "That was before."

"Before what?"

Isn't it obvious? I didn't want to scare her more by dropping the real word on her, so I softened it. "Before I fell for you." When Nina didn't say anything, I kept going. "I'm not going to leave you." I moved closer, her silence stretching on. "I'm not going to hurt you." My fingers curled around the edge of the shower curtain, her silence deafening. "I'm not going to betray you."

I couldn't take one minute more before sliding the curtain open just enough to look inside to make sure she hadn't disappeared. Nina felt like more of a dream than reality, and I wasn't sure what I'd do when I was forced to finally wake up.

I found her sitting on the shower floor, curled up into a ball, her whole body shaking as the shower pounded down on her.

"Nina . . ." My voice was tight from the way my vocal cords were collapsing from seeing her this way, knowing I was responsible for it.

"Just go, Max. Please." Her voice was shaking too.

Stepping inside the shower, suit and shoes and all, I kneeled beside her. The water pummeled the side of my face, saturating my jacket instantly. "Didn't you just hear what I said? I'm not leaving you. Ever."

When my hand slid a sheet of hair back from her face, she flinched. "Everyone leaves me. Everyone."

I scooted closer, blinking through the water. "Not me."

As my hand moved back to her face, sliding the last wet ribbon of hair from her cheek, her hand lifted slowly until it was covering mine.

"Not me," I repeated as she tangled her fingers through mine. "Never."

Now that I could see her face, I could tell she was crying. It should have been impossible to tell the difference between tears and shower water, but it wasn't. Not with Nina. I could have pointed out every last tear her eyes had shed.

Her hand slid mine down to her lips, holding it so she could kiss it. She didn't stop. She continued to kiss my hand until she'd touched every part of my palm, then she twisted it to kiss the backside, lingering along each knuckle.

My chest felt on fire. With relief. With awe. With dedication. She'd let me past her walls. She was opening up in the way she feared most because . . . she trusted me.

My jaw tightened when that hit me. Nina trusted me. She was proving it right this moment as her lips continued up my wrist, her body relaxing and opening up to me. It might have gone against every instinct life had equipped her with. It might have gone in the face of every warning firing in her. It might have scared the shit out of her the way it did out of me, but together, we were moving beyond the fear of our pasts to embrace the hope waiting in our futures.

Leaning closer, her mouth captured mine as her hands settled around my neck like she wasn't going to let me leave.

My mind switched streams then. Going from wanting to say and do anything to make her know I wasn't going to hurt her, to just wanting her. Here. Now.

Always.

The shower rushed down on us as our kisses became more insistent, our bodies joining in.

Nina's mouth broke away from mine, dropping outside of my ear. Her breaths were rushed, fogging against my ear. "I need you."

Her words had a direct line to my own need, firing it to life in a way that felt as though it could rip me in half if I didn't satisfy it. My arms wound around her as I lifted us from the shower floor. Nina's legs wound around me, her arms doing the same as her mouth found mine once more.

Backing her into the wall, I rocked my hips into her, desperate to be inside her before that fire consumed me.

It took a moment for me to be reminded that I was still fully clothed. In my favorite suit. In my favorite shoes. Totally drenched inside the shower with Nina's wet, naked body wrapped around me.

Well, fuck.

I didn't give a shit about ruining the shoes or the suit; all I cared about was her. Giving her whatever she needed, my body being her present request.

Lowering one arm below her ass to get a good hold on her, my other hand lowered to my zipper. Normally I would have taken the time to undress because Nina's body against mine while I moved inside her was the closest thing to heaven a man like me would ever experience. But right now, a minute was too long to wait. My need was as insistent as hers. Our desires collided in a way that made it difficult to remain standing.

Making quick work of freeing myself, I positioned myself outside her. When I felt how wet she was, how her hips drove down as soon as she felt me close, a gravelly moan rolled up my throat.

Right before I drove her body down over me, I paused, just long enough to let some rational thought wind its way back into my consciousness. "I don't want to hurt you. After last night . . ." My forehead dropped into the wall beside hers when she managed to wiggle down on me a little more.

"I can take care of you a different way, Liebling. I can give you what you need without hurting you."

My hand dug in her backside as she continued to fight me, taking more of me into her body. The muscles of my back were quivering from holding back.

Her head tipped toward me, her mouth winding up outside my ear. "You won't hurt me, Max."

Her words weakened me just long enough for her to lower her body down the rest of mine, until I was buried so deep inside her, Nina's lap was pressed into my open zipper. She didn't move after that, just kept her body settled on mine, arching her back against the wall as she seemed to struggle to regulate her breathing.

I was still trying to wrap my head around the fact that I was balls-deep inside Nina while still fully dressed, inside her shower, minutes after being convinced I'd lost her for good.

"Please, Max." Her body tightened around me. "Please."

When her hips circled my lap, making me see my own kind of stars, my body fired to life, primed and ready to give her what she wanted. Reaching around to mold my hands around her backside, I rocked out of her until I broke our connection. Her face creased as her chest rose and fell hard between us, her back so arched away from the wall that her tits were pointing at the ceiling.

Rocking closer, as soon as I felt her wet opening, I pitched hard and deep inside her.

Nina's cries reverberated around the small room, awakening the animal buried inside me. It took every shred of my willpower to keep from rutting into her like the savage animal begged to. It took everything inside me to keep from coming inside her right then because I could have. My body was that lost in hers. From the way I felt her pulsing around me, I knew hers was the same.

But not yet. I could never forget how close I'd been to losing her. How close I'd come to driving her away.

"Eyes on me," I ordered when her eyes stayed closed. "Eyes"—I breathed as I started to pull out of her—"on me."

When her eyes opened, they looked as wild as I imagined mine did. Her own animal had risen from its slumber and was only focused on one thing. Her hips bucked against me as I continued to withdraw. "Please, Max."

"I'm not going to leave you." My hand moved to her throat, gently winding around it as I looked in her eyes. "I'm not your parents. I'm not them, and I'm not going to leave you." I leaned closer, licking the water from her lips. "Say it," I whispered against her mouth before my tongue pressed inside.

She moaned when our tongues tangled, her hips pumping against mine. When her moans sounded agonized, I gave her what she wanted. I drove into her, her back slapping against the wet shower wall.

"Say it."

"You're not going to leave me." When my hand tightened just enough around her throat, she opened her eyes. "You're not going to leave me." She stared right into my eyes.

My dick throbbed inside her, from the way her words and body made me feel. "Now I want you to tell me the same thing."

Her chest was moving so hard, with every breath, her breasts spilled around my arm winding up to her neck. With every exhale, they dropped. The feel of her like this was enough to make my balls draw up inside my stomach.

"I'm not going to leave you." Her whisper evolved into a moan when my shaft disappeared inside her. "Never." This time, I didn't have to give her a throat a squeeze before she remembered. Her eyes opened into mine. "Say it."

My pace picked up. "You're never going to leave me, Nina Burton." My forehead fell into the wall beside her head as I continued to thrust into her. "Because I'm never, ever going to let you."

She made little moaning noises as I moved faster.

"You're going to come for me right now, Liebling. Right now." Her tits were bouncing from my rushed pace, her hips slapping against the shower wall as I ground into her. "Because I can't wait another second to come inside of you, and I want to feel you going off when I do."

"God, Max," she breathed, keeping her eyes on me the whole time as I rocked her against the wall. "Why are you so bossy when we fuck?"

My mouth dropped to her chest, her bouncing tits teasing me for long enough. I sucked her hard, lashing her firm nipple with my tongue before releasing her with a loud pop. Her back arched like she was inviting me to continue. "Because I'm the one who knows what he wants."

"I know what I want. You." When my mouth did the same with her other tit, punishing this one even harder, Nina cried, "I want *you*."

"You have me." My hand curled deeper into her backside as I tipped her higher to give myself better access. "Now give it to me, Nina. I want all of you, but right now, I want your orgasm. Give it to me." Looking down at our combined bodies as I rocked in and out of her, I felt my own orgasm driving up through me. "Give it to me, Liebling. Get me off."

Seating myself as deep inside her as I could, I rocked into her in quick, shallow thrusts until I felt her orgasm cresting. Her head rolled back against the wall, but her eyes never left mine as screams spilled past her lips when her release found her. At the first clench of her orgasm, I lost myself. It was the most powerful thing I'd ever felt, and my release seemed to have no end as I continued fucking her against the wet tile wall, in my wet suit, with my hands on her ass and throat.

Nina's body was still spasming around mine when I finally collapsed into the wall, my lungs feeling like they were about to burst.

I let the shower rain down on us while I kept my hold on her. I wanted to be there to catch her when she fell. I wanted to be wrapped around her if the fear and confusion made its return. I wanted to be there to chase it away and remind her just how much I wanted her.

"I'll never leave you," I whispered in her ear, winding my arms around her back.

She draped her body over mine, her arms finding their way around my neck. "I know, Max. I know."

We stayed like that for a while, letting the warm shower soothe us, letting our bodies stay connected.

"Are you okay?" I asked as she started to unwind her legs from around me. They were trembling from what we'd just done, and I kept my arms braced around her to make sure she didn't fall.

Nina locked eyes with me. "I'm okay." A smile started to form. "Nothing like a good fuck to pound some sense back into a girl."

When I felt confident she could stand on her own, I lifted my hand to her face. "I'm not leaving you. I mean that."

"I know. I knew that last night too." She kissed my thumb when it brushed across her lips. "It was just a lot to deal with all at once. I let the demons get the better of me. The fear. My past. I trust you, Max. I trust this." She lifted our combined hands, giving mine a squeeze. "But one day at a time, okay? Don't rush this. Don't rush us. I'm already marrying you. I just gave you my virginity. Please don't push anything else yet. Let's get used to what this is like before moving on to anything else."

Holding her stare, I knew what she was alluding to. The exchanging of three words. She'd made me promise not to fall in love with her weeks ago, since she seemed to view love and commitment between a man and a woman as the kiss of death. Given her background, I could understand why. Given what I had in mind for our future, I had to change her mind on the subject. Eventually.

I didn't want to rush her. I didn't want to push her away. I didn't want to lose her. But more than that, I always wanted to do right by Nina Burton. Her first, me second. Forever and for always.

"Okay. One day at a time." Kissing her forehead, I started to open the shower curtain. I had to take care of something. Now. "I've got to do something really quick. Will you be okay if I step out?"

Nina lifted a brow. "Well, I did start this all out wanting to take a shower, so yeah, I think I'll be okay." She reached for a bottle of shampoo and squirted some into her hand.

As I watched her start to wash her hair, I got the urge to just grab a chair and watch her. I was already hard from watching her wet body as she washed her hair, the signs of our love-making rolling down her legs. Giving my head a shake, I stepped out of the shower and closed the curtain before the animal took over again, and she wound up on the shower floor on her knees and palms.

"Max?" she called as I moved for the door. "You might want to change before you take care of whatever it is you have in mind."

My mouth twitched. Nina's voice was back to normal—the hint of humor with the undercurrent of busting my balls. She was back. She was good. Whatever dark place she'd woken up in this morning, we'd managed to bring her back into the light by working out our issues in the shower.

"Okay," I replied before closing the door, but I had no intentions of changing first. I needed to get this done. It couldn't wait another minute.

With every step I took down the hall, I left a trail of water drops behind me. My suit clung to my body, water running down my face from my hair, and I made squishing sounds as I moved toward the front door. My briefcase was on the antique table against the entryway wall, and I paused there long enough to pull out what I needed. Then I threw open the front door and stormed out onto the porch.

Dad was still stationed at the grill, lazily tending to the bratwurst, a fresh bottle of beer in his hand.

"*Scheisse*, Maximilian!" He gaped at me dripping wet and steaming up the cool night air.

"How much?" I approached him, opening my checkbook and cocking a brow. "How much will it take for you to leave?"

His eyes dropped to my checkbook. He wet his lips. "This isn't about money."

Clicking the end of the pen, I dropped it to the amount box. "Of course it is. I know that. You know that. Now, let's settle this like businessmen." I moved closer until we were almost butting chests. "How much?"

"Your mother and I are just looking out for you, Max." He set his beer on the porch rail. "Nina's a sweet girl, but what's a woman like that see when she looks at a man like you?"

The blood heating in my veins chased away the chill of the fall air. "It sure as shit isn't the same dollar signs you see when you look at me."

He lifted his hands. I'd never realized until now that I was taller than my dad. He'd always seemed so big, so imposing, but now, eye-to-eye, I'd crept above him. I stood above where he did.

"Max . . ."

My nostrils flared. "How. Much?"

Dad's gaze lingered at the spot where my pen was pressed into the check. "There's this new business venture I've been presented. It's a strong one. One that could really turn things around for me." He paused and, for a moment, I wondered if that was shame in his eyes. It passed so quickly, I'd never know. "I'd buy in on my own but—"

"You wasted millions of dollars on a different business venture?"

He exhaled. "I never meant to . . . if I could redo it all, I would."

My patience was wearing thin, and all I was concerned about right then was Nina. No matter my parents' intentions, I would not let them wedge themselves between her and me.

I couldn't let them hurt her. I'd made her a promise that I never would, and that meant I wouldn't let those close to me hurt her either. "And yet you can't, so what the hell do you want?"

Dad backed up a couple of steps. "There's a lot of zeros after that one I have in mind."

The water dropping off of me was puddling around my feet, and I wanted to get back to Nina. I wrote the one, waiting for the number to fill in the zeroes. "And yet it will be worth every one to have you out of this house and out of our lives."

I glanced at my dad. This time, I knew it was shame in his eyes because it was everywhere else on his face too. He was ashamed of asking for money from his son—but that didn't keep him from lifting the number of fingers he had in mind for those zeroes.

I couldn't look at him another moment. Scribbling down the zeroes, I filled in his name, signed mine, then ripped out the check.

"I want you gone tomorrow morning. You'll leave Nina alone and stop trying to upset her. You won't say a thing to her unless it's kind, you hear me? You'll let go of the whole reason you flew you and Mom over here, and you will never revisit that agenda again." I held the check out, pinching it between my fingers. His eyes widened, his arm already moving toward it. "If you can do that, this is yours. If you can't, I'll find some other way to take care of you because, by god, I will not let you come between Nina and me. I will not let you hurt her. I won't let you near her if you keep trying, you hear me?"

He didn't pause to think about it. He didn't stop to let the shame dig in a little deeper. He just nodded then snatched the check from me. It was folded up and buried in his pocket a moment later.

"Good-bye, good riddance, and safe travels." I turned around and headed for the front door. "You'll get the wedding invitation in the mail."

TWENTY-THREE

Nina

"So? Pool table?" Max smirked as he waited for me to finish my shift at The Busy Bean.

"Best waste of space ever," I said, replaying this morning's round of insanely hot sex. On top of his pool table. I never knew green felt could feel so good scraping my back as I got fucked.

"Glad we agree on this." Max checked the window again while I restocked the cups and lids for the next shift. I'd agreed to let him pick me up because I was so tired, I didn't want to waste the extra time taking the bus tonight.

"You heard from your parents?" I asked.

"The last I heard from them was last week when Mom let me know they'd arrived back home."

"Strange how suddenly they left. I was starting to think they were going to take up permanent residence," I said as Max wandered over to help me stack rows of fresh cups.

"They had to get back to where they belong." He shrugged. "Plus, I think they came to realize that whatever their hopes were for breaking us up or slowing things down or drawing up some serious prenup, it wasn't going to work."

"Why not? Your dad seems as stubborn as you are. He doesn't strike me as the kind to give up easily." When I wiggled by Max to refill the beans, he made sure I had to wiggle extra hard to get by. As tempting as it was and as many times as he'd offered, I would not be one of those people who had sex in their place of employment. Especially not some decaying shack called The Busy Bean.

"Because they could see how I felt about you. They could tell that you and me"—his finger wove between us—"this is real."

"Glad our fake relationship seems so real." When I smiled at him, I found Max was not amused. "Sorry, I didn't mean it like that. You know what I mean. Right?"

It took a minute, but Max got back to stacking new lids. "I know what you mean."

Good. Because this was confusing enough without having to explain anything else to Max. Our relationship had been convoluted from the start, but now, having feelings for one another yet still going forward like we'd planned as a "couple of convenience," it was a damn web of complicated.

I had to keep our agreement separate from our feelings. That was important to me. I couldn't let my feelings get in the way of what I'd promised Max, and I couldn't let what I'd agreed to get in the way of my feelings. In the spirit of separating the church and the state, I was separating the feelings from the arrangement.

"Haven't heard from Elena either?" I asked gently, checking to make sure he wasn't about to explode because I'd spoken her name.

"Not one word," he replied, appearing cool and collected.

"Wow. So your family went back home after a predominately uncomplicated visit, and your ex, who you were under the impression sustains herself on destruction and demise, has left us both totally alone for almost two weeks." When he gave me a warning look, I gave it right back to him. "All of that worry for nothing."

"Better to worry too much and be pleasantly surprised than worry too little and get taken advantage of." Without me asking, he wiped down the espresso machine.

Watching Max clean anything in that nice suit of his made me wish I had my camera so I could capture the moment. Perfection. "You know, if this whole stock market thing gets old and skyscrapers lose their appeal, I think you have a promising career as an espresso stand barista."

Max kept cleaning, pausing just long enough to snap the wet towel in my direction. "Good to know." His gaze shifted toward me. "What about you? Have you ever considered what other opportunities are out there for you?"

Once I finished loading five pounds of fresh beans into the machine, I leaned into the counter. "Only a few dozen times a day."

"And what opportunity sounds most appealing a few dozen times a day?"

Checking the clock, I found that I still had five minutes before Devon would be here for her shift, which was more like ten since she ran five minutes late every shift. I couldn't stall or avoid his question for ten minutes unfortunately.

"I'd like to go to college, I guess. Enroll in a two-year program first to make sure it's really what I want to do, then transfer to a four-year close by." To distract myself, I grabbed the broom and started to sweep the floor I'd just swept an hour ago.

"What's stopping you from doing that now?" Max tossed the cleaning rag aside and turned to watch me.

I was about to reply with *shortage of cash flow* when I stopped myself. Money might have played a factor in why I wasn't in school, but it wasn't the only one. I knew I could apply for grants and loans that would help. I knew plenty of programs catered to plenty of schedules.

"I don't know," I said instead, concentrating on the floor. "I guess I just got stuck or something. I was planning on it in high school, I even sent out applications my senior year, but then Grandma started getting sick and I couldn't leave. So I stayed."

"You could have gone to one of the schools around here," Max suggested gently, still watching me sweep a clean floor.

"I could have, and I probably could have even made it through my first couple of years, but I would have had to drop out when she got really sick. During that last year of her life, I could barely leave for the grocery store, let alone for half a day to go to class." I locked eyes with him. "It was worth it. I wouldn't change anything if I could go back and do it again. Putting my life on hold to spend what was left of my grandma's with her was worth a lot more than a lost dream."

Max's eyes softened. "Who says that dream has to be lost? Why can't it be right here in front of you, found?" He waved at the space in front of me like my dream flashing was right there at my feet.

"I'm a little busy marrying some foreigner right now. Working a couple of jobs. Not sure college is a good idea until I've cleared my schedule some." Fighting a smile, I got back to sweeping.

"Marriage isn't about forfeiting your dreams, Nina. The real kind or fake kind, just in case you were about to ask." Max peaked his brow. "It's about having someone to share them with. Someone to help you reach them. Someone to stand at your side or pull you up or kick your ass when you need it. Don't let me be the reason you keep putting this off. If you're worried about money, I've already told you I am happy to—"

"It's two in the morning, Max. I've been up for nineteen and a half hours. Think we could tone down the depth of the conversation by about twenty-five rungs?" When I moved to unlock the door to sweep out the two specks of dust I managed to wrangle up, Max bolted toward me.

Moving in front of me, he put himself between the door and me as he pulled it open, checking to make sure the coast was clear. "You want to change the subject?"

"Yes, double please."

Taking the broom from me, Max swept the two particles of dust outside. "Okay. So how do you think this is going?" Max tipped the broom handle between us. "You and me?"

My forehead pinched together. "You and me the plan? Or you and me the surprise?"

Max's brow answered my question.

"And this topic is what you consider not-so-deep?" I nudged him and moved to finish stocking syrups.

"All I'm looking for is a simple estimation. Since we were just talking about school, give us a grade for how you think this is going."

"A grade? Like A, B, C, D, F?"

"Exactly like that."

I shook my head. "Did you have a rough day at work today? Lose an Olympic-size swimming pool of money or something? Are you needing your daily ego stroking to come from somewhere else today?" When I glanced back at him, I found Max leaning into the door he'd relocked, arms crossed and waiting.

"Our relationship is unique," he said. "Intricate. I'm asking not because I need my ego stroked, but because I care. If I need to make some changes, I'm willing to. Anything you need, whatever you want, that's what I'll give you. But first, I have to know how I'm doing."

If a man could get a woman pregnant from a piercing stare and a collection of words, I'd just gotten myself good and knocked up. With twins.

"You know how it's going," I said, trying to focus on the syrups instead of what—or who—I wanted to focus on.

"I know how I think it's going. I'd like to know how *you* think it's going."

My mouth went a little dry. Having these kinds of talks was hard for anyone—they were next to impossible for me. "Well, you haven't gone and confessed your undying love or scared the hell out of me by asking me to be your baby mama, so you're keeping your promise to take it nice and slow." When he gave a mini bow, I rolled my eyes. "Not to mention you aren't too shabby in the sack, you don't leave dirty dishes in the sink, and you share the remote well."

Max's face went flat. "Not too shabby?"

"Oh, please. You know how good you are. Stop fishing for compliments." A flush crept up my neck as I thought of the most recent evidence to support that theory.

A slow, crooked smile spread across his face. "I want a grade."

"Like comprehensive? Or broken down by category?" I was stalling, and Max knew I was stalling.

"You're making this way too difficult," he grumbled.

"An A minus," I said abruptly. "I'd give you an A minus."

"Why not an A plus?"

I kept my head turned so he couldn't see my smile. Only Max Sturm would be outraged by an A minus. "Because there's always room for improvement. And I wouldn't want it to go to your head, that's why not an A plus."

The door creaked when he shoved off of it. He made no move to tame the way he was checking me out, leaning into the counter as I organized the syrups. "Something's definitely going to my head."

My gaze roamed his zipper region. Insatiable. "I was talking about the one north of your neck."

"And I'm talking about the one at the end of my dick. My, at present, *hard* dick, thanks to you." He came up behind me, fitting himself against my backside as his hands moved around to work on my jeans.

"Max," I protested, my eyes closing a second later when his dick nuzzled deeper into my ass.

"Nina. I'm taking your body. Here. Now." His chest pressed into my back as he lowered my zipper. "Accept that so we can move on to the next part."

"The windows. Someone could see us," I whispered, feeling my own need building with his body wrapped around mine the way it was.

His mouth slid outside of my ear as his fingers moved inside my underwear. A groan rumbled in his chest when he felt how ready I was for him. "That's why you're going to get on your hands and knees for me."

I was already agreeing with a nod when my next protest slipped past my lips. "Devon will be here any minute."

Max lowered his zipper and pointed at the floor in front of him. "All I need is a minute."

I couldn't have lowered to the floor faster, leaning forward and spreading my palms on the cool linoleum. *What am I doing?* My silent question was hushed when Max lowered behind me, tugging my jeans and underwear down my ass as he moved between my legs. One hand dug into my hip and the other guided himself into position.

"Oh, god," I moaned, already on the cusp of an orgasm from the sheer thrill of the forbidden.

"Let's see if you're still claiming 'not too shabby' when I finish fucking you the way I'm going to." He didn't slide inside me gently then—he plunged inside with the kind of force that lifted my knees into the air. "Let's see if you can even stand when I've had my way with you."

"Max . . ." I moaned, giving my body over to his, letting him give me the pleasure only his body could.

"That's right, Liebling, you keep saying my name." Max's hand found its way around to my ponytail and gave it a rough pull as he felt my orgasm start to throb around him. "You know I like my name on your lips when I come inside your body."

That night, on the freshly swept floor of The Busy Bean . . . I became one of those girls.

TWENTY-FOUR

Max

I thought the one thing I was missing in life was my green card. I'd learned the one thing that had been missing was her.

Nina was curled around my body in her bed, having fallen asleep hours ago, but sleep held no interest for me tonight. Not with the things I had to get sorted out before our wedding in two days.

Nina was going to be my wife. I wanted that so badly I could taste it. But not for the same reason I'd originally entered into our arrangement. I didn't want to marry her so I could get a piece of paper telling me I could spend the rest of my life in this country; I wanted to marry her so I could spend the rest of my life with *her*. She was my home. I'd been wrong about it being a place on a map.

When I'd tried explaining how I felt before, I had either failed to find the right words or Nina hadn't caught the depth of my meaning. We had feelings for each other. She knew that as well as I did. What she didn't know was how deep my feelings for her ran. What she didn't know was that I didn't *just* have feelings for her—I loved her.

Nina was going to marry me in two days, no matter what. To her, she'd made me a promise she intended on keeping. Her word was her honor. But I didn't want her to marry me because she'd made me a promise. I wanted her to marry me because she felt the same way about me as I did for her.

I wanted her to marry me because she loved me too.

And I wasn't sure if she did. Love was the enemy to Nina, and if I flat out told her how I felt, she would move me into the same position. I didn't want to be Nina's enemy.

I wanted to be her husband. The real one, not the pretend one she thought she was marrying.

When Nina shifted below me, moving into a position that would make my arm even more numb than it already was, I didn't budge. Having Nina any way I could have her was more than I had a right to—numb arm included.

Taking a moment to admire her hair spilling across my arm, I sighed. I knew Nina wasn't in the same place as me mentally. I knew if we'd met under different circumstances and my green card wasn't a factor, she'd be nowhere close to exchanging vows like I was. I wasn't sure if she'd ever be ready really.

It wasn't the expression of love or commitment of marriage she shunned—it was the labels. You didn't have to call it love to express it . . . and Nina did. She "loved" me better than anyone ever had. From her concern to her care to her compassion, Nina embodied love without designating it so.

She expressed commitment better than those I'd seen married for decades. She embodied the soul of love and marriage, but she was vehemently against the labels.

Given her history, I could understand. That was why I had to do right by her. No matter what I wanted, her needs had to be put first.

Nina had agreed to marry me because she'd been out of choices. Would she still agree to it if I gave her one? Would she marry me not because she felt she had to, but because she wanted to?

Those were the questions taking up my mental real estate tonight. The questions I needed to force answers to.

Before I worked anything else out, I lowered my mouth to Nina's ear. My numb arm curled her tighter to me. "Ich dien stein," I whispered, wondering if I'd have the courage to say those same three words to her when she was awake.

Courage or not, I'd have to.

TWENTY-FIVE

Nina

I felt like I'd just been sitting across from him for the first time, taking the first look at my future husband, and in a few minutes, he would officially be my husband.

The two months since our engagement had made up the best weeks of my life. I couldn't wait to see what waited for us after today. Max and I had stuck to our commitment to take each day as it came, never veering too far into the future—for fear of it overwhelming us—or rushing whatever was waiting for us, and this approach had worked better than either of us could have hoped.

Neither of us talked about the plan for after the wedding or that date two years in the future when he'd leave the marriage with a green card, and I'd leave it a million dollars richer. I thought the main reason we didn't discuss it was because it didn't concern either of us. We cared for one another, and whatever came, we'd deal with as it dropped in our laps.

In short, life was idyllic in a way I hadn't guessed it could be. At least for me.

Another check of the clock on the wall revealed we were T-minus ten minutes. I sighed and checked the sky from the window of the room I was waiting in. It wasn't just gray up there, it was moody—dark charcoal swirling through light ash. A storm was brewing. I hoped it would control itself for another half hour so we could get through the outdoor ceremony without being power-washed by nature.

I was probably the least nervous bride in history, I thought as I took a seat and waited patiently for the time to pass. After crawling into bed last night, I'd fallen asleep and stayed asleep until my alarm woke me. No butterflies had found their way into my stomach. Cold feet had stayed away. Second thoughts and hesitations had steered clear too. Even checking my pulse revealed that everything was normal.

That probably had a lot to do with the nature of Max's and my arrangement, but I also knew it had something to do with Max. I wasn't just marrying some guy who thought commitment was something to lie about when he wanted to get a girl into bed; I was marrying the kind who knew what a promise meant and how to keep one.

I was ready to get married and move on. To whatever was waiting for us.

Since nothing about our relationship was traditional—right down to the way it had started—we'd decided to go with the same when it came to our wedding.

I was wearing the same dress Max had gotten me for our engagement since he was a big fan and if he wasn't going to let me return it, I might as well get some use out of it.

Plus, it did look pretty fantastic on me. Max would be wearing one of his classic blue suits because when he had asked me what he should wear, I just couldn't picture him wearing anything else waiting for me in front of an altar.

We were getting married at 5:40 at night, the flowers from my "bouquet" were handpicked wild roses from Grandma's garden in the backyard and tied together with a bit of twine, and the menu tonight certainly didn't fall into the elegant category—German fare combined with an array of American favorites like a nacho bar, sliders, and chili fries.

The menu pretty much looked like an adolescent boy had gotten his hands on it, and the rest was like a group of little girls had been set loose on the place.

It wouldn't be a large wedding—we'd sent out thirty invitations, almost all of those going to Max's family, friends, and acquaintances, and were expecting fifty people to attend. We'd picked a charming event center that overlooked the river where we could hold both the ceremony and reception and, at Max's request, made sure it was close to the hotel he'd booked for our wedding night.

We'd done it. We'd made it here.

I was ready.

A knock sounded at the door, but before I could invite whoever it was in, the door opened and in came my soon-to-be husband. I stood, my hand moving to my hip.

His eyes found me, going wide. "Holy fucking heart attack, Nina." Max leaned into the door, his hand dropping to his chest.

My eyebrow quirked. "I'm going to assume you mean that as a compliment."

His head shook as his eyes roamed me once more before landing on mine. "No, I mean that as there never has been and never will be a more beautiful bride than mine."

He was in my favorite blue suit. The one he'd worn the day in the shower. *Holy fucking heart attack exactly.* "It's bad luck to see me before the wedding."

His head shook slowly. "Seeing you could never bring me bad luck."

I pointed at the clock I'd been monitoring for the past fifteen minutes. "You're supposed to be in front of an altar in two minutes."

"I need to talk to you." He was smiling as he moved toward me, but the corners of his eyes started to crease.

"Can it wait until after? I think we're paying the minister by the minute." When I took a good look at his face, I felt the blood in my veins chill. Something was wrong.

"It can't wait." He took a few more steps toward me, swallowing. "I can't marry you today, Nina."

My grip tightened on my bouquet, trying to figure out what he'd just said. Or what he was saying. I couldn't decipher either. "Funny. Get out there already." I smiled, clinging to the hope that he was just teasing. Because he had to be. Right? This whole thing had been his idea. He'd picked the date and everything.

Nothing about his expression looked as though he were teasing. "I'm serious, Nina."

My heartbeat started echoing in my ears. "So am I, Max. Get your butt out there."

As he let out a breath, his hands slid into his pockets. "I can't marry you."

My stomach churned, confusion surging in my veins. "What are you talking about? This is the day we planned on, and now you come in here and say 'I can't marry you to-day'? What does that even mean?"

His finger moved between us. "I can't marry you like this."

"Like what we agreed upon?" I wasn't sure if it was the room or me or my head that was spinning, but something was definitely reeling.

He stopped moving closer, looking like he had to force himself to keep his eyes on mine. "No."

"But . . ." My hand moved to my forehead as I tried to make sense of what was going on. Nothing like how I'd planned this day would go. "But . . . why not?" That was all I had. A hundred other questions were floating in my mind, but that was the only one that mattered.

Max took a breath. Then he let it out. "Because I love you."

And just like that, the air left my lungs. "Max . . ."

He held up his hands like he was trying to buttress against an avalanche coming for him. "I know I wasn't sup-posed to fall in love with you, I know we weren't going to rush into anything, but it happened, and I can't take it back or wish it back." He lifted his shoulders. "I love you, Nina. This wasn't part of the plan, but this is what happened."

Rubbing my forehead, I focused on what to say. I knew we had feelings for each other, but I hadn't guessed he had this kind. Not yet. Love was a big deal, not something you threw around with someone you'd met months ago for some sham marriage.

"I don't understand why you can't marry me though. You still need your green card." Reason, that was what I needed. No more of that emotion stuff that was making me feel a myriad of things I couldn't put a name to.

"I don't need my green card." Max's jaw set. "I *need* you."

Need. Love. I hadn't shown up prepared to discuss these topics when I expected to be walking down the aisle toward a man who'd essentially hired me to marry him. I wasn't ready. Not yet. With time, maybe, but not so soon. This was why people fell apart so quickly—they let feelings and chemistry and emotions trick them into thinking a relationship was more than it was.

"This isn't what we agreed on." My head shook. "This wasn't how it was supposed to happen."

Max tugged at his tie, loosening it. Why was he loosening his tie when we were supposed to be getting married? That, more than anything else, made me realize that he really had no intentions of exchanging vows with me today.

"I'm sorry," he said. "I should have told you before now, but it took this long to work up the courage to tell you. I don't want you to marry me because you said you would. I want you to marry me because you love me too."

My vision was going blurry. It took me a moment to realize I was tearing up. "That's not fair."

He nodded slowly. "I know, but things have changed. My feelings for you have."

Roaming back to the window, I watched the first drops fall out of the sky. I'd known we were facing one storm today; I hadn't known there'd be two. "We agreed to do this. This was your whole idea."

"I can't marry you, Nina. Not if you don't feel the same as I do." He stayed frozen in the same spot, just barely in my peripheral vision. "I won't do that to you."

My arms wrapped around my body. I felt like I was falling apart from the core outward. "You said you were never going to leave me."

"I'm not leaving you, Nina. I'll be right here whenever you need me." He was trying to keep his voice even, but it wobbled every few words. This was hard for him. "I mean that. Whenever. Whatever. I'm here. I always will be."

I wondered if it was as hard for him as it was for me. I wondered if this storm would stay with him as long it would stay with me. I doubted it. He might claim today that he loved me, but tomorrow was a new day.

"If you're not leaving me, then what's going on?" I whispered at the window.

"I'm setting you free."

From the corner of my eye, I noticed Max move closer. My body tensing at his approach stopped him.

"I love you too much to make you go through with this."

"Go through with this?" My eyes narrowed. "I *agreed* to it."

"I don't want you to marry me because you agreed to it. I want you to marry me because you want to."

My lip quivered, so I bit it. I didn't want to feel weak in a moment when I needed to be at my strongest. "This is so truly unfair. You know how I feel about all of that."

I heard his footsteps move closer. He didn't stop until he was right beside me. "Do you love me?"

My skin chilled. "Max."

"It's a simple question," he said softly.

"Nothing's simple about love."

"Everything's simple about it. You either love me or you don't."

When his hand curved around my elbow, I reacted like he'd just shocked me. Dropping his hand, he stepped back to give me some space.

He gave me a minute. Then he gave me two.

The whole time, I stayed quiet. *You either love me or you don't.* Was it really that straightforward? Was there really no in-between? God, thinking about this was impossible when he was standing right here in front of me and the clock had just hit 5:40 on the dot.

Max glanced at his watch, exhaling. Then he gave me a sad smile. "And if you have to think about your answer, that's an answer."

My throat tightened. I thought we'd been good. I thought we were both okay with the way our relationship was evolving . . . but I'd warned him about the L word. I'd pleaded with him not to push it or force it or do whatever it was he was doing right now. Moments from when we were supposed to be exchanging vows.

"Max, I don't know what to say," I choked out. "I'm sorry."

He was in pain. He was hurting. He was fighting the same army of emotions I was. Through it all, he managed to hold his smile.

"I'm not," he said, backing toward the door. "This is what love is—doing what's best for that person and forgoing what's best for yourself."

That was when I felt the first tear rain down my cheek, in the spirit of the storm outside, in response to the storm inside.

Do you love me?

That question cycled around in my head, my answer confusing me.

Do you love me?

"Good-bye, Nina," Max whispered as the door closed behind him, sealing me alone with nothing but the storm to comfort me.

TWENTY-SIX

Nina

"*A*re you sure you don't want a piece of cake? I want to take a bath in this blackberry ribbon stuff," Kate called from the kitchen sometime closer to sunrise than sunset. Officially April first—or April Fool's Day.

It was kind of poetic since I felt like a fool. Sitting here in my wedding dress for the wedding that had never happened, twirling an engagement ring around my finger even though the guy who'd given it to me had decided he didn't want to marry me like we'd planned.

Well, I guessed that wasn't entirely fair. He would have married me if . . .

I didn't like conditions. We'd had an arrangement, we'd had a plan. He'd shot that all to hell, but somehow, I felt guilty. The hurt I'd felt earlier had melted into the current anger I was stewing in.

Do you love me?

That question had been playing on repeat in my head ever since those words had spilled from his lips. It was so unfair for him to put me on the spot like that, two and a half minutes before I'd been ready to walk down an aisle to exchange vows with him. Especially when he knew my history. Especially when he knew I did have feelings for him.

I'd felt a lot of things for Max, but love was forbidden territory. It was securely reserved for fairy-tale land, only pulled from the pages of a storybook if someone wanted to ensure an unhappy ending. Love was not something I threw around glibly, if at all, but especially not seconds away from marrying the person expecting me to confess it in return.

"I brought you a piece since you were unresponsive. But if you don't want any, it will be an extra for me when I finish mine." Kate held a piece of cake out for me, waiting.

I didn't take it. I didn't even look at it.

"Don't think of it as wedding cake. Think of it as mind-blowing sex in confection form." When my gaze met hers, she set the cake on the coffee table instead. "Good, more for me. I was looking to go up a jean size by lunch anyways."

Dropping to the floor, Kate curled her legs beneath her and stabbed her fork into the cake, but she didn't take a bite. I knew she was trying to make me feel better, but nothing short of waking up from this nightmare would do that.

After Max had left me, he'd announced to everyone that the wedding had been canceled. Of course, Kate made a beeline my way, getting me out of there before I had to face any of the guests or Max. She hadn't said anything—just wrapped her arm around me and led me out to her Honda to get the hell out of there.

It was almost like she'd known this would happen, or at least she wasn't surprised it had.

She'd been warning me against this whole thing from the beginning. She was the one who'd told me that if I let

Max get in too deep, he'd ruin me. If only I'd taken her warning more seriously. I knew I'd let him in—I just hadn't realized how far I'd let him burrow until I felt the emptiness now after losing him.

I felt like I was made up of more hollow spots than whole pieces.

Do you love me?

"Wanna talk?" Kate was still in her bridesmaid dress, looking up at me like she was another unresponsive minute away from calling the professionals in the white coats.

My head shook. "Wanna forget."

"What happened?"

My ring twirled around on my finger. Why did I still have it on? "He said he didn't want to marry me."

Kate's brow lifted. "Max said he didn't want to marry you?" It went higher. "Max?"

"Yes, him. That guy I'd been planning on marrying to-day." The doubt on her face and in her voice rubbed at my frayed nerves, making me sound snappier than I'd intended.

"The same Max who—"

"Approached me about getting his green card?" I interrupted, throwing my arm in the air before letting it flop back down into my lap. "Yep. That's the one."

"Actually, I was going to say, the same Max who's so crazy about you I guessed he was going to find you in your next ten lifetimes so you could be together."

My eyes closed. Not Kate too. I needed someone on my side to get why this was so wrong. Someone who understood that no matter what feelings we'd developed for each other, we'd agreed to marry today.

"Well, he didn't want to be with me in this lifetime, so I think you can cross the next-ten theory off your list."

Kate shoved the cake aside and leaned into the coffee table. "Why didn't he want to marry you?"

"Because he didn't."

Her eyes lifted. "He had a reason. I want to hear it."

My tongue worked into my cheek as I stalled. I'd stayed quiet because I'd been dreading this point in the conversation. The why. Kate knew how I felt about the whole love topic and would call me out on it. I didn't want to be called out on it. Not tonight.

"I'm only going to assume the worst if you don't tell me," Kate added.

"Then you'd be correct," I grumbled.

"He's in love with a traveling polka singer named Gustav?"

Slumping deeper into the chair, I decided to tell her. She was going to find out anyway. Where there was a Kate, there was a way.

"Worse." I took a breath. "He's in love *with me*."

Kate let that settle between us, keeping her affect flat. Then she cleared her throat. "And you were surprised by this?"

I waved at myself, lost and a mess. "Obviously."

Kate bit her lip like she was trying to figure out a diplomatic way to say something. "And I'm going to assume that the reason you're sharing your wedding night with me instead of him is because you didn't say it back?"

"It's not my wedding night," I grumbled.

"Your what-could-have-been wedding night," Kate edited, taking another stab at the cake with her fork. "Okay, so he freaked you out with the L word. I get it. A freak-out was totally warranted. But . . ."

I sighed—I knew there'd be a *but*.

"You two have been together, as a *real* couple, for a while. You seemed happy, did the whole melty eyes around each other." Kate shrugged. "Isn't love kind of a natural progression from all of that greatness?"

"You know how I feel about that. He knows how I feel about that." I found myself staring at the wedding cake.

"Love isn't the enemy, Nina."

"This casualty of it disagrees."

"Wounded combatant." Kate lifted her finger. "Pull yourself up, dust your bum off, and get on with it."

"Get on with what?"

"Figuring out if you love him too."

Do you love me?

"I don't know," I said, my answer finally materializing. "I don't know if I love him."

TWENTY-SEVEN

Nina

"How did I let you talk me into this again?" I muttered as Kate and I shoved through the doors of one of downtown's nicer hotels.

"I didn't so much talk you into this as I pretty much just forced your ass out the front door."

"Ah, that's right."

Kate detoured through the lobby toward the restaurant. "It's been almost a month. You can't just mope the rest of your life away inside that big, empty house."

"I haven't been moping. I've been thinking."

Kate rolled her eyes. "Come up with any answers yet? With all of that thinking, you should have arrived at the solution to patching up the ozone layer. Should at least have been able to figure out if you love Max or not."

"It's not that easy."

"No, it's an easy enough thing to figure out. It's you who brings the difficulty into the equation." Kate gave a name to the hostess, who searched her book before leading us into the restaurant.

"I don't know," I hissed at Kate when she threw me a look over her shoulder.

"No, you know. You just think you don't. Either you know you don't love him and are afraid to tell him. Or you know you do love him and are afraid to tell him. Of those two possibilities, which is the most likely?" Kate spun around, tapping her chin, as we moved through the restaurant. "It's obvious to me."

Ignoring her comment, I waved her into the booth the hostess stopped at. I wanted an outside seat for a quick escape.

"You should sit on the other side," she said.

"I will *not* sit on the other side." I slid in beside her, and my leg started to bounce as I stared at the empty booth seat across from us.

"Come on. Relax. It's just a double date, not a bikini wax." Kate nudged me. "This will help, trust me."

"How's this supposed to help me again?" As I took a sip of the water, my gaze moved toward the entrance. I needed to know my escape route.

"Dean is a totally great guy. He works at the same firm as Carter, went to a good school, has his own place, and volunteers every other weekend at a soup kitchen. He's date potential gold."

My brow lifted at her. "And you know this because you've been dating his friend for all of three and a half weeks?"

She gave me a tight smile. "I know this because I have a keen sense for these kinds of things."

"And how is Date Potential Gold supposed to help me decide how I feel about Max?"

"Because if you can't feel anything for Dean the stud, that tells us something."

"What does it tell us?" I grumbled.

"You can't move on from Max."

I blinked at her. "And this tells me what?"

She scooted down so she'd put some space between us. "That you love him." She was just bracing for my punch when she locked on something at the restaurant entrance. "And how's that for good timing?" Shooting her arm up, she hailed the two guys hovering there over.

My throat turned into a tube of sandpaper. This was not what I needed right now, no matter what Kate's reasons were. Some other guy wasn't going to help me figure out how I felt about Max.

"You've still got your engagement ring on," Kate hissed when I reached for my water glass.

"I can't get it off," I whispered.

"Can't? Or won't?" As the two approached, she smiled like we weren't talking about anything more serious than what appetizer to order.

"I've tried butter, ice water, everything. It won't come off." I glanced at the ring still on my hand. It was like my hands had decided to swell ever since the wedding day. Short of yanking off my finger or having the ring cut, I'd tried everything to remove it. The darn thing was stuck.

"Just keep your hand under the table then." Kate grabbed my hand and stuffed it into my lap right as the guys stopped at the table. She leaned over the table to give Carter a kiss as he slid into the booth.

Dean hovered beside me, shifting like he might have been as uncomfortable as I was. "This is my first one of these and I'm probably going to mess something up, so you have my permission to just splash your drink in my face when I do, 'kay?"

Whether it was the self-depreciation or the discomfort he was smothering under, I found myself relaxing. A little. "I'll probably do the same, so that permission thing goes both ways."

Dean smiled as he slid into the seat across from me, nodding hello at Kate. He was cute—I guessed that was the word for it—and dressed more like a college kid than the lawyer he was, but I couldn't help comparing him to Max. From the drink he ordered when the waiter came to the table, to the way his laugh was loud, like it was for everyone to hear instead of just the person he meant it for. He was shorter, slouched his shoulders a little, hands weren't as big—not one thing I observed about Dean didn't make me think of Max. If Kate's plan had been to fuck with my head, she'd nailed it.

"So what do you do, Nina?" Dean leaned into the table, putting his elbows on it. Max never put his elbows on the table.

My jaw ground. Enough Max for one night.

"I actually just enrolled at PCC for summer quarter to get some basic classes out of the way before I transfer to a four-year. But to pay the bills in the mean time, I work a few nights at a coffee stand across the river and walk dogs during the day."

"Nice. I got my AA at PCC. It's a great school. What do you want to do after?" Dean took a sip of his beer, looking genuinely interested, but I couldn't help thinking about how Max had been appalled when he found out where I worked late at night, instead of replying with a *Nice*.

"I don't know yet. We'll see when I get there. One step at a time." My eyes wandered the restaurant, searching. I wasn't sure for what.

"Kate told me you got out of a serious relationship pretty recently. How are you doing?"

Kate had started swiping her hand across her neck at Dean the second "serious" came out of his mouth, but he missed it. He didn't seem to realize his question was hitting sensitive ground until he took a good look at me.

Dean set down his beer as Carter shook his head. "And this is why I'm single. I have no filter for what's acceptable first date conversation and what isn't."

Clearing my throat, I started to slide out of the booth. It wasn't so much what he'd said that had upset me; it was how being in front of a different man made thinking about him that much more painful.

"Excuse me for a minute." When Kate started to slide out with me, I shook my head. "I just need to grab a breath of fresh air. I'll be right back."

Dean turned in his seat as I left, regret creasing his forehead, but thankfully he stayed at the table. I needed to be alone. Just long enough to catch my breath and reconnect with reality.

The lobby was busy with people, but I kept my head down and focused on making it to the doors. Fresh air was less than twenty feet away. I'd just made it to the door I was about to pull open when someone else opened it from outside.

He didn't notice me at first; he was holding the door open for someone who I thought was me at first. But then I realized he wasn't looking at me—he was looking at someone else.

As the woman passed Max, she gave him a smile that looked like it wasn't meant to be seen by anyone else. She passed me in a swirl of silk and skin. She was the female version of Max—commanding, confident, and striking.

Trying to duck my head and turn so I could save us both this awkward run-in, I didn't make it a step.

"Nina?" Max's voice rolled over me, making me feel a hundred things all at once.

Lifting my shoulders, I turned back around. "Max."

"What are you doing here?" He stepped in front of me, looking like the man I remembered but a roughed-up version. His eyes looked duller and his suit didn't look so pristine, but that might have had to do with the way he was holding himself—less like he was unbreakable and more like he'd tried to restack the pieces after crumbling.

"Eating dinner." My thumb went over my shoulder toward the restaurant. I tried to ignore the woman I could feel lingering behind me, waiting for him. "What about you?"

"Dropping someone off," he said, still looking at me like he couldn't quite decide if it was really me standing in front of him.

"Oh, well, since you're coming in and I'm going out"—my hand flashed between us—"I'll let you go. Good seeing you."

God, Nina. Could you sound any less moronic?

"You haven't cashed the check yet." He slid a hand into his pocket and shrugged. "Why?"

A one-million-dollar check had been sitting in a blank envelope on my dining room table the morning after the wedding disaster. No note. No explanation. Just a check with a hell of a lot of zeros.

It was still tucked in the cupboard above the fridge. I had no plans of ever cashing it, so I didn't know why I hadn't ripped it up or burned it already.

"Because we had a deal and that deal fell through."

"Because of me. You would have held up your end of the agreement if it wasn't for what I did that day. You deserve that money, Nina. I insist you cash it."

Having him close like this was dangerous. I could smell the spicy hints of his aftershave, see the flecks of silver in his light eyes; I could almost feel the warmth of his hands on my body. That pull toward him was just as strong as ever, weeks later, even after what he'd done.

"Your stuff. You know you can swing by and get it whenever you want." I stepped back to give myself a cushion of space.

Max erased that cushion. "You mean you haven't thrown it out in the street yet?"

When he tried to smile, I tried with him. "Not yet."

"Surely the pool table's been hacked into pieces though?"

When I shook my head, Max's brows rose.

"Good memories, I guess," I said right before I remembered one of the creative ways we'd found to use a pool table. "You know, good memories playing pool. Playing with sticks . . . balls . . ."—*just shut up already*—"scoring." When Max's mouth twitched in amusement, I groaned. "And shutting up now. I need to go. Before I say anything else stupid."

Max moved with me when I started to leave. "I miss you, Nina."

"Max—" I warned, shaking my head. I couldn't do this. Even though I missed him and this awkward conversation was the height of my month, I couldn't. He knew how he felt, or at least how he *had*. I didn't know. I wouldn't put either of us through more pain until I knew for sure.

"I'm sorry," he breathed, his forehead creasing when he saw the look on my face. "I shouldn't have said that. I'm sorry."

Before I could say anything, Max's eyes locked onto something on my hand. My left hand. His brow furrowed.

Curling my hand around the door handle, I started to shove it open, not missing the woman still hovering in the lobby. "See you around."

"She's my cousin," Max said suddenly as I stepped outside. His gaze flickered to the girl hovering in the lobby, waiting for him. "She wanted to come visit the States, and I told my aunt and uncle I'd look after her. She's my cousin."

My chest shouldn't have felt like a boulder had just been lifted off it, but it did. "Oh." I was chalking up the brilliant responses one after one.

"Yeah, I just didn't want you to think I was that guy who was on the rebound that soon after . . . you know." He swallowed. "I wouldn't want you to think I could just move on so quickly after everything." His gaze dropped as something pulled at his face. Looked like pain.

Say something, Nina. Something. Anything. Everything.

When his eyes returned to mine, I saw the same question in them I'd heard the day of our wedding that never happened.

Do you love me?

The suddenness of my answer shocked me.

That was when I noticed a familiar face come around Max. Could his timing really be that terrible?

"Hey, Nina, I'm sorry. I feel like an idiot." Either not acknowledging Max or not noticing we were having a conversation, Dean placed himself between Max and me. "Please come back to dinner. I promise not to say anything unless I run it through a dozen different filters first."

I wasn't looking at Dean—I was watching Max. Darkness shadowed his expression, which was replaced by something else a moment later. Something I'd never once seen on Max Sturm's face—defeat.

"I better move on," Max said briskly, turning away. "It appears you already have."

TWENTY-EIGHT

Max

The feeling of knowing you're in a nightmare but can't wake up because you're already awake—that's been my existence for the past two months. Ever since the day I told Nina how I really felt. Ever since the day Nina wouldn't tell me how she really did.

Nothing had gotten easier with time, my feelings hadn't dimmed from separation, and my life hadn't gotten back to normal. I still felt a crater had been carved out of me and I no idea how to fill it back in.

Staring into my untouched drink, twisting the glass around in my hands, I ran through the maze of what-ifs like I did every day. What if I'd told her sooner and given her time to think about it? What if I hadn't told her at all and she'd figured it out on her own instead? What if we'd kept to the deal, despite my confession? What if extra time was all Nina needed to realize she felt the same way?

What I'd come to accept from making frequent visits to the realm of what-if was that I'd done what I had for Nina, not for me.

It was the least selfish thing I'd ever done. It was also the hardest. Because I'd lost her.

But I'd also set her free.

I'd given her the freedom I was planning to exchange one million dollars for. She was free to do what she wanted without the worry of financial burdens and without the strain of being tied to a man she didn't want to be with for the next two years.

I'd done the right thing.

I'd never felt so wrong.

Time to take that first drink. Before my thoughts became any darker. My face puckered when I took a sip. The finest scotch in this kind of place was a little different than the best scotch in the places I was used to ordering a drink at. I didn't even know why I'd stepped into this sports bar. It was loud and swarmed by young kids drinking beer and cheering the mix of games playing on the dozen televisions staggered around. I looked to be the only person in a suit, and certainly the only one in a foul mood.

Sitting at a tall table positioned into the back of the place, my jaw ground when another group of rowdy college-types shoved through the front door, laughing and behaving like life was one big party. Bracing myself for the taste, I drained another sip of the "scotch."

I needed to get out of there. The whole reason I'd stepped inside was because I'd hoped all of the noise would help drown out the noise in my head. For whatever reason, it only made it worse. With the increase in volume outside, the volume inside dialed up too. This had been a bad idea.

Nothing could drown out the regret and heartache. Nothing other than her, but since I hadn't heard from Nina once in two months' time, and the one time we had run into each other had been when she'd been with someone else, the chances of Nina coming back into my life were slim to non-existent.

The rowdy newcomers found a table more toward the front of the bar, but their noise still echoed around the big space. Happy people pissed me off. It didn't used to be that way—it never had—but now when I saw someone who appeared happy, I fought the urge to flip them my middle finger.

The booze must have been working, because where my conscience usually reined in my impulse, this time, it fell short. Lifting my arm, I raised my middle finger and waved it at the loud group just getting their drinks.

At the same moment, I felt it. That feeling of someone whispering my name in a packed room of people. The shock of electricity that felt as though it were coiling around my spine.

Nina.

My gaze had just found her when she saw me—her face that same screen of shocked I imagined mine was. That was when she noticed my finger. Shock faded to ire.

Dammit, Max. Now you're going to have to go over there and apologize and try to explain yourself. Glaring into my drink, I was just shoving out of my stool when she stopped at my table.

"What was that for?" Nina's hands were on her hips, her eyes glazed over from what I guessed was, in her case, one sip too many. Besides appearing tipsy, she looked beautiful. The kind that made breathing difficult.

"It wasn't you I was flipping off—"

"Yes, it was. You were looking right at me." She tapped the table with her palms. "And I wasn't the one who called off the wedding. That merit badge belongs to you."

"Nina—"

She waved me off, her hand flying back to her hip. "You know, you want to flip me off for trying to hold up my end of our agreement? Fine. Go ahead." She held out her arms, swaying enough I knew she was likely more than just tipsy. "I'll flip *you* off for not holding up *your* end of our agreement." Lifting her arm between us, she waved her middle finger in my face.

I shouldn't have smiled, but I did. I didn't have a choice. Having her close, acknowledging me—garnering some kind of feeling from her—was the best moment I'd had in two months. And my happiness was thanks to the girl I still loved holding her middle finger two feet from my face in some crappy bar where she was drunk enough she probably wouldn't remember any of this in the morning.

Without another word or gesture, she marched back to the group she'd arrived with. The shadow of a smile stayed on my face as I watched her walk away. Nothing had changed between us, but I'd gotten to see her and exchange a clipped conversation—these days, that was a win.

I'd been planning on leaving once I'd forced down the last of my drink, but now that she was here, I wasn't going anywhere. Being in the same space with her, loud and packed as it was, was infinitely better than anything else I had to look forward to tonight.

Watching her made me happy. Happy to see her out with other people, talking and enjoying herself. I'd been worried about her living alone in that house with no one other than Kate checking in on her. But there she was, out on a Friday night, with a group of friends, drinking and laughing.

Nina was resilient. She'd be okay.

At least one of us would be.

The guy I'd seen her with in the hotel that night wasn't there—that might have been the first thing I'd checked after the shock of seeing her had worn off. I didn't know who he was or how serious Nina was about him or if they were even still together—it didn't matter. If I'd seen him beside her tonight, I would have said or done something I'd regret.

It was only about ten minutes before Nina made her way back to my table. At least, this time, she didn't look as pissed as she had the first time.

I tried not to notice the way her hips moved when she walked. I tried not to think about the way they felt in my hands when I made love to her body. I tried not to think about how she was everything I needed . . . and couldn't have.

Like she could read the tenor of my thoughts, her face softened as she stopped across from me. "I'm sorry about earlier. I shouldn't have yelled and flipped you off." As soon as her eyes met mine, they shot away.

I folded my arms across the table and leaned forward. "In your defense, you thought I'd done the flipping off first."

"Well, you had."

"But mine wasn't *at* you. Yours was definitely at me."

Nina sighed. "You were defending me a dozen words ago, and now you're back to accusing me."

Lifting my glass, I shook it so the scotch sloshed around. "I blame it on this."

"I'm surprised this place serves the 'good' scotch you like."

"They don't." I tossed back the last of it and braced myself. "This tastes like aged piss."

Nina was fighting a smile. "Then why are you here? This is not your kind of place." She waved around the loud room.

"My kind of place is wherever I can get the quickest drink whenever the need arises. This happened to be that place tonight." When I caught the female bartender's attention, I raised my empty glass. "Do you want something?" I asked Nina.

She swallowed. "Yeah."

My brow lifted as I waited.

"Something strong."

I lifted two fingers at the bartender, who'd already grabbed the bottle of aged piss from the "top shelf."

"So?" Nina pulled out the barstool across from me, but she didn't take a seat. She was nervous, which was unusual for Nina. I couldn't help but wonder about the cause of her nerves. "How have you been?"

My brows drew together. Was she making small talk or did she really want to know? I guessed the former. "Fine. How about you?"

She nodded. "Fine." Then a long pause. "I enrolled in some courses at Portland Community College."

This smile came naturally. "Good for you. How's it been so far?"

"Good. Easier than I thought it would be. I've made some friends already, survived my first tests." She lifted her shoulders. "So far, so good."

My eyes went to the table she'd been at. College friends. It felt like a lifetime ago since I'd hung out at a bar with college friends.

"So cut the bullshit, Max." The Nina I remembered appeared from behind that nervous one for a moment. "How are you really?"

That was when our drinks arrived, which was perfect since I was going to need one to answer her question truthfully.

"Max?" Nina prompted before taking her first drink. Her face puckered the way mine had.

"I'm surviving, Nina." I sighed, claiming her eyes with mine. "That's all any of us can expect of life anyways, so I'm on par with the billions of others on the planet."

She didn't say anything right after that. I guessed the tension that followed my little tirade required some silence to diffuse. Sliding onto the barstool, she drank the rest of her drink in one gulp.

"Easy," I said when she waved her empty glass at the bar. "You're going to need your brain cells to get through college. Don't waste them on shitty scotch." When she reached across the table and grabbed my glass then drained that in one drink, my eyes went wide. "Nina, I'm serious. Slow down."

I didn't care about her taking my drink or running up my bill or any of that, but I didn't want her getting sick or waking up tomorrow feeling like a machete had been lodged in her skull. I didn't want her to experience any more pain than she already had.

Her eyes lifted to meet mine. "I'm sorry, Max," she said, her forehead wrinkling. "I'm sorry for what happened that day. I'm sorry I couldn't say back what you said to me.

I'm sorry I couldn't give you what you wanted. I'm sorry I couldn't be *who* you wanted. I'm sorry I hurt you." Her voice broke, but she kept going. "I'm sorry for everything."

I was quiet for a moment, not knowing what to say. I'd never expected to hear this from her. It was me who'd broken our agreement. It was me who'd confessed my love moments before our wedding. It was me who'd put this whole thing into motion in the first place.

"I'm sorry too, Nina." My hand instinctively reached for hers and found hers reaching back. When our fingers wound together, the ache inside me receded just enough to let me breathe again.

We sat like that for a minute, saying nothing, looking out the windows, our only connection our palms pressed together. It took me a while to figure out what the hard, cool object circling her finger was. At the same moment my eyes dropped to her finger, she seemed to realize I'd acknowledged it.

"You're still wearing it?" My voice came out quiet, almost breathless.

She bit her lip, looking away. "I can't get it off. It's stuck."

Twisting the ring around, I slid it up her finger. She was right—it didn't budge past the knuckle. Seeing the ring on her finger had made me feel hopeful, and that hope was crushed the next moment. She wasn't wearing it because she couldn't let go—she was wearing it because she couldn't get it off.

"I'll send you my jeweler's contact information." I let go of her hand to pull my phone from my pocket. "I'm sure they can find a way to remove it." I guessed they'd probably have to cut it off, but I doubted Nina cared if they had to crush the entire thing just so long as she would be free of it. I was surprised she'd waited this long to do something about it.

"A jeweler? You bought a fake diamond at an actual jeweler's?"

My jaw tightened as I debated if I should tell her. What the hell; it wasn't like she could leave me a second time. "No, but you do have to visit a jeweler to find a real diamond."

Nina inhaled. "You didn't . . ."

"Of course I did." I pulled at my tie and shrugged. "There was no way in hell I was putting some fake ring on your finger."

"I guess I shouldn't be surprised." She sighed, staring at the ring like she was seeing it for the first time.

When her drink showed up, I was in the middle of forwarding her the jeweler's information and didn't move fast enough to keep her from upending this one in record-breaking time.

Her face didn't pucker up and her body didn't shiver from the burn of it rolling down her throat. She chugged it like water then slammed the empty glass on the table, looking around like she was waiting for her next.

"No, you're cut off," I said as she tried to get the bartender's attention.

"No, I'm just getting warmed up." She was starting to sway on her stool, which was no big surprise since she was petite and had an alcohol tolerance so low it was practically non-existent.

"You're not drinking another sip unless it's water."

Fire lit up her eyes. "Stop ordering me around. You're not my husband. You're not my boyfriend. You're not even in my life anymore. You just disappeared. Poof. One minute you're everywhere—the next one you're nowhere. You don't get to boss me around." Her words were starting to draw out, her face especially expressive. She was good and drunk.

"Because even if I was your boyfriend or husband, you'd be okay with me ordering you around?" My brow lifted at her.

"No, I wouldn't. Because people who care about you don't boss you around. Or tell you what to do. Or break their promises. Or tell us things we don't want to hear or aren't ready to hear." As Nina slid off of the stool, she almost slid all the way to the floor. I shoved out of my seat and got to her just in time. She pushed against my chest as she shoved out of my hold. "Real friends don't tell each other they can't have another drink when they really fucking need another drink."

My eyes lifted to the table of people she'd shown up with. It was empty. "Do real friends also just up and bail on you without sparing thirty seconds to let you know?"

Nina's head whipped around. When she saw the empty table, she scanned the rest of the bar like she was expecting to find them. They were gone, probably too drunk to even recall they were leaving with one less than they'd arrived. The thought made me violent. If I hadn't been there and Nina had disappeared to the bathroom for a few minutes and come out to an empty table, I didn't want to think about what might have happened to her.

Then again, she probably wouldn't have been so drunk if it wasn't for my presence.

"Friends don't mind when other friends come and go. They don't make conditions on their relationship." Nina started for the door.

I followed right behind her. "Are we still talking about your 'friends' or are you taking hits at me now?"

"Don't flatter yourself. I'm talking about my friends."

I waved at the empty table as we moved by it. "The friends that left you alone in a bar on a Friday night? Awesome friends. Know where I can find myself some just like them?"

Nina ignored me as she shoved out the door, trying to power away from me, but for every step forward, she stumbled one to the side.

"Come on, Nina. Those aren't friends. Those are people you share a drink and a laugh with, that's all."

She huffed, still struggling to walk a straight line down the sidewalk. "Please. What do you know about friends or caring about people? You were drinking alone in one of the biggest cities in the country."

I caught her arm before she staggered into a light pole. "I know enough to accept I'd rather be alone than surrounded by a bunch of people I have to pretend with."

She broke to a stop and whipped around to face me. "I wasn't pretending. I like those people. They like me."

I crossed my arms and nodded. "That's obvious."

"What makes it obvious? Since I know you're dying to tell me?"

I steered her aside as a group of loud, frat-looking guys passed by. They smelled like they'd been bathing in a vat of beer for days. After they'd passed, I lowered my face until it was level with Nina's. She was glaring at me, but at least she was looking.

"People who like us tell us what we want to hear. People who love us tell us what we need to hear." I paused to let that settle in. "Since you clearly like to hear what you want to rather than what you need to, it's safe to assume you 'like' those people very much."

Somehow, her eyes narrowed even more. I wasn't trying to piss her off—I was trying to be honest with her. But I knew from experience that being honest with Nina was a good way to upset her.

"Then you must have really, really, *really* loved me because you sure told me a whole lot of stuff you thought I needed to hear," she shouted loudly enough to earn a few head turns from people wandering down the sidewalks.

"You did need to hear it. All of it." When she spun around to keep trying to move down the sidewalk, I grabbed her hand to keep her from leaving. "And right now, you need to hear that you are too drunk to go out on your own and get home safely by the end of it. You're shit-faced and not in any condition to go anywhere alone."

I pulled on her hand, leading her to where my Tesla was parked up ahead. She was struggling against me, but along with dulling her inhibitions, the alcohol had dulled her strength.

"And while I'm on a roll, let me just say that I think the whole reason you acted so appalled and upset that day of the wedding was because some part of you knew you felt the same way as I did. You knew you might have loved me too and that scared the shit out of you." I broke to a stop, turning to face her once we were in front of the car. She looked like she was ready to slap me, but I didn't care. "That's why you couldn't say it back. Because you were scared."

Her hand shook in mine. From the look on her face, I guessed it was from anger. "I am not scared of anything," she seethed, nice and slow. That, she didn't slur in the slightest.

She was better at telling lies than sharing truths. That was the nature of a person who'd been battered by life. What I wanted to tell her was something different from what I needed to.

"Nina, please, you are scared of everything." I softened my words as much as I could.

Her face fell for the briefest moment. Then she looked at me like she'd never despised the sight of a person more than she did me. "I hate you, Max Sturm."

When she tried to yank her hand free again, my grip tightened. "Of course you do. Because hating me is less terrifying than the thought of loving me is."

She froze for a moment, something hitting her. It passed as soon as it had come on. "Let me go," she ordered, pulling against me again. "Leave me alone."

"Fine." I opened the passenger door of the Tesla. "After I make sure you get home."

"Stop, Max." Her free hand kept shoving at my chest, but then she lost her balance and kind of fell into me. When I caught her again, it only seemed to make her madder. "I hate you. Leave me alone. Did you just miss all of that?"

My arms gently folded around her and pulled her to me. I held her close so she wouldn't fall again and kept her close because I couldn't bear the thought of letting her go again.

"No, I didn't," I said, lowering my mouth to her ear. "But here's the thing. I care about you, no matter what you say or do to try to make me feel otherwise. I care about you, and I will look after you in whatever way I can, and tell you what you need to hear, and force you into my goddamn car so you don't wind up naked in some ditch tonight."

She was shaking against me, crying. I'd never wanted to be the cause of Nina's tears, but at the same time, I knew the only way to really move on from something was to properly mourn it. This was my final gift to Nina. My good-bye gift. So once the tears had dried up, she could bury us in a box and move on.

"I will always do what's best for you, even if it means you wind up hating me. Because that's how much I love you," I said.

After I got her in the car, I drove her home, carried her into her house, and tucked her into bed. I stood there and watched her sleep for a minute. She'd passed out before I'd pulled away from the curb outside the bar, and I guessed she'd wake up tomorrow and feel the exact same way about me as she had tonight. And that was okay.

Nina Burton might very well spend the rest of her life hating me.

But I'd spend the rest of mine loving her.

TWENTY-NINE

Nina

*e*very morning I rolled out of bed with the goal to move on from Max. Every night I crawled into bed swearing I'd try harder the next day. It was a sick cycle I felt powerless to overcome.

It had already been three weeks since the night I'd run into Max at that bar. It had been three weeks since I'd seen or heard from him. I didn't remember much about that night—at least not much after that quart of scotch I'd chugged hit my system.

I remembered arguing with him, but not what the argument was about. I remembered yelling at him about something, but not what had preceded that. I did remember shouting at him, "I hate you."

That was what I woke up the next morning remembering—those three words. That was all I could recall as the night's events struggled to materialize. He'd driven me home. He must have carried me into the house and laid me on my bed. He had to have taken off my shoes and tucked the blankets over me and left the bottles of water and aspirin on my nightstand.

He must have stayed all night and made his escape once he'd heard me stirring, because when I padded out into the living room that morning, I'd just caught a glimpse of his car disappearing down the road. His body's impression was still molded into the leather chair he must have spent the night in.

He'd left so he wouldn't have to face me, and really, I couldn't blame him. Not with the words I remembered shouting at him.

He'd done the right thing, as only Max could, and then he'd left. I'd succeeded at pushing him away—if I hadn't already the day of our failed wedding when I couldn't say three words to him.

Instead, I'd given him three different words.

My mind never strayed far from those trios of words—the ones he'd spoken, and the ones I had.

I love you.

I hate you.

I didn't hate Max. I never could. I'd lied.

The love part was more confusing. I'd seen it abused by too many people. I'd perverted it too much on my own. I'd convinced myself it could never be experienced within the confines of a romantic relationship. A mother could love a child. A son could love his father. But a man could not love a woman. A woman could not love a man.

That had been my belief for years, but all of that was starting to crumble, the first crack punched in it the day Max professed his love for me.

So that was my life now. Crumbling walls that had kept me protected now exposed me, leaving me feeling naked and scared. That was probably why I'd sought solace here this afternoon.

This was the most peaceful place I'd ever been. Maybe that was because the residents here had permanently made their peace with life, forced or otherwise.

It had been a while since I'd visited Grandma's grave, but today I'd woken up and known a visit was in order.

I'd been sitting here for a while, just staring at her headstone, searching for answers on the marble face. I'd read the inscription hundreds of times, maybe thousands— I'd committed it to memory the first time I read in her will what she wanted on her headstone.

It was simple and concise, but still, there was comfort in reading that handful of words over and over. *Margaret Louise Burton, May 24th, 1939 to January 8th, 2015.* Below that was only one word. *Love.* No famous quote, no scripture verse, no "Beloved Grandmother." Nothing besides that one word.

If it had been up to me, I would have added that "Beloved Grandmother" part, but this had been her request, and it had seemed more important to honor that than to make sure anyone who passed her headstone knew she had been a beloved grandmother. I knew she had been—and so had she. There was more permanence in that than in some words etched into a big piece of stone.

Love. Of all the things to leave as her final message to the world, this seemed both perfectly fitting and off. At the same time Grandma had been love's greatest giver, she'd been one of its greatest victims as well. She'd been scalded by it in as grand a measure as she'd bestowed it.

I'd always assumed Grandma held a sort of love-hate relationship with love, as familiar with its sting as she was with its healing powers. But was I wrong?

That was the question I was wrestling with as I continued to study those four large letters staring back at me. Love.

Do you love me?

My heart ached at the question, giving its answer. My mind rallied, offering a different one.

Love. My grandma's last manifesto to the world and the word she'd chosen to summarize seventy-six years of life.

What did she mean by it? Love more? Love was the answer? Love was the theme? Love was a verb? Love was a noun?

I'd never given so much thought to love before. I'd never agonized over one word so much in my entire life. How could a person choose as her parting word to the world the very thing she'd been betrayed by?

Love.

Of all the life she'd lived, all of the lessons she'd learned, was that the one thing it all boiled down to? Was, perhaps, this one word meant for me and me alone? Had Grandma somehow predicted this day I'd fall in front of her grave, looking for answers, and realized this was the one thing I needed to read?

Was this her way of telling me that instead of spending the rest of my life running from love, I should spend the rest of it chasing love? Instead of avoiding it, embracing it? Instead of fearing it, searching for it?

Love.

The storm of confusion receded.

Do you love me?

THIRTY

Nina

My feet had taken me out of the cemetery—my heart had taken me the rest of the way. For the first time in years, I felt like I was finally moving forward, instead of spinning in circles in the same small space.

My fear of being hurt and abandoned by someone I loved had been responsible for driving away a person who cared about me and who I cared about in return. My fear of being alone had created that very reality. No more.

Fear had no place in my life.

Love was not the enemy.

This was what I reminded myself of when the urge to turn and run hit me every few steps. Those sentences played on a loop as soon as his office building came into view and fear really tried to send me running. But no more. I was exhaling fear and inhaling love from this moment on.

In the elevator on the way up to his office, I tried to focus on what I was about to say instead of who I was about to see. If I thought about him, I might chicken out.

When the elevator doors slid open on the top floor, I stepped out into his office. It was dark, all of the lights off, nothing but the glow from outside filling the expansive space.

Rounding down the hall toward his office, my body shook from the emotions charging through me. I didn't know what I was going to say. What he'd say. I wasn't sure what I'd do when I saw him or what he'd do when he saw me.

I just knew I needed to be there.

Instead of knocking, I shoved the door open and stepped inside. Max was sitting in his chair, staring at his computer screens with an absent look. He hadn't shaved in days. His eyes looked flat, almost lifeless. The rest of him kept with the same theme.

When I moved inside his office, his eyes slid in my direction. Emotions that made my throat tighten drew hard lines on his forehead.

My heart was slamming against my ribcage, its beat echoing in my ears. "You were right," I said slowly, forcing myself to look him in the eyes. "About me being scared."

Max swallowed, his gaze suggesting he was trying to ascertain if I was really standing in front of him. "Being scared of what?"

At first, the words stuck in my throat. On the second try, I got them out. "Falling in love with you."

His face pulled into a wince. "Why?"

I absently twirled the ring still on my finger. Having him close, in a confined space, and looking at me like he was made it hard to breathe, let alone speak.

"Because when you give what you feel a name, a name like that, it's real." I moved a few steps deeper into his office. "When it's real, it means you've got something to lose, and in my experience, something like love is a guarantee that I'll lose it. I didn't want to lose you."

Max's chair rolled back from his desk. "I didn't want to lose you either, but I couldn't make you marry me because you'd signed some agreement. I couldn't marry you because you felt it was some kind of duty. Because, for me, marrying you would have been my greatest honor."

My throat burned as I watched him put together words that seemed to cause him physical pain. I'd never intended to have feelings for Max Sturm, but I'd developed them. They'd carved their way deep into my being, settling into the empty places that had been hollow for so long, I'd forgotten they were there.

By walking away on our wedding day, I'd fooled myself into believing I'd left Max behind. But I'd never be able to leave him behind because every step I took, I carried him inside me. He'd nestled into my empty spaces and filled them with the kind of permanence that didn't crumble with time or absence.

He was part of me. I was part of him.

"I wanted to marry you, Max. God, I wanted to, but when you told me how you felt, it scared me." My feet kept moving closer to him.

His brow arched. "But you're not scared anymore?"

"I'm terrified," I breathed, "but I'm not letting my fear guide my life any longer. I'm letting something else."

He shifted in his chair. "What else?"

An invisible force coiled around my throat, constricting my vocal cords. But I beat it back.

"Love," I said a moment later. "You asked me a question. I didn't answer it honestly last time, and I'd like the chance to answer it again. If you still want to know my answer."

At the same time his expression cleared, Max shoved out of his chair. "Do you love me?" His whispered words filled the empty space.

Willing my eyes to stay on his as he came around his desk, I felt my heart beat for what felt like the first time in months. "I do." When he reached for me, the warmth of his hand enveloping mine chased away the rest of my fear and pain. "I do love you."

EPILOGUE

Nina

(Two years later)

I t was divorce day.

Or at least it was according to Max's perfectly planned schedule. We'd burned both copies of our original arrangement a couple of years ago, along with the rest of the pages in the folders. We'd burned them the day before our wedding, and this time, we made it to the altar. This time, we exchanged vows, and when he whispered he loved me during our first dance, I said it back without hesitation.

Since today had been the original date we'd set as the day to go our separate ways, it seemed kind of poetic that we were sitting at the Immigration office, in front of the officer giving us our interview for Max's green card.

We'd lingered in the waiting room for over three hours with other couples awaiting their interviews, but that had been the easy part. Ever since we'd crossed into Officer Cranky Pants's office, I'd felt as though we were in some interrogation room and being investigated for being double agents or something.

Officer *Cranburg* looked like the type of person who had seen it all and been disappointed by it all. He looked close to retirement, but from the way he held on to a perpetual frown, I thought he had another decade of hell to endure before getting out.

From the start, he'd acted as though there was a shortage of green cards and he was the one gatekeeper who ruled them all. Like the only way to get one would be to pry one from his dead fingers.

Everyone was guilty until proven innocent.

At least that was the feeling I got as soon as I sat down in front of his desk, Max sliding into the chair beside me. My smile was met by his frown—maybe his smile muscles had atrophied and smiling was a physical impossibility now. Max's attempt at a handshake was met by a cocked brow.

We'd already been sitting here for over thirty minutes, answering question after question clearly intended to confuse us or catch us in a lie. From the looks of the officer, he was only getting warmed up.

"How many guests were at your wedding?" His droll voice filled the small office once again.

Max and I glanced at each other.

"Forty-five, wasn't it?" he checked with me, his brows coming together.

"Forty-four," I corrected. "Your cousin had to cancel at the last minute, remember?"

"That's right." Max snapped his fingers. "Forty-four."

It was a miracle those forty-four people had been able to attend with as short of notice as we'd given everyone. Especially since our first attempt at becoming husband and wife had wound up a no-go.

"What food was served at the reception?"

I slumped a little farther in my chair. The questions were never going to end. Max and I had answered them all honestly, and this guy was still looking at us like he was just itching to call the authorities.

"We didn't exactly hang around long enough to find out." A grin stretched across Max's face as he leaned forward in his chair. "If you know what I mean."

"I'm sure I don't." Officer Cranky Pants scratched something down on his notepad. "What side of the bed to you sleep on, Mr. Sturm?"

Max's grin stayed in place. "Whatever side I roll off on." My elbow jutting into his ribcage dimmed the grin some. "Usually the right side though."

"What was the reason for the last fight you got into?"

Max ran point on this one as well. "Nina had ridden the bus home late one night. Again," he muttered at me.

The officer's forehead creased as he shuffled through the stack of paperwork we'd assembled for the interview. Everything from wedding pictures to original birth certificates to bank statements. It was the financial stuff he was riffling through now. "Mrs. Sturm rides the bus?"

I lifted my finger. "Mrs. *Burton*—Sturm rides the bus sometimes."

Officer Cranburg's forehead creased deeper as he skimmed the financial statements. Probably didn't make a lot of sense that the wife of a man who'd made a small fortune would utilize public transportation.

"I like the bus," I explained with a shrug. Why was that so hard a concept for people to wrap their heads around?

"Mrs. *Burton-Sturm*"—the officer looked at me over his bifocals—"if I'm to understand this correctly, you were in a grave degree of debt when you and Mr. Sturm first met. Is that correct?"

Max's hand tightened around mine. Not enough for the officer to notice, but enough for me to feel its reassurance.

"That's right." I nodded, remembering not to add anything more. Max and I had been prepping for this interview for months, and I knew not to say anything that didn't need to be said. Unless I was asked why I had been in so much debt, I didn't need to tell him. Keep it brief and honest. That was our plan for the interview.

"And Mr. Sturm was a man of substantial means at the same time, correct?"

My ankles crossed. I didn't want to fidget, but I needed to move. "That's right."

The officer was quiet after that, letting the implications and accusations settle in the air.

Across the desk from him, Max and I stayed quiet as well. He couldn't break us with a couple of loaded questions and a few minutes of bloated silence.

Max and I might have started our relationship on one foot, but that wasn't the reason we were there now. Our love might have been fake at the start, but now . . . it didn't get any more real than this.

Our relationship was a testament to the strangeness of love. How it worked in unusual ways. How it cropped up when you least expected it. How it appeared when it was the last thing you thought you wanted.

"You know, this might be a good time to bring this into the interview."

Max looked at me as I riffled through my purse for the item I'd stuffed in there earlier today.

Pulling out the white stick, I held it out for the officer.

At first, his face creased with surprise, like he had no idea what I was holding. Then I tapped my index finger just outside the window that showed two pink lines. The officer's nose curled as he shoved back in his chair. That this surly old immigration officer was grossed out by a pregnancy test was all kinds of funny.

Max had moved so close to the edge of his seat, he was lucky he hadn't fallen out of it. Grabbing my hand, he turned it so the stick was facing him.

The look on his face? Priceless.

We hadn't talked about getting pregnant, and we sure as hell hadn't been trying, but kind of like the majority of our relationship, it had sneaked up and surprised us.

"What . . ." Max had to shake his head a few times, blinking like he was making sure he wasn't seeing things. "Does that mean . . ."

"I'm pregnant," I said, leaning in to give him a kiss. He was still frozen, which made me laugh. "You're going to be a dad. In seven and a half months to be exact."

Dropping the stick in my lap, I fitted my hand around the side of his neck. His face was kind of pale and he even felt clammy, but a smile was stretching into place. One of those bewildered smiles.

"A dad?" His voice matched his expression.

When he swayed in his chair, I roped my arm around his waist so if he did pass out, he wouldn't hit the ground.

He kept staring at me, his eyes swimming with a million different things that all reduced down to one thing—love.

"Your green card's approved," the officer announced, stamping Max's passport. "You'll receive your official one in the mail in a few weeks."

My head whipped toward the officer, but Max's attention stayed centered on me. All of it.

The officer must have noticed the surprise in my expression because one of his shoulders lifted as he waved the stamp between Max and me. "No one can fake the look on their face of finding out they're going to become a parent." He circled the stamp at Max's face a few times. "Congratulations." Clearing his throat, Officer Cranky Pants almost cracked a smile. "On both subjects."

Laughing with excitement, I found Max still reeling in his seat. The words *a dad* were still whispering on his lips. What a dad he'd be too. If he was half the dad he was a husband, our child would never lack for love.

After shaking hands with the officer, Max threw me into his arms and carried me out of the room. He carried me through the waiting area and down the hall and out the front doors.

It wasn't until we were outside on the sidewalk that he set me down.

I stared up at him, the man I'd planned on marrying before I even met him. The same one I was planning on staying married to until the day I left this world. I loved him. Hate had been wrong. Hate was love not ready to be realized. Hate came from fear and doubt and burned at the same degree as passion. Consumed as much thought space, required as much energy to feel, dominated as much mind space.

Our hate story had become a love story.

"Come on." He took my hand and started down the sidewalk. "Let's go home."

My gaze locked on his and my hand tightened around his. "I am home."

The End

Thank you for reading HATE STORY
by NEW YORK TIMES and USATODAY
bestselling author, Nicole Williams.

Nicole loves to hear from her readers.
You can connect with her on:

Facebook: Nicole Williams (Official Author Page)
Twitter: nwilliamsbooks
Blog: nicoleawilliams.blogspot.com

Other Works by Nicole:

CRASH, CLASH, and CRUSH (HarperCollins)

UP IN FLAMES (Simon & Schuster UK)

LOST & FOUND, NEAR & FAR, HEART & SOUL

FINDERS KEEPERS, LOSERS WEEPERS

STEALING HOME, TOUCHING DOWN

COLLARED

THE FABLE OF US

THREE BROTHERS

HARD KNOX, DAMAGED GOODS

CROSSING STARS

GREAT EXPLOITATIONS

THE EDEN TRILOGY

THE PATRICK CHRONICLES

44381473R00197

Made in the USA
San Bernardino, CA
13 January 2017